THE ONLY WAY TO COPE

If she let herself, she'd drown in a world of pain. But she can't let that happen, she simply wouldn't be able to handle it, not *that* kind of pain. Thankfully she knows how to prevent such a thing.

Willow reaches into the pocket of her robe, feeling for what she knows is there.

She never takes her eyes off of them as she slices into her flesh. The blade bites so deeply that she almost swoons, but still, she never stops looking at David and Cathy.

Her blood spouts as voluptuously as David's tears. It drips unchecked, down her arm and onto the floor as Willow watches Cathy dry David's eyes with her long, long hair.

Willow knows that she should leave. At any moment they could look up. But she can't leave, she can't move. She can only slice deeper and deeper.

The razor doesn't hurt her. Not really.

Not like some things could, anyway. Willow savagely swipes at her wrist.

Not like some things could.

OTHER BOOKS YOU MAY ENJOY

Because I Am Furniture	Thalia Chaltas
Dreamland	Sarah Dessen
Hold Still	Nina LaCour
If I Stay	Gayle Forman
Jerk, California	Jonathan Friesen
Looking for Alaska	John Green
Looks	Madeleine George
The Outsiders	S.E. Hinton
Speak	Laurie Halse Anderson
Wintergirls	Laurie Halse Anderson

WILLOW

JULIA HOBAN

speak
An Imprint of Penguin Group (USA) Inc.

For Henry Grayson and Charles Grodin:
Two of the eighteen

Speak
Published by the Penguin Group
Penguin Group (USA) Inc., 345 Hudson Street, New York, New York 10014, U.S.A.
Penguin Group (Canada), 90 Eglinton Avenue East, Suite 700, Toronto, Ontario, Canada M4P 2Y3
(a division of Pearson Penguin Canada Inc.)
Penguin Books Ltd, 80 Strand, London WC2R 0RL, England
Penguin Ireland, 25 St Stephen's Green, Dublin 2, Ireland (a division of Penguin Books Ltd)
Penguin Group (Australia), 250 Camberwell Road, Camberwell, Victoria 3124, Australia
(a division of Pearson Australia Group Pty Ltd)
Penguin Books India Pvt Ltd, 11 Community Centre, Panchsheel Park, New Delhi - 110 017, India
Penguin Group (NZ), 67 Apollo Drive, Rosedale, North Shore 0632,New Zealand
(a division of Pearson New Zealand Ltd)
Penguin Books (South Africa) (Pty) Ltd, 24 Sturdee Avenue,
Rosebank, Johannesburg 2196, South Africa

Registered Offices: Penguin Books Ltd, 80 Strand, London WC2R 0RL, England

First published in the United States of America by Dial Books,
a member of Penguin Group (USA) Inc., 2009
Published by Speak, an imprint of Penguin Group (USA) Inc., 2010

5 7 9 10 8 6 4

THE LIBRARY OF CONGRESS HAS CATALOGED THE DIAL EDITION AS FOLLOWS:
Hoban, Julia.
Willow / by Julia Hoban.
p. cm.
Summary: Sixteen-year-old Willow, who was driving the car that killed both of
her parents, copes with the pain and guilt by cutting herself, until she meets
a smart and sensitive boy who is determined to help her stop.
ISBN: 978-0-8037-3356-5 (hc)
[1. Self-mutilation—Fiction. 2. Guilt—Fiction. 3. Grief—Fiction. 4. Orphans—Fiction.]
PZ7.H63487 Wi 2009
[Fic]—dc22

Speak ISBN 978-0-14-241666-2

Printed in the United States of America

CHAPTER ONE

Maybe it's just a scratch.

Willow Randall stares at the girl seated opposite her. Some might notice the girl because she is pretty. Others because of her flaming red hair. If the guys in the class were looking, they would see that the outline of her bra is clearly visible beneath her shirt. But Willow's eyes are riveted by something else: an angry red welt, about three inches long, that runs from the girl's elbow to her wrist. If Willow squints hard enough, she can just about make out a few flecks of dried blood.

How did she get it? She doesn't look the type.

Maybe she has a cat. A whole bunch of kittens.

Yeah, that's it. Playing with her kitty. That's probably how it happened.

Willow slumps down in her seat. But her scrutiny hasn't

gone unnoticed and the girl turns to one of her friends and starts whispering.

Sshshhsh . . .

What are they saying?

Willow looks at the other girls uncertainly. She has a bad feeling that they're talking about her, and she's pretty sure that she knows what they're saying, too.

She's the one without parents.

No. She's the one who killed *her parents.*

Their whispers remind her of the rustling of dried leaves. Willow has always hated the sound. She fights the urge to clap her hands over her ears, reluctant to call any more attention to herself. But she can't stop the river of noise that flows out of their mouths. *Shhhhsshhhsh . . .*

The sound engulfs her. Threatens to overwhelm her.

Only one thing can make it go away.

Willow stands up abruptly, but her shoelace gets tangled with the chair leg and she pitches forward. Her books fall to the floor with a crash. She grabs the desk with both hands, barely managing to stay upright.

Dead silence. *Everyone* is staring at her.

She can feel her face burning and glares at the two girls who were whispering.

"Willow?" Ms. Benson sounds alarmed. She's clearly concerned, and not just pretending. She's a good teacher.

She's nice to the fat kids, the pimply kids, so why not the orphan kids? Why not the killer kids?

"I just . . ." Willow straightens up slowly. "Just—the bathroom." Her blush deepens painfully. She's ashamed of her clumsiness. Ashamed at the way she looked at those girls . . . And couldn't she have come up with a *different* excuse?

Ms. Benson nods, but she looks doubtful, as if she might suspect.

Willow couldn't care less at this point. All she's thinking about is making a quick getaway and leaving those smirking faces behind. She picks up her books, grabs her bag, and as soon as she's out the door she starts running down the hall. Wait. No running in the halls. She slows down to a walk. That's the last thing she needs, to get busted for something as stupid as running in the halls.

The bathroom smells like smoke. There's no one around. Good. The door to one of the stalls swings free. Willow kicks it shut behind her and lowers the toilet seat before sitting down.

She rummages through her bag. Getting frantic because she can't find what she so desperately needs. Did she forget to get more supplies? Finally, just when she's given up hope, when she's about to start howling like a dog, her hand closes on smooth metal. Her fingers test the sharpness of the edge. Perfect. It's a fresh blade.

The girls' voices rustle in her head. Their clamoring pushes out all rational thought. She rolls up her sleeve.

The bite of the blade kills the noise. It wipes out the memory of those staring faces. Willow looks at her arm, at the life springing from her. Tiny pinpricks of red that blossom into giant peonies.

Peonies like the ones my mother used to plant.

Willow shuts her eyes, drinking in the quiet. Her breath

deepens with each dip of the razor. Silence reigns, not like when she tripped, but perfect and pure.

You couldn't really say that something that hurts so badly feels good exactly. It's more that it just feels right. And something that feels so right just couldn't be bad. It has to be good.

It is good. Better than good.

Better than anything with any guy ever.

Better than mother's milk.

CHAPTER TWO

"No, that's out till the twenty-sixth," Miss Hamilton says with a brisk professional smile. Willow stands next to her behind the circulation desk, stifling a yawn. She's tired. Thank God her shift at the library is almost over. She steals a glance at her watch. Well, not quite over; another forty-five minutes.

Willow knows she should be grateful for the job. After all, her brother had to pull enough strings to get it for her. Three afternoons a week she helps out in the university library. It brings in some cash. Not enough, but still, more than she would have made back home working in the local Häagen-Dazs scooping ice cream.

Of course, back home any money she made would have gone straight into her own pocket. Things are a little different now. Now she works to help her brother out with expenses. Now she has to worry about things like the electric bill. But that's not really so bad, at least not compared to the rest of her life.

"I think we can get that for you on interlibrary loan," Miss Hamilton continues. "Willow, will you set that up?"

Miss Hamilton looks at her sharply, ready to pounce if she makes a mistake. She's not a bad soul, not really. She's nice enough to everyone else, she just doesn't like Willow invading her library. Most of the other people who work there are graduate students, and those who aren't have chosen the library as their career. Suffice it to say, Willow is the only high school student there.

It's just like everything else these days. She simply does not belong.

Willow takes the card that the guy's filled out in his shaky, spidery handwriting. He's looking for some obscure work on twelfth-century philosophers. She glances up at him. An older man. Way older. Probably in his seventies. It's always interesting to see the different types that wander in.

"That should get here in a couple days," she says as she keys the call number into the computer. "You wrote your phone number down?" She looks at the card again. "Perfect, we'll let you know when it comes in."

"Wonderful," he says with real enthusiasm. Willow notices what a friendly smile he has. She bets that he's a retired professor who still likes to read. His eyes positively gleam at the prospect of getting his hands on the book. Her father would have been like that in another twenty years or so. Just the thought of some monograph about a little-known tribe in New Guinea would have been enough to make him drool.

Would have been.

She's blindsided by a wave of despair, it's hard to even stand. She grips the edge of the circulation desk so hard that her knuckles turn white. She simply cannot afford to lose it in here. Is there any way, any way at all, that she can excuse herself, go and do what she has to, without Miss Hamilton getting angry at her?

Willow can see her bag with all her supplies underneath one of the chairs. Just the sight of it calms her a little. She moves her hands away from the desk and rubs her arms, relishing the way the cotton irritates her fresh wounds. That will have to do for now.

"Willow!" Miss Hamilton's voice is sharp; clearly this isn't the first time that she's said her name.

"I'm sorry!" Willow is so startled that she practically jumps. She forces herself to look away from her bag and focus on Miss Hamilton's scowling face.

"I need you to go up to the stacks."

"Okay." She nods, even though she hates the stacks. They're filthy, positively caked in dust. They're scary too. Willow's heard rumors about ghosts. Not that she believes in ghosts, but still. . . .

"This young man forgot his ID, you need to go up with him."

Willow switches her attention to the guy leaning against the circulation desk behind Miss Hamilton. Now, *this* guy isn't any seventy years old. He's probably only a few years older than she is, if that. He flips the hair out of his eyes and flashes her a lazy smile.

Willow knows that she should smile back, but it's no good, she's lost the knack.

"I'll take him up in a second." She turns back to Miss Hamilton. "I just have to finish . . . " Willow makes a vague gesture toward the computer.

Miss Hamilton nods and turns away, but the guy doesn't. He keeps on looking. She can feel his eyes following her as she finishes taking care of the interlibrary loan.

Willow is sure that she's just being paranoid, but his scrutiny is terrifying. It reminds her of the girls back at school. She doesn't like the thought of going up to the stacks with him at all. Just to delay things, she takes more time than is strictly necessary to fill in all the information fields.

"So how about it?" he says after a minute or two. He's starting to get impatient. His fingers drum along the counter and his voice has a distinct edge. He doesn't seem so interested in her anymore.

Willow sighs in relief. *This* she can handle.

"Yeah, okay. Just a second." Her voice matches his.

"Why don't you let me do this for you?" Carlos says, taking the twelfth-century man's card from her. Carlos is one of the graduate students, he's almost as old as her brother. Willow likes him—well, as much as she can like anyone these days. He's nice to her, he's covered for her more than once.

"Thanks," she says under her breath. She wishes he would let her finish at the computer and take this guy up to the stacks instead.

"Well, c'mon then." Willow marches ahead of him toward the elevator.

"Do you know where this is?" she asks, looking at the card he's filled out. "Never mind, I got it." She steps into the elevator and punches the button for the eleventh-floor stacks. The doors close and they're alone. Willow stares straight ahead at the illuminated numbers.

"I'm Guy," he says after a moment. "What's your name?"

"Willow."

"Willow . . ." He trails off, obviously expecting her to respond. "Willow?" he prompts, after a second. "What's your last name?"

Willow can't think of any way, short of being downright rude, to avoid answering him. "Randall," she says.

"Are you related to David Randall?" He eyes her curiously. "I thought you looked kinda familiar. I took anthropology with him last year. He's great."

"He's my brother," Willow answers in a tone meant to discourage further conversation. His chatter is starting to make her nervous.

"You're not a student here, are you?" He frowns. "You look a little young. How did you get this job?"

Willow doesn't respond right away. The questions he's asking are making her a little uncomfortable. She starts counting the floors under her breath. She can't wait for the ride to be over.

"They usually only hire students," he continues. "Otherwise I'd try and get a job. I'd love to work in the library." His expression is pleasant and his voice is good-natured. If he notices that she's being slightly standoffish, it doesn't seem to bother him.

"If you're not a student, what are you doing here?" Willow is confused.

"My high school has this program where you can take college courses for credit," he says. "So what about you, how *did* you get the job?"

"I'm living with my brother right now," Willow says after a moment. "He worked it out." The elevator stops and they get off.

The stacks are dark; the lights are on a timer, which Willow quickly presses. She blinks rapidly as her eyes adjust to the dim lighting. Their gazes catch and for a moment she feels herself respond the way any normal girl would if she were standing next to a cute guy. She's a little flustered, a little embarrassed, and a little attracted too.

Willow steps away from him, as far as she possibly can. She can't deal with anything like this right now.

"Hey, watch it." Guy reaches out with his hand to steady her as she bangs against the metal stacks.

Willow jerks her arm away, stunned by how much his touch affects her. In a way his hand is as searing as the razor . . . only the effect is something quite different. The razor numbs her, makes her forget, but this . . . well . . . She shivers and rubs her arms convulsively.

"You cold?" He raises an eyebrow.

"I'm fine, thanks. I . . . C'mon, let's get your book, okay?" Willow checks the call number again, then turns and heads over to the shelves.

She finds the volume easily and is about to hand it to him, when she glances at the title and stops, transfixed.

"Everything okay?" Guy frowns as he watches her.

"Oh, sure, I just . . ." Willow trails off. She can't stop staring at the book. Well, she shouldn't be so surprised. He did say something about anthropology, and it is a classic.

"Do you know this book? I mean, have you read *Tristes Tropiques* before?" he asks as he takes it from her hands.

"Yes, a couple of times, actually," Willow says after a few seconds. She closes her eyes for a moment and pictures her parents' study with its wall of books. *Tristes Tropiques*, third shelf, second in from the left.

"I've never met anyone else who's read it!" Guy looks impressed. "It's amazing, isn't it?" he says as he flips through the pages. "I guess your brother must have told you about it, right? If it wasn't for this book I wouldn't have even taken his class."

"What do you mean?"

"Well, last year, right before I started classes here, I was wandering around downtown, trying to decide what I should take. I figured I'd end up doing something like chemistry or math, since those would look pretty good on my transcript and maybe help me get into a fancy school or something. Anyway, it started to rain and I ducked into this used bookstore. This literally fell off the shelf while I was looking for something else. I opened it up and four hours later I was still there reading. That's when I decided that I had to take anthropology."

"Really?" In spite of herself, Willow can't help being interested. She too has never met anyone else—anyone her own age, that is—who's read the book, let alone been so captivated by it.

"Really." Guy nods. "It's like an adventure story, isn't it?"

"That's it exactly!" Willow's face lights up. Just for a second she forgets that *Tristes Tropiques* was her father's favorite book. She forgets about sitting on the window seat in the living room on rainy Saturday afternoons working her way through *all* his favorite books. She forgets that she doesn't *have* a father anymore, and she even forgets to be unhappy. "It is like an adventure story," she says. "But you know what's funny? Remember how on the first page he goes on and on about how he doesn't even like adventure stories?"

"Right." Guy laughs. "And then he pretty much goes ahead and writes one."

The lights click off suddenly and they stand in the darkness for a moment before Guy reaches out and presses the timer. Then he sits down on the floor as if it were the most natural thing in the world, as if the only thing that he could possibly want to do with his time is talk to her.

Willow is a little unsure of what to do. She feels comfortable talking to him, but the way she felt when he touched her, that wasn't comfortable at all. She searches his face. He doesn't look as if there's anything on his mind besides books.

After a second Willow sits down next to him.

"Why do you need this?" She gestures toward *Tristes Tropiques*. "What happened to the copy that you bought at that used bookstore?" Of course she doesn't really care about what happened to his copy, and it's kind of a stupid question, stupid and boring, but she doesn't know what else to say, and she doesn't feel relaxed enough to sit there with him in silence.

"Lost it on the subway." Guy shrugs. "I should buy another, but I'm kind of low on cash right now. Do you know the place I'm talking about?" He puts the book down and turns to look at her. "I figure your brother's had to have dragged you down there about a thousand times. It's always packed with professors whenever I go."

Willow thinks for a minute. "Is it way downtown?" she asks. "And even though it's huge, it's really cramped, right?"

"Right." Guy nods. "There's hardly room to move. It's like the books have taken over. They've spilled off the shelves and there's so many piled all over the floor that it's almost impossible to walk."

"And it kind of smells," Willow says. "But not in a good,

old, bookish sort of way, but in a kind of . . ." She pauses for a second.

"A kind of unwashed and dirty way," Guy finishes.

"That's right." Willow laughs. "And the staff are really rude."

"If you ask them something, they act like you're bothering them."

"And it's almost impossible to find anything on your own, because they don't arrange things in any logical order."

"And the whole place is so far out of the way to begin with, you wonder why anyone even bothers to go there. But still, it's actually really . . ."

"Fabulous," Willow chimes in.

"So you do know it." Guy smiles. He stops talking and studies her face carefully. Willow shifts uncomfortably. She's suddenly acutely aware of how quiet the stacks are, how quiet and how empty.

"You don't really look that much like your brother," Guy continues after a few moments. "I mean, I don't think that's why I recognized you."

Willow isn't sure where this is leading, but she does know that she feels distinctly less relaxed than she did a few minutes ago.

"I'm such an idiot!" Guy exclaims. "I can't believe this. You go to my school, don't you? That's why I know you. I've seen you around the halls. You just transferred there this year, right?"

Willow is much too startled to answer this. They go to the same school? He knows her? Does he know *about* her?

She scrambles to her feet. "I have to go," she says in alarm. "I shouldn't have been up here this long anyway."

"Well, sure." Guy stands up and starts to follow her as she practically runs to the elevator.

Willow can't bring herself to look at him. She stares at the elevator floor, the ceiling, anything but his face. It's as if their pleasant little interlude had never even occurred. She feels used. Used and *stupid.* Had he known all along? Had that entire conversation been some act so he could report back to his friends at school that he'd actually managed to talk to the new girl? The *strange* girl, the girl who *killed her parents*?

The desire to cut is palpable, even stronger than it was back at the circulation desk. She has to get away from him. She has to be alone.

"So listen, do you think . . ."

"I have to *go,*" Willow says. She bolts out of the elevator, leaving Guy behind, and rushes toward Miss Hamilton. For once her scowl is welcome.

"You certainly took a long time." Miss Hamilton seems suspicious.

"I . . . I had a hard time finding what he was looking for." Willow joins her behind the desk.

"You need to be more familiar with the call numbers," Miss Hamilton says. Excuses carry no weight with her.

"Hey, c'mon, it took me forever to figure out the stacks." Carlos flashes Willow a sympathetic smile.

"I suppose." Miss Hamilton looks back and forth between the two of them. "All right then, you're done, Willow. I'll see you in a few days."

Willow glances at the clock in surprise. She had no idea that her shift was over. Miss Hamilton was right, she had been gone for a while. She didn't realize that their conversation had lasted that long.

Well, that's one more day I don't have to live through again, she thinks as she grabs her bag and dashes out the door.

Willow pushes past the students clustered around the library entrance, filthying the air with cigarettes, and heads toward the rack where everybody stows their bikes. It takes her a second to remember that she doesn't have a bike anymore, that it's still back in her parents' house, leaning against the garage wall. Too bad, really—it would make the trip back and forth from work much easier.

But why should her life be any easier anyway?

She heads off campus and onto the street. Just two blocks and she'll be in the park. Somehow the trees make her feel better.

But not good enough, she thinks as she pats her bag. *Never good enough.*

Without a bike it takes about twenty minutes to walk to her brother's apartment. Her brother, his wife, Cathy, and their baby daughter's apartment. It's not such a bad place. David, Cathy, and Isabelle live downstairs and she has David's old office, the maid's room at the top. It's much better than it sounds, actually. Her room is very small, but kind of special, like something out of a fairy tale, or a movie about Paris. It's got a great view of the park, and Cathy made it pretty just for her, hanging lace curtains and painting the walls a pale apple green, not that Willow really cares about things like that anymore.

"Which way are you going?"

Willow whips around in alarm. She had no idea that Guy was behind her. Has he been following her? Hoping to hear more, maybe get her to tell him some juicy details?

"Are you headed toward the park?" he asks, his steps falling into place beside hers. "I always walk that way."

Willow wants to ask him what he knows about her, but she's not quite sure how. She wants to ask him if he was deliberately stringing her along before, or if he truly didn't recognize her at first. She supposes that it's possible—after all, she didn't recognize him. But she's been lost in her own world. Nothing makes any kind of impression on her these days. As the new girl in school, she's bound to be noticed, even if she didn't come with a scarlet letter *K* embroidered on her chest.

"Hey, Guy, hold up!" a tall dark-haired student calls to Guy from across the street. He hurries over, a pile of books under his arm.

"Adrian, what are you doing up here?" Guy stops for a second.

"Looking into some AP stuff." Adrian glances back and forth between Willow and Guy.

"Oh, sorry, Adrian this is Willow. She goes to our school."

"Oh yeah?" Adrian smiles at her. "Are you new? I haven't seen you around before."

"Yes. I'm new," Willow says. She looks at him carefully. He seems like he's being straight with her, and she feels a little better. Maybe she doesn't stand out quite as much as she thought she did.

"We should definitely talk if you're thinking of taking classes here. I've already picked out a couple of possibilities." Guy hands Adrian a piece of paper scribbled all over with course numbers and descriptions.

"Yeah, you know, I probably should take one of these."

Adrian glances at the paper. "But on the other hand, the idea of a really easy senior year is pretty appealing."

The spotlight's off of her. Willow breathes a sigh of relief. She should go now, while the going's good.

"Listen, I have to get out of here." She offers a glimpse of a smile.

"Oh, sure. Adrian, I'll call you later." To Willow's surprise, Guy says good-bye to his friend and continues walking with her. "So, where are you off to now?"

"I'm going home." Even as she says the words, Willow is struck by how misleading they are. Her brother's apartment may be her home now, but it doesn't feel like it. It doesn't feel like it at all.

"Want to stop on the way and get some coffee?" Guy asks.

No.

She does not want any coffee. She wants to be alone. Still, Willow can't help thinking that any of her friends from back home would be thrilled to have someone like Guy ask them out. She wonders how she would have felt if he made the offer, say a year ago. Would she have been flattered? Would she have liked the idea? Would she have liked *him*? Willow squints trying to see herself as she'd been the fall before. *Of course* she would have liked him. Why not? Cute and reads books too. Too bad last year's girl is dead.

"So how about it?" He shifts his backpack to his left shoulder and flashes her a smile. "There's a great place a few blocks from here. Best cappuccino you've ever had, and the pastries aren't bad either."

First coffee, then a movie. Then a few more walks in the park. Willow knows how this kind of thing works. Then *feelings.* Just the thought of it makes her flesh crawl. She's done with feelings. She doesn't ever want to feel anything again.

"No thank you." Even to her own ears her voice sounds cold and unfriendly. Perfect.

Guy shrugs. He looks a little disappointed.

Life's full of disappointments, Guy. Willow kicks a stone out of her path.

"Okay, sure, maybe another time." But he doesn't say goodbye, he just keeps walking alongside her.

Why doesn't he go away? Willow thinks fretfully. *Maybe he likes what he's been hearing. Maybe he just likes a challenge.*

She wonders briefly what he would think if he saw the blade marks on her arm. Would that be enough of a challenge for him? She's never shown anyone, and he certainly won't be the first. Still, how can she get rid of him?

"So how come you're living with your brother?" Guy asks. "Are your parents on sabbatical? Because I remember your brother saying that they were in the field too." He smiles again, completely unaware of the effect he's having on her.

Is he like Adrian? He really knows nothing about her? Or is it that he wants to hear her say the words?

In any case, he's given her an out. She knows how to get rid of him now.

"They're not on sabbatical." Willow's voice is hard. She stops walking and turns to face Guy head-on. She looks him straight in the eye. So closely, she can see the brown flecks in among the hazel. His eyes are beautiful, but that hardly matters to her. He returns her gaze. He's not smiling now, but looking at her just as deeply. Anyone passing by would take them for a romantic young couple. They must make a pretty picture as they stand facing each other under the leafy bower of trees.

"But your parents are profs, right?" He breaks the silence. "Your father's in anthro and your mother's an archaeologist? Because I once went—"

"They're dead." Willow says the words coolly, dispassionately. She enjoys seeing Guy's face turn pale. "They're dead," she repeats just to make sure he gets it. "And I'm the one who killed them."

CHAPTER THREE

How come you're living with your brother?

But your parents are profs, right? Because I once went . . .

Guy's questions ring in her ears. His pleasant voice is distorted by memory into something querulous and insistent.

But your parents are profs, right? Because I once went . . .

All right, all right, set it to music already!

Willow rolls onto her stomach, the book she's been trying to read for the past half hour tumbles to the floor as she buries her face in the pillow in a vain attempt to shut out the chattering in her head.

But it's useless. His questions keep repeating themselves and far, far worse than any question he could think to ask, is her own response:

I'm the one who killed them.

How many times throughout the coming years will she be called upon to say those words?

She can barely even remember it. It was raining, that's all

she knows. They'd been out to dinner and her parents had wanted to have a second bottle of wine, so they decided that Willow should be the one to drive. She remembers her father tossing her the keys, the slickness of the road, and the sound of the windshield wipers.

Sometimes in her dreams she hears the sound of the rain.

Willow turns her head listlessly to look out the window. There's a faint breeze stirring the lace curtains. The dying rays of the sun filter through them and make beautiful patterns on the floor.

The view outside her window is particularly nice, and if she could bring herself to be interested in anything, it would be that. In the morning and evening the park is filled with joggers. In the afternoon young mothers take over and there are always plenty of lovers winding their way down the leaf-strewn paths. It's like a living painting. Back before the accident, when she used to care about things, Willow used to spend a lot of time doing watercolors. Back then she would have liked nothing more than to sit by this window for hours and try to capture the changing scene outside.

Willow glances over at her desk, at the box of watercolors and assortment of brushes that Cathy bought for her. Like her bike, like most of her things, she'd left her painting supplies at home. It was incredibly thoughtful of Cathy to replace them for her, and she should repay that thoughtfulness, by at least attempting to use them, but somehow she can't summon the energy.

Of course Cathy has been kind in so many ways. She'd worked hard to make this room nice for Willow, and with its soft colors and pretty furniture, it is especially lovely. Far nicer than anything she had at home. At home she'd moved into David's old room because it was the biggest. The walls were black, a leftover from his heavy metal days, and Willow and her mother had always promised each other that they'd get around to changing them.

Who knew that four black walls could feel so safe?

Willow sits up abruptly, opens the window, and sticks her head out. The air is soft with just the slightest breeze that ruffles the hair around her face. This is her favorite time of day, just before the evening becomes the night.

If she were back home now, she'd probably be talking on the phone with one of her friends. That's the way things usually went: She used to hang out with her friends after school, come home and get her work done, gossip on the phone before dinner, or maybe, if she didn't have a lot of homework, go for a bike ride on the trails behind her house.

Now the pattern of her days is different. She sleepwalks through school, has no friends to speak of, goes to the library, tries and *fails* to do her homework, and eats whatever Cathy orders in—all to the accompaniment of the razor.

She's left her old friends behind as surely as she's left her old life. They all belong to another world, one she has no intention of visiting again. She never takes their calls, deletes their e-mails, and one by one they've all stopped trying to get in touch with her. The only person who still makes an effort to contact her is Markie, her best friend, and Willow knows that it will only take a few more unanswered messages before she too stops trying.

She shuts the window with a sigh. If she does nothing else, she should at least make an effort with her homework.

Willow picks up the book she'd been reading. *Bulfinch's Mythology*. She's supposed to get through fifty pages for tomorrow. After that she has to get started on a paper for the same class. It should be easy too. The book is one she's read a thousand times before. She flutters the pages of the cheap paperback as she recalls the first edition that used to rest on her father's desk, the flyleaf inscribed by him in his favorite deep blue ink.

Of course it's probably still there. The house stands just as it did, it hasn't even gone on the market yet.

At first Willow had thought that she would be staying there, that David, Cathy, and Isabelle would join her. In some ways it would make the most sense. After all, this cozy apartment, while just the right size for two adults and an infant, feels somewhat cramped now that she's moved in. But David had vetoed the idea from the start, claiming the commute would be too difficult. Willow's parents took the train in for over twenty years, but that was only twice a week, and while David's teaching schedule is similar, Cathy's job would require her to make the trip every day.

Still, as uncomfortable as things sometimes get, Willow has to agree with her brother. Although their house may be large and roomy, living there would be far from easy, and not because of the traveling involved. The house is simply too crowded with memories and reminders. It is too crowded with ghosts.

She's only been there a handful of times since the accident. The first occasion had been when David wanted to pack up their parents' books and move them to the apartment. That had proved to be a disastrous idea, which they abandoned before they even got halfway through. In fact, that excursion had affected David so badly that he refused to enter the house again. So the next time they went, he and Cathy waited outside in the car, while Willow, feeling like a refugee, a displaced person, fleeing her country for unknown territory, had run around grabbing whatever clothes would fit into her backpack. Now she wishes that she had taken the time to think about what she was packing. Her bag hadn't held much, and she's constantly borrowing things from Cathy anyway. Wouldn't she have been better off taking some of the books that she cared about instead of three pairs of jeans, a couple of shirts, and a skirt? She would love to be reading her father's copy of *Bulfinch* instead of this flimsy paperback that she bought at one of the chain bookstores around the city.

Willow doesn't know why her throat hurts. She can't understand the way her eyes are prickling all of a sudden.

It's just a book!

She throws the paperback across the room, where it hits the wall before landing on the floor with its pages all askew.

"Mouka touka hashatouka . . ."

Willow is stunned. Her face turns white and she grips the corner of the candlewick bedspread as her mother's voice floats up the stairs. It takes her a moment, then she realizes that it's Cathy singing to Isabelle. David must have taught her the song, an old Russian lullaby that their mother used to sing to them.

She gets up from the bed and walks into the bathroom to splash some cold water on her face. She stares in the mirror for a few seconds, looking at herself as if she were a stranger.

Who is this?

She supposes that to anyone else she looks exactly the same as she always did, except for her hair, that is. She doesn't have the energy or inclination to fuss with it like she once did, so she just wears it in a braid that hangs halfway down her back.

But *she* doesn't recognize herself. Maybe her face isn't any different, but the look in her eyes is. Worse than dead, their expression is simply blank. She reaches out a hand to cover them in the mirror. She remembers the reflection that used to stare back at her. Those eyes weren't dead.

Willow had never known that she used to be happy. It had simply never occurred to her that her life had all that she would ever need or want.

The one thing that can make Willow laugh these days is how much she used to take things for granted. In the past, little hurts, like doing badly in school, or getting dumped by a guy, really used to throw her. How was she to know what was lying in store for her? She shakes her head at how foolish she used to be, getting upset because her favorite dress got lost at the cleaners, or something equally stupid.

Stupid!

She has an urge suddenly to smash her head against the mirror. Wipe that silly expression off her face. She knows she can't, though. Not here, not now. Not with Cathy downstairs, and David just coming in the door.

Instead, she regards herself calmly, then screws up her mouth and spits at her reflection with as much venom as she can muster.

Willow knows she's being melodramatic, but so what? The

spit trails down the mirror and she's confronted, once again, by a pair of dead eyes.

Who are you?

This isn't the Willow that she's lived inside for the past seventeen years. This is someone else.

A killer.

A cutter.

Willow turns away from the mirror. Spitting at herself. That's juvenile, straight out of a B movie, and really, accomplishes nothing. But cutting, that's something else again.

She stares down at her arms for a moment. If someone were to look carefully, the angry red marks underneath the fine cotton of her blouse would be clearly visible. But nobody ever does look carefully.

She rolls up her sleeves and examines the most accessible cuts, then opens the medicine cabinet and takes out a tube of disinfectant. She's scrupulously careful not to let her wounds get infected. She doesn't need the complications. Already Cathy's been giving her strange looks. She keeps asking why Willow wants to borrow long-sleeved shirts when it's such a beautiful, mild Indian summer. She doesn't understand that Willow, who used to be so concerned with what she wore, now selects her outfits with one criterion only: Will her clothes cover her scars?

Taking care of her stuff isn't the easy task it once was either. She can't just toss her dirty things into the communal laundry hamper. The other day she had to bury one of her own bloodstained blouses in the park. She simply can't risk leaving things like that around. Losing the shirt didn't bother her, but she hated digging around in the dirt. Later on, when she was walking home, she was sure that she saw a Rottweiler playing with it.

Willow hears the phone ring. It's just about Markie's favorite time to call. Quickly, without thinking, she reaches behind her and turns on the shower.

"Willow?" Cathy calls. "Phone for you! Markie."

She leans out the bathroom door. "Yeah, sorry, I'm in the shower!"

That should take care of that. She leaves the shower running, takes off her jeans and shirt, and sitting down on the floor of the bathroom, she spreads some of the antiseptic cream on a particularly nasty-looking cut.

It takes a while, at least ten minutes, but finally she is done ministering to her wounds.

"Willow?" David calls. "Dinner!"

"Coming," Willow calls back as she turns off the shower. She puts her clothes on, wincing a little as her jeans stick to the cream. Of course it would make much more sense to bandage all of them, but the gauze would look too bulky under her clothes.

"Hey." She tries to look lively as she enters the kitchen.

"God, your hair dries fast." Cathy smiles at her.

"Oh, yeah, uhh . . . Shower cap, didn't even bother to unbraid it." Willow smiles in return. It's something of an effort. Just the thought of sitting down and eating dinner is more than enough to wear her out completely, because it's the one time of day that she can be sure of coming face-to-face with the only other surviving member of her family.

It shouldn't be like this. Seeing her brother should be the lone bright spot in the otherwise bleak landscape that is her life, and yet it simply isn't so. Because somehow, that rainy night last March didn't just end her parents' lives. Somehow—as surely as if he had been in the car with them—she lost her brother that night too.

This feeling is with her always. Their relationship has been so fractured that for all intents and purposes she could be living with a stranger. In a way it is almost more difficult to bear than the loss of her parents, they are dead and gone forever. But to be in constant contact with her brother, to the person that she was once closest with, to the single person spared her—to see him, talk to him, and yet have no connection with him whatsoever is more painful than she could possibly have imagined.

Sometimes Willow tries to convince herself that things will return to normal between them. After all, there have been times in the past when they didn't get along. He is ten years older than she is, and that age difference hasn't always made for an easy relationship.

Willow thinks back to when she was five and he was fifteen. Back then David didn't like having a little sister. He wanted to be out doing his own thing instead of babysitting, and Willow hadn't liked him much either. But things had changed as they got older. Sometime around when she turned ten or eleven, things had evened out somehow, he'd become her confidant, her friend, her protector. Suddenly it had been fun to have a brother who was so much her senior.

If Willow tries hard enough, she can pretend, for moments at a time, that she isn't living with David, that she is merely visiting the way she might have last year, say whenever her parents' attention threatened to become suffocating, when their involvement in her life felt oppressive rather than comforting. At times like that she would stay with David and Cathy for the weekend, much to the envy of all her friends.

Willow spends a lot of time thinking about those weekends, about what things had been like then. David had just been finishing graduate school. He and Cathy had been about to become parents. Everything had seemed perfect.

But Willow has smashed her brother's picture-perfect life as surely as she smashed her parents' car. Cathy didn't want to go back to work. She *had* to go back instead of staying at home with Isabelle like she had planned to. Instead of preparing for his classes, David has to worry about money all the time. He has to worry about how he's going to make ends meet. He has to worry about Willow.

In many ways this is a burden that he appears to accept easily. He is so strong, so considerate, so capable, his treatment of her is so unfailingly correct that to the outside observer it must seem as if nothing is amiss. He is absurdly polite to her, it as if she is a stranger whose welfare has been entrusted to him, and he handles that responsibility with the utmost seriousness. But there is a wall of glass between them.

David never, *never* talks about the accident. His conversations with her are limited to the minutiae of her daily life. Even when they are forced to discuss logistical things, like how much of her library salary has to go toward household expenses, or when they should put their parents' house on the market, he manages to avoid any suggestion of how it is that they've found themselves in such an extraordinary situation.

At first Willow was sure that it was just a matter of time. That David would eventually confront her. She kept waiting for him to yell at her, scream, shake her, do anything but treat her with such aloof courtesy. But as the months wore on, it became increasingly clear to her that he had no intention of ever talking about what had happened.

She doesn't feel like she can broach the subject on her own either. If David doesn't want to talk about it, it can only be because of how painful the topic is, and Willow refuses, absolutely refuses, to hurt him more than she already has.

Still, his coldness toward her upsets her terribly; it is the worst condemnation that she could endure. And yet she is fully in accord with his assessment of her: She is no longer his little sister, she is their parents' murderer. Why should she expect any other treatment? Why should she even expect him to be as kind as he is?

"How was school today?" David asks as she sits down. Cathy passes her a cardboard container of cold sesame noodles. Obviously tonight is Chinese.

"Fine," Willow says. She dumps some of the noodles onto her plate with a sigh. She knows that that answer isn't good enough, that David expects a complete and full accounting of everything that she did, but she's so tired of lying to him, she just doesn't have the strength anymore. She stares down at her plate. The noodles look like worms.

"Uh-huh. Well, I don't really know what *fine* means. Why don't you tell me what's going on in your classes? Didn't you just have a quiz in French? How did that go?"

A quiz? The only thing Willow can remember about French class is seeing that other girl with the scratches on her arm—that, and the fact that she'd run out of class so that she could indulge in her extracurricular activities.

But she can hardly tell David about *that.*

Oh right, the quiz. . . . They did have one the other day, Willow realizes. She must have mentioned it to David at one of their nightly grilling sessions.

"We . . . I didn't get it back yet. I answered everything, at least." This happens to be true, but it was the merest stroke of good luck that she'd been able to finish the quiz, given that she'd barely even opened the textbook.

"All right." He nods thoughtfully. "What about your other classes? Is there anything special I should know about?"

Sigh.

Willow wishes that Cathy would interrupt him, change the subject somehow, but she's busy feeding the baby some noxious-looking concoction, so Willow has no choice but to answer.

"No—well, I do have this paper to do for that class I'm taking with the *Bulfinch*. . . . You know, the one about myths and heroes. . . ."

"Well, that should be easy enough for you," David says. "Do you have a topic picked out already? When is it due?"

"Uh . . . no. No topic, not yet. . . ." Willow avoids his eyes. She has a topic, all right, and not one of her own choosing. How can she tell her brother that the teacher has asked her to write about the themes of loss and redemption as shown in the relationship between Demeter and Persephone? She can't, she just can't look him in the eyes and talk to him about another motherless child. "It's not due for three weeks anyway, so I have some time to come up with one. . . ."

"What about the library? How was that today? Any better? Is Miss Hamilton being nicer to you? Do you want me to talk to her?"

"No! I mean, thank you, but no. She's fine, really. . . ."

An idea occurs to Willow. David wants to know how things went at the library? Maybe she should tell him about that guy she met, well, *Guy*, in fact. She wonders if possibly, just *possibly*, his reaction to this piece of news will be different from the way he responds to her daily recitations regarding school and homework. The responsibility of being in charge of her education may be new to him, but this kind of thing, well . . .

Willow remembers a time last year when she went to meet David at one of his classes. A fellow graduate student, not realizing that she was a sophomore in high school, had asked her out. Their father had not been at all amused, but David had thought it was hilarious.

"I . . . I met someone in the library who was in one of your classes last year." Willow says this tentatively. She's floating the idea out there, kind of like a test balloon. She wants to see how he'll take it. She wants to believe that somehow, some way, he's capable of unbending toward her, and that perhaps, talking about the kind of thing he used to tease her about might just be the key.

"Really?" Cathy says. She sounds interested and she glances at Willow as she continues unsuccessfully to try to get Isabelle to eat. "What was their name?"

"Male or female?" David says at the same time. He looks at her over the rim of his glass. His tone is anything but lighthearted.

Oh boy. . . .

"It's a guy. . . . Well, actually, his name *is* Guy. I thought that was kind of funny."

And nice too. It's a nice name.

"Guy?" David is thoughtful. "I think I remember Guy—he's still in high school, isn't he? I guess that's all right. . . ."

Oh for God's sake!

"He was taking my class to get some college credit," David continues. "He's very smart, and a lot more hardworking than most of the regular students I get. Believe me, I wish I had more like him. So what did he have to say for himself?"

Now that sounds a little bit like the brother she used to know. Maybe this was a good idea after all, except even as she thinks this, Willow realizes that she herself is no longer capable of lighthearted conversation. How can she even answer such an innocuous question? What can she possibly say?

He asked why I was living with you and I told him that I killed Mom and Dad.

Of course they did talk about other things, but those topics are also off limits. Maybe last year Willow would have felt free to tell David that Guy likes that bookstore downtown, but now she can't. She can't because any mention of that place—which David loves—would trigger too many memories of their father. He was the one who had first taken them there.

"Umm, I think he said that we looked alike. . . ." Willow looks at her brother in despair. It's impossible not to notice how tired he is, how worn, how empty his own eyes are.

She wishes so much that she could take that emptiness away.

But then she remembers something else Guy said. Something that it *won't* hurt her brother to hear, and she grasps at it like a lifeline.

"Oh, you know what, I almost forgot." She tries to sound enthusiastic. "He thought that you were a great professor, I mean, he kind of went on about that." It's not much, it won't bring their parents back, it won't make his life easier in any appreciable way, but it's the best she has to offer.

"Really?" David says slowly. Maybe he's not bowled over by the news, but he does seem a little interested, his eyes look a little less dead.

"Really." Willow is emphatic. She tries to think of something else to say. Some way that she can elaborate, expand the compliment. "I think he said that he was seriously thinking of going into anthropology, I mean, major in it when he gets to college. He said that your class had convinced him that's what he should be doing."

Of course he'd said nothing of the kind. Willow has no idea what he wants to do. And anyway, if anything had influenced him, it was *Tristes Tropiques*, not her brother. But still, she can't help feeling a glimmer of satisfaction as she watches David's expression change.

"Oh come on!" Cathy exclaims suddenly. She puts the spoon and the jar of baby food down in frustration. "I can't get her to eat anything."

"Well, what do you expect?" David asks as he picks up the jar and examines it closely. "Organic strained peas? Who *would* like that? She has good taste, that's all." He gets up and lifts Isabelle out of her high chair. "Wouldn't you rather have some spare ribs?" he asks the baby.

"Oh David, please!" Cathy gives him a look.

"Okay, I'm not being serious. But how about ice cream? She can eat that, can't she? There's nothing wrong with ice cream—we even have some too."

"There's a lot wrong with it," Cathy says, exasperated.

"But you'd like it, wouldn't you?" He holds Isabelle above his head as he talks to her. "I can tell that you're going to be a girl who likes her chocolate ice cream. Oh c'mon." David turns back to Cathy. "It would be kind of fun to see if she likes it."

Willow isn't jealous of her niece, not exactly, and she certainly has no desire for her brother to talk to her the way he does to an infant. But as she watches the way that David plays with Isabelle, as she sees his face finally light up, it is borne in on her, for perhaps the thousandth time, that she has *lost* her brother.

❋

Willow pushes the *Bulfinch* away listlessly. It's one in the morning and in spite of the fact that she's been sitting at her desk for the past four hours, she's managed to accomplish almost nothing. Not only has she gotten no work done, not only is she too restless to fall asleep, but she's starving, hardly surprising since she barely touched anything at dinner earlier.

Maybe she should go downstairs and get something to eat, maybe then she'll be able to focus on her work. She gets up from her chair, walks to the door and opens it a crack. The apartment is completely dark. Good. Willow steals down the stairs slowly, careful not to make a sound. But as she nears the bottom she is dismayed to see that she is not, after all, alone. David is in the kitchen, sitting at the table surrounded by dozens of papers. He's extinguished all of the lights but one.

Well, she has no desire to go into the kitchen now. She can only imagine how uncomfortable it would be for both of them, but as much as she wants to go back upstairs, she can't help staring at her brother. There's something not quite right about the way that he's sitting there.

David's head is in his hands. Is it because he's laughing? But what would he be laughing about? She's heard him complain about grading undergraduate papers enough to know that he doesn't consider it the most amusing task. Besides, he's hardly making any noise. And then Willow realizes why his shoulders are shaking that way, and the reason is so shocking, so disturbing that it literally takes her breath away. She barely has the strength to stand.

Her brother is crying, he is wretched and broken. Though his sobs are barely audible, he is weeping with absolute and total abandon. She's never seen him like this. She's never seen *anyone* like this. Such a naked display of emotion is both alarming and frightening.

Willow clutches the banister with an unsteady hand and lowers herself to sit down on the stairs. She knows what she's doing is wrong, that she should allow David his privacy. But she feels compelled to watch.

Willow stares at him in astonishment. She herself could never do such a thing, she could never give way to her grief like this. Willow wonders if she should go to him. But she knows she can't. Because she is the one who has put him in this position, it is her actions that have given him this pain.

As she's thinking this, Cathy comes up behind David. He doesn't see her, but Willow does. Her dark hair flows down her back, interrupted by the pink shawl that she's thrown on over her nightgown.

Cathy wraps her arms around David. Without turning, he grips her forearms, pulling her closer.

Willow is transfixed. The longing and need that are stamped across David's face are riveting. She watches as Cathy holds him tighter, as tightly as possible, then bends her head to kiss him.

Willow feels like a moth, inexorably drawn to the flame. How would it feel to cry like that? How would it feel to be comforted like that?

If she let herself, she'd drown in a world of pain. But she can't let that happen, she simply wouldn't be able to handle it, not *that* kind of pain. Thankfully she knows how to prevent such a thing.

Willow reaches into the pocket of her robe, feeling for what she knows is there.

She never takes her eyes off of them as she slices into her flesh. The blade bites so deeply that she almost swoons, but still, she never stops looking at David and Cathy.

Her blood spouts as voluptuously as David's tears. It drips unchecked, down her arm and onto the floor as Willow watches Cathy dry David's eyes with her long, long hair.

Willow knows that she should leave. At any moment they could look up. But she can't leave, she can't move. She can only slice deeper and deeper.

The razor doesn't hurt her. Not really.

Not like some things could, anyway. Willow savagely swipes at her wrist.

Not like some things could.

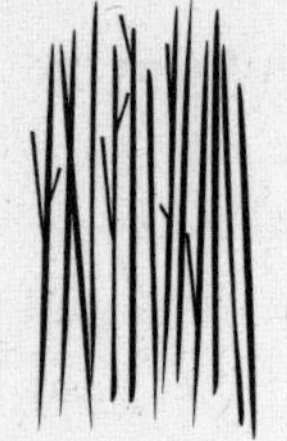

CHAPTER FOUR

Willow leans back against the linden tree in the school garden and closes her book with a deep sigh. She's been trying to read for the past half hour, but it's hopeless. She just can't focus. Instead of seeing the pages in front of her, she just keeps seeing her poor brother.

She's afraid of what will happen the next time they talk. Will her face give her away? She knows that he wouldn't have wanted her to witness that scene. There was something so profoundly . . . well, *intimate* is the only word she can think of—something so intimate, both about his misery and the way that Cathy comforted him.

For once it had been a relief to go to school in the morning. She'd left the house extra early just to avoid running into either of them, hoping that if she didn't have to confront David's red-eyed face over the breakfast table, then she'd be able to forget about what she saw.

Yeah, right!

Missing breakfast had accomplished nothing beyond an empty stomach. Because in spite of the fact that it's a beautiful day, in spite of the fact that she has a free period with nothing else to do but sit outside and read, she simply can't stop thinking about David. She'd known that he was in pain, *of course* she'd known, but to see him like that . . .

Even now she can hardly believe it happened. Since the accident, David has been so contained, so reserved, that to witness him in such a state, shattered and broken, well, it still doesn't seem credible.

Her stomach turns a little as she thinks of how she'd tried to cheer him up over the dinner table with some manufactured compliments. How could she have been so naive, so stupid? How could she think that anything she had to offer, anything that she could give, could help him after the horror that she's put him through?

She hates herself for what she's done to him. But even more than that, she hates herself for being so selfish. Because, after seeing his breakdown, she knows that her primary concern should be for him. But instead all she can think of is that if he can let go like that . . .

Then why is he always so cold and distant with me?

Willow looks up, momentarily distracted as a group of students come into the garden. She recognizes a few of them from some of her classes.

"Hey Willow, what's going on?" one of the girls calls over to her.

"Not much." Willow smiles a little at the other girl. Her

name is Claudia. Willow doesn't know much else about her, but she does know that this girl has been friendly to her once or twice before, and she is grateful for her kindness.

"You want to hang out with us?" Claudia sits down on the grass. She tilts her head to one side and gives Willow a pleasant smile.

No. Willow does not want to join them. She wants to stay under the linden tree and try to read. But she hasn't had much luck with that, and anyway, how can she say no? Claudia's being friendly, it would look odd to reject the overture, and she has a bad feeling that she looks *plenty* odd already.

Willow gets to her feet and slowly walks over to the group. She's a little unsure of what to do or say to these girls. If this had been a year ago, she wouldn't have even waited to be asked. It would have been the most natural thing in the world to go right over to Claudia and introduce herself to everyone else. But now . . . It's not that she's shy exactly, it's more that she doesn't know how to behave around people anymore.

There's something else too, she thinks, as Claudia shifts to make room for her. She wonders if this invitation is as innocent as it seems. Everyone knows that there's something different about her. Well, aside from everything else, she's new, and by itself that's enough to raise questions, even of the most innocent kind. But Willow is sure that the interest she's aroused is more sinister than that. There *must* be a million rumors floating around. There have to be some people who know what happened. There have to be some people who know she lost her parents. There have to be some people who know she *killed* her parents. So far nobody's asked her anything directly, but she can tell that they all want to know her story.

It's hard for Willow not to feel anxious as she sits there. By joining them she's opening the door. Any moment now and the questions she's been dreading could start. So instead of relaxing and enjoying the sunshine and the innocent chatter of the other girls, she waits, tense, to see what will happen.

"If I get into my first choice I'm coloring my hair red," the brunette sitting next to her says.

"Excuse me if I don't get the connection," another girl responds. Willow recognizes this one. This girl *is* already a redhead, she's the one that Willow had been staring at so intently the other day, right before her spectacular pratfall. She's the one with the scratch on her arm. The one that Willow thought might have been a kindred spirit. "And anyway," the redhead continues. "Why do you want to change your color?"

"Well . . ." The brunette lies back on the grass and shields her eyes with a baseball cap. "If I get into my first choice, my parents will be so happy that they won't care if I color my hair, and besides, I like red hair. You should be flattered."

"Yeah Kristen, it's so attention getting." This is from Claudia.

"Did you bring anything to eat?" the brunette under the baseball cap says. Willow can see her name written on one of the books that rests by her side: Laurie.

"I have a day-old Luna bar somewhere," Kristen says, and roots around in her bag.

"Thanks, but I'll pass." Laurie laughs.

"What about you. It's Willow, right?" Laurie lifts the

baseball cap off of one eye and looks at her. "I don't suppose you have anything more appetizing, do you?"

"No, I . . . Nothing . . ." Willow trails off.

"You want to cut out and go for croissants?" Claudia glances at her watch.

"I don't have enough time." Kristen shakes her head. She looks at Willow to see what she has to say about the matter.

Willow tries to smile, but it comes out sort of funny. More like a grimace. She avoids Kristen's gaze and stares at her shoes instead.

"So Willow," Claudia says, fanning herself with her notebook. "What classes are you in, besides history, I mean." She and Willow share fourth-period history.

"Oh, who cares?" Laurie complains from underneath the baseball cap. "I mean, no offense, Willow, but I've had it up to here with school." She makes a slashing motion with her hand at the base of her throat. "You're not a senior, are you? School is all I think about these days. Where will I go next year? What should I do for my last semester of extracurricular to look good on my transcript? I've had it. Can't we just gossip or something?"

"Just making conversation," Claudia says mildly. She nudges Laurie with her boot. "I was trying to be *polite,* you know, Laurie, find out about *Willow.*"

"Oh sure." Laurie nods. "Don't think I'm not interested in you, Willow. I'm dying to know if you think I'd look better as a redhead."

But Willow is saved from answering this by the real redhead—Kristen.

"Oh, c'mon Laurie, you're *always* up for talking about this kind of stuff. You're just over it now because your first choice is already a missile lock. You've got the highest SATs of anyone I know." Kristen has found the Luna bar and bites into it. "You've got *nothing* to worry about."

"That's not all it's about," Laurie protests. "I'm not a legacy at any of my top choices. These days it's about a lot more than just grades and scores."

"Kristen's right, Laurie," Claudia says. "Your scores are so good that those other things don't matter. Besides, you've done so much other stuff it's like the Pope sprinkled holy water on your transcript. I'm the one in trouble here." She frowns for a second as she gathers her hair into a ponytail. "I mean, not only are my scores not that great, but what else have I done?"

"Maybe you should retake the SATs," Laurie suggests. "What about you, Willow? Are you taking any prep courses this year?"

"They're so worth it." Kristen nods.

Willow knows that she should say something. Anything. She feels more and more uncomfortable sitting there and not joining in, but what *can* she say? An SAT prep course? Nothing could seem less important.

Of course, if things hadn't changed so much for her she probably would be thinking about taking an SAT prep course. But things have changed. College? How about the moon? If she's thought about life after high school at all, it's only been to wonder whether David will have put the house on the market by the time she graduates—otherwise they won't be able to pay for college.

There's an enormous gulf that separates her from these girls. She knows, because she used to be on the other side along with them. She wishes—desperately—that she could connect with them, but she's simply forgotten how.

Willow casts about for something, *anything,* to say. Then Kristen crumples up the Luna bar wrapper and stretches out her arm to put it in her bag. For a second the red mark that Willow saw the other day is visible.

"Are you a cut—" Willow blurts out before she can stop herself. Her voice is much too loud, but even worse . . .

What am I saying??

"I mean, are you a cut—"

God almighty!!

Can she save this? They're all looking at her expectantly, she's got to do *something.*

Cut, cutters, cutting, what the hell can she spin out of *cut*?? Willow looks around at them, looks at Kristen and remembers. . . .

"I mean a *cat* . . . A cat person . . ."

Better than cutter, but just barely.

"What I mean is . . ." Willow pauses and closes her eyes for a second. If she stays like that, will they all just get up and go away? Forget it. She doesn't have that kind of luck, she'd better just finish this thing. "Do you . . . Do you . . ."

What?? Does she what??

"Do you have a kitten?" she finally manages after a few more seconds. The girls look at her in stupefaction.

Good God!

Willow can feel that her face is flaming. To think, she'd only sat down with them because she hadn't wanted to seem strange!

"No," Kristen says after a few moments. "I'm way too

allergic. Which reminds me." She turns to Laurie. "That lotion you told me to try gave me the worst rash." She rolls her sleeve up all the way and starts to rub her arm vigorously, and Willow can see that the mark she'd been so fascinated by is in fact *just a scratch.* Absolutely nothing more. Most probably brought on by the way Kristen is irritating her skin. Even as she watches, the other girl clearly raises a welt or two. Unlike the cuts that score Willow's arm, this girl's abrasions are perfectly innocent. She is no more a kindred spirit than anyone else in this little group. Than anyone else *anywhere*. "How come you want to know if I have a kitten?" Kristen fixes her shirt and looks at Willow. "Were you . . . Were you maybe thinking of getting one?" She says this slowly, as if she were talking to someone who doesn't speak the language very well. She's trying to be nice, but clearly, she thinks that Willow is an idiot.

Even worse, it's hard to miss the bemused glances that the other girls are sharing.

"Well," says Laurie. She removes the baseball cap and rolls over to rest her head on her hand. "My sister volunteers at a pet shelter if you need me to set you up with a kitten."

Willow nods. She can tell they all think she's weird. They'll try to be nice, offer to help with kittens, but behind her back they'll roll their eyes and thank God that they're not crazy like she is. Maybe they'll tell other people that they've hung out with the new girl. No, they don't know the whole story, but she is *strange,* all right. . . . Maybe they'll add a few rumors of their own.

"Excuse me." Willow scrambles to her feet. She can't sit there with them anymore. "I have to . . ." To what? She can't think of anything to say. But it doesn't really matter. Is it her imagination, or do they look relieved to see her go? The invitation had only been out of politeness anyway.

"See you in history," Willow manages.

"Right." Claudia nods.

Willow moves as fast as she can out of the garden and into the building.

She still has some time before her next class. But she doesn't know where she should go. Neither the library nor the cafeteria holds any appeal.

She doesn't know where she should go, but she knows what she wants to do, all right.

She's a little worried about the practicalities of it, though. Her arms have so many marks on them—you could almost play connect the dots. She's going to have to wait until some of the cuts heal before she can start working there again. What about her legs? She's wearing jeans—can she even get to her legs? If she does it on her stomach, will her sweater stick to it? Willow shakes her head. She should have planned for eventualities like this. Tomorrow she'll wear a button-down shirt.

Still, as desperate as she is, just thinking about the details helps to calm her down, makes her forget the embarrassment of what just happened, of how awful she sounded when she asked about the kitten. It almost makes her forget how sad it is that she *won't* be taking a stupid SAT prep course.

Willow heads for the bathroom with a sense of purpose, but she's in for a letdown, because the bathroom isn't empty. Two girls are smoking in there. Another illicit activity, only much more acceptable.

Willow isn't quite sure what to do. She could wait until they leave, but there's no knowing how long that will take. As

Willow considers this, the girl closest to her stubs out her cigarette in the sink and lights up another one.

"Want one?" she asks, offering the pack to Willow.

Willow shakes her head. She knows how ironic this is, she might as well smoke, why not? But cigarettes, while damaging, are pleasurable too, and besides . . .

Nicotine, that takes years before it hurts . . .

She backs out the door and it swings shut behind her. Willow looks up and down the hall, which is blessedly empty.

Willow starts walking. She doesn't know where she's headed, she's not even sure where this particular hall leads to, she just knows that she has to move, or she'll explode.

She's moving faster and faster, her legs hurt, she realizes suddenly that she's running, hurtling down the hall, rules be damned. Her ribs ache, both from the labored breaths that she just manages to draw and the way that her backpack is slapping against her shoulder.

But that's good. All of that is good. Not as good as a razor would be, but uncomfortable enough to distract her.

Unfortunately, the halls are only so long, and Willow only has so much stamina. She's furious, *furious* when she reaches a dead end and she finds herself staring at a brick wall. If it weren't such a cliché she'd start pounding the brick with her fists.

If it weren't such a cliché, and bruised hands weren't so hard to hide.

Instead she collapses against the wall, her lungs screaming, even if she herself is silent, and tries to focus on how badly her ribs hurt, on whether or not running that way opened up some of the cuts on her legs.

She moves one sneakered foot gingerly up and down her calf, rubbing, feeling if there are any open sores.

A hit! Willow looks down. A small bloodstain is creeping through the denim of her jeans. Not much, not something that anyone else would notice, but . . .

There's a hand on her shoulder. An inquiring voice. Willow looks up to see the face of her physics teacher, Mr. Moston.

He looks alarmed.

Willow doesn't want to talk to him. She wants to focus on the way that the wound on her leg feels. She wants to make it feel even worse by worrying it with her shoe. But unfortunately she can't. Somewhere in the back of her mind she knows that if she doesn't pull it together right now there'll be repercussions: a conference with a guidance counselor, a lecture. Maybe her brother will be called in. Most *probably* her brother will be called in. Just the thought of that is enough to shock her back into reality.

"Willow? Are you all right?" His manner is sympathetic, gentle, solicitous. Is it sincere? She can't tell anymore. There have been so many people over the past seven months asking her if she was all right in just that tone.

Willow has come to hate that tone.

"Are you all right?" He repeats the question, and Willow has to fight not to laugh at how absurd he sounds. Why is it that people only ask if somebody is all right when it's obvious that they *aren't*?

"Is there anything I can do to help?" he continues.

Willow is worried that his next move will be to offer to take her to the infirmary, or maybe worse, to get in touch with David. She'd better start talking, and fast.

"No. Thank you," she says finally. "I'm okay, really. I'm fine now. I was just a little . . ." She trails off uncertainly, hoping that Moston will be so relieved that she's actually responding that he won't demand more convincing answers.

"Do you want to come and help me set up in the physics lab?" Mr. Moston asks. He says this as if she were five years old and he was offering her an ice cream cone. It's clear he means well, but this is beyond him. He's young, probably younger than David. Willow's heard that this is his first teaching job. She's sure that he's never dealt with a student in her condition before.

Willow doesn't care that he's completely unable to offer anything in the way of real help, she's just glad that he doesn't really know what's going on with her. He probably just thinks she's fragile. Maybe he's already gotten the heads-up about her in the teachers' lounge: *Give her time, don't press her, she'll need a little breathing room. . . .*

"Okay," Willow manages to say after a few seconds. "I'll help you set up." After all, physics is the next class on her schedule, and there's nothing else for her to do. There's no place else for her to go.

Willow straightens up. She can feel a thin line of blood trickling its way down her right leg and she concentrates on that as she follows him to the physics lab.

Moston pushes the door open and Willow enters the musty room behind him. Class hasn't started yet, but there's already another girl puttering around in there.

"Hey, Vicki, how's the experiment going?" Moston asks.

The girl looks up with a start. "Um, well, not perfect yet," she stammers, clearly nervous, "but I think I can get it to work out this time."

"All right then." Mr. Moston nods. "I'll leave you to it in that case." He riffles through the papers he's carrying, a frown on his face. "Willow." He looks up. "I thought I had last week's corrected homeworks with me, but apparently I left them in my office. Do you want to come with me, or are you okay waiting here?"

"I'll be fine," Willow assures him, but she's embarrassed. He's made her sound like some kind of special case, which she guesses she is, but he doesn't have to advertise. She glances over at Vicki, but thankfully she's too busy with her own stuff to be paying them much attention. She probably didn't even hear.

Willow dumps her bag on the table. Mr. Moston leaves, and she sits down on one of the stools with a sigh. Now she can get back to exploring the cut on her leg.

She props her chin in her hands and watches idly as Vicki bustles around. It's important to keep her face clear, not to give anything away with her expression. She has to look like there's absolutely nothing going on underneath the table. She has to look like she's not trying to open the cut further, she has to look like she's not smearing the toe of her sneaker with blood.

She feels like a woman playing footsie with her lover at a fancy dinner party.

Her leg hurts. It's extraordinary that a two-inch cut could be so painful. It's easy to do, really, just open it up before it's healed, take something blunt like the toe of a sneaker and try to enlarge the cut up to three or four inches . . .

Now that she has her fix, now that the pain is flowing through her blood like a narcotic, Willow is free to think about other things. She tries to follow what Vicki is doing, but the experiment she's working on seems totally unfamiliar. She wonders if she should recognize what's going on. Maybe she's behind in this class too.

"What are you working on?" Willow asks. "That's not supposed to be part of this week's homework, is it?"

"Oh, no." Vicki scribbles something in her lab book without looking up. "I'm just doing this for extra credit. I . . . I barely passed last year, and I've really got to bring up my grades this semester." She flushes a little as she says this. "Moston said that doing some independent experiments was the way to go." Vicki snaps her notebook closed and narrowly misses knocking over some equipment.

"What's the experiment?" Willow asks. Her leg hurts enough that she can leave it alone now.

"Oh, I'm trying to figure out this thing about acceleration under gravity. I mean, who cares? I just want to— Hi, Guy," Vicki interrupts herself to say as the door swings open.

Willow knows before she turns around that it has to be the same Guy that she met in the library. Of course there *could* be others. He's not in her physics class, so there's no reason why it has to be him, but she knows it is. So what? She has nothing to be ashamed of with him. She didn't ask *him* about any kittens.

"Hey, Vicki, Willow." He smiles at them. "Is Moston around? I wanted to drop off this lab report."

"He should be back in a minute," Vicki says. She attaches a weight to a length of metal tubing and sets it to swinging back and forth.

Willow can't help thinking that it's no wonder Vicki has to do extra credit projects. The girl's completely clueless—anyone can see that the way she's set things up is extremely precarious. The little metal weight is swaying dangerously close to a group of glass beakers, some filled with fluid, clearly part of another experiment.

She's about to suggest that Vicki move the apparatus away from the glasses, when the weight smacks into one of them. Willow watches as several of them tumble to the floor with a loud crash, all shattering beyond repair. A nasty blue liquid starts to seep across the tiles.

"Oh, Christ!" Vicki exclaims.

"It's not that bad," Guy hastens to reassure her as he hurries over to inspect the damage.

"Not that bad?!" Vicki looks at him in disbelief. "Are you crazy? It's disastrous! I'm only doing this stupid experiment because I'm so far behind! The last thing I need is to wreck someone else's! He's going to kill me!"

"We should probably clean it up before he gets back," Willow says as she joins them, hobbling slightly. "Here." She grabs some sponges sitting near the sink and tosses one to Guy. "We need something to take care of the glass." She gets down on her hands and knees and starts wiping up the blue fluid.

"Oh, what's the use?" Vicki wails. She's practically wringing her hands.

Willow is shocked to see that she's on the verge of tears. Doesn't this girl know that a couple of broken beakers and a failed physics experiment are nothing to cry over? Willow sits back on her heels, the sponge dangling uselessly from her hand, and stares at Vicki. Doesn't this girl realize how *lucky* she is that the worst thing in her life is some broken glass?

Tears, actual tears, start to form in Vicki's eyes and roll down her cheeks.

Over some broken glass?

Willow is stunned. She can't help it, maybe she should be more charitable, but she simply can't bring herself to feel anything but contempt for someone so weak.

"What's going on?" Mr. Moston has come in. He stands behind Willow and looks at the mess on the floor.

None of them say anything for a few minutes. Vicki has managed to avert her face so that Moston can't see that she's crying.

Willow can see that Vicki is screwing up her courage to tell Mr. Moston what happened.

"My fault. Totally." Willow is surprised to hear her own voice.

She tosses the sponge on the floor and stands up to face Mr. Moston.

"I asked Vicki to show me the experiment," Willow continues, deliberately avoiding looking at Guy and Vicki. "I was trying to adjust the weight, and while I was doing it, well"—Willow waves her hand toward the mess on the floor—"everything just kind of smashed. . ."

Willow isn't quite sure why she came to Vicki's aid. Maybe it's because she knows that as the new girl she won't get in trouble. Maybe it's because she knows that Moston is already so worried about her that he wouldn't dare give her a hard time. Or maybe it's because if she's honest with herself, she knows that she *doesn't* really feel contempt for Vicki.

She feels jealous.

Because now that she thinks about it, *really* thinks about it, is it so awful that the worst thing in Vicki's world is some broken glass? Isn't that actually just the way things *should* be?

It wasn't that long ago when some smashed beakers would have been the worst thing that could have happened to her . . .

"All right." Moston nods slowly. "Don't bother cleaning this up, I don't want you getting hurt by the glass. It looks like you already have a cut on your leg, Willow."

Willow is startled. She must have opened it up even further than she thought. She hopes that he isn't going to suggest that she see the nurse. "Uh, it's nothing, honest, I got that before—shaving," she stammers, and immediately starts blushing.

Shaving???

"If you say so." Moston looks dubious. "Still, I don't want anyone else getting hurt. I'll find a maintenance man to take care of this. Guy, can you come with me?" He takes the lab report from him. "I don't want to keep you from your next class, but I need help carrying some equipment."

"No problem," Guy answers Moston, but Willow can feel that his eyes are on her. "I have a free period anyway."

The two of them leave, and Vicki and Willow are alone again.

"I can't believe that you did that," Vicki says. Her eyes light up with something like hero worship.

Willow didn't take the blame in order to win this girl's admiration. But the expression on Vicki's face, well, it's hard not to feel at least a little bit good about that. . . . It's been a long time since someone looked at her without pity.

"Forget it." Willow shrugs. "I knew that I wouldn't get in trouble." She smiles at Vicki as she walks back to her seat.

"Oh, sure, I know," Vicki says, following her. "I mean, forget the fact that you haven't been screwing up in here like I have, Moston would never give you a hard time. He's got to be feeling bad for you, I mean, you having no parents and all."

"Excuse me?" Willow is rifling through her bag for a Band-Aid since she doesn't want anyone else to notice her leg, but she stops and turns back to face Vicki.

"Well, I mean you're an orphan, aren't you? Your parents just died like last year or something? Right? You can probably play on that until you graduate."

Willow feels like she's been slapped. Vicki's casually delivered sentence crushes the little good feeling that was starting to bloom. She's as disenfranchised from this girl as she was from the other ones.

But she shouldn't be angry, not really. Vicki isn't speaking maliciously. She's simply too insensitive to know any better, as clumsy with words as she is with equipment.

Mr. Moston and Guy come back carrying a load of equipment. A group of students enter with them. It's time for class to start.

Willow watches Guy as he helps Moston set up. She thinks about the way he reacted to what she'd told him.

He'd turned pale. He didn't come out with some platitudes. He didn't say anything callous. There was nothing to say and he had the sense to know it.

Willow is so grateful as she remembers this that she almost wants to go up and thank him, to follow him as he leaves the classroom, and tell him how much his consideration meant to her.

For a moment their eyes meet. Willow can feel herself

blushing again, but she's not sure why. He can't possibly know what she's thinking, and anyway the moment's passed. She has no intention of thanking him, or even talking to him. She's learned her lesson. It's probably best to not talk to *anyone* at this point.

She can't talk to people anymore, and clearly, they have just as hard a time talking to her.

If she does speak to Guy again, maybe he won't be so nice. Maybe he'll have heard things about her that will make him change his mind, or maybe that's just the way he felt like acting on that particular day.

Whatever. She'll never know. Still, as she watches him leave, she can't help feeling a small pang. She thinks that he must be the only person she's met in the past seven months who didn't say something stupid or insensitive about the fact that her parents are dead.

And the only one she talked about *Tristes Tropiques* with too.

CHAPTER FIVE

Couldn't she talk just a little more quietly? Willow thinks as she rolls over onto her stomach and buries her head deeper in her book. She's still struggling with the *Bulfinch*; at least she has a couple of weeks before the paper is due. Ordinarily more than enough time, but things are far from ordinary these days, and the other girl's chattering is hardly making her job any easier.

"He *said* he'd call. . . ."

Willow tries to tune her out, but it's a losing battle. She'd cut out of school early and come up to the campus hoping to get some work done, but instead of concentrating on the *Bulfinch,* she keeps being distracted by everything that's going on around her. She'd had to move twice already to avoid being hit by a Frisbee, and then finally, just when she'd gotten herself settled, this girl had plopped down right next to her and started talking, *very loudly,* on her cell phone.

"It's been two days already! But you know what? He had

this really big test to study for, you *know* how stressful that is. I bet that's why . . ."

Willow closes the book with a sigh. It's futile to even try to read. At least eavesdropping promises to be entertaining.

All of a sudden Willow is overcome by a wave of loneliness. She wishes that she could to talk to Markie, that she was *capable* of talking to Markie. Rewind seven months and it could have been the two of them gossiping this way. They wouldn't have sounded any different really. After examining the phone call problem from every possible angle, they'd move on to skin care, and then . . .

"You should see how fried my hair is getting . . ."

Oh, okay, split ends, not skin care, close enough. Willow smiles a little. Maybe she can still follow these things after all. Maybe every time she opens her mouth it doesn't have to be an unmitigated disaster.

"I tried doing my own highlights and it was a complete catastrophe."

Catastrophe? Willow sits up and stares at the other girl in disbelief. *That's her idea of a catastrophe?*

She'd like to show her some pictures of the accident.

Maybe she should have stayed at school, but really, was listening to this any worse than listening to Claudia and Laurie talk about SAT scores? At least up here no one expects her to join in; besides, she likes hanging out on the campus lawn. Back when her parents were alive she used to come into the city all the time and read on the grass while she waited for their classes to end. Then they'd pick up David and Cathy and go out to dinner.

Willow shakes her head. Ridiculous that she thought it would be the same now. After all, nothing else is.

She doesn't want to hear any more. She doesn't want to lie around on the lawn anymore. There's only one thing she wants to do. Odd really, because until this moment she hadn't even thought of doing any razor work.

Willow isn't stupid. She knows what's going on. Listening to this type of conversation is like a window onto her past. The actual crash, the angle of her mother's collarbone, the way her own hair was soaked in her father's blood, those things are too difficult to process. But trivial things, they get her *every* time.

She'd been foiled in her attempts at cutting the day before. Maybe she'll have more luck today. The campus is big, much bigger than school, and if she can't find a place on the grounds, there's always the park. . . .

But it's still daylight. She doesn't want to take the risk of someone seeing her in the park. Willow rummages through her bag in search of her library ID. Even though she hates going up to the stacks alone, they would be a good place, except it looks like she left her ID at home.

Of course she has everything else that she needs. She'd never think of leaving home without her supplies. But she has to be careful, exercise a little discipline. Do it too often and things could get tricky. Each time she indulges, the chance of someone finding out, the chance of infection, even the possibility of her losing too much blood increases. She's going to have to start rationing her sessions. Think about the razor the way other girls might think about ice cream.

Not only that, but concealment is getting more and more

difficult. It's just so hard to remember everything, all the little details that she has to keep on top of if she's going to keep her secret. Take a few nights ago, when she saw David crying. After Willow had finally fallen asleep, after the bite of the blade had soothed her like a lullaby, she'd awoken with a start, knowing something was wrong. Willow had tossed and turned for a good half hour racking her brain until she realized that she hadn't wiped up the blood that had dripped from her arm and onto the floor.

What if she'd forgotten to clean it up? What if Cathy had seen it in the morning?

The girl with the cell phone is getting ready to leave. Willow won't have to listen to her anymore. But she doesn't care, it's too late. If only she could find that stupid library pass. She digs a little deeper.

"Hey, how's it going?"

Willow is startled by the interruption. She jerks her hand out of her bag as if she's been caught stealing. Her heart is beating as fast as if she's just run a marathon.

It's Guy. Well of course. Who else would it be? He's the only person that she's talked to around here.

"Hi." She scrambles to her feet, wiping her palms, which are slightly sweaty, against her jeans.

"You headed over to the library?"

"No." Willow shakes her head. "I don't work today."

"Oh, are you meeting your brother then?"

"I . . . No." Willow almost laughs. She's gone out of her way to avoid David ever since she witnessed that little scene in the middle of the night.

"Okay." He considers this for a second. "Did you just come

up here to read then? 'Cause I do that all the time too. I find it a lot easier to get work done here than at school." Guy sits down next to her as he says this. He puts his backpack on the grass and, using it like a pillow, lies down with one arm across his face to shield his eyes from the sun.

Willow doesn't know how to answer. She's too busy trying to figure out how she can get away, so she can keep her date with the razor.

"*Bulfinch*?" Guy picks up the book. "You must be taking Myths and Heroes. I had it last year." He starts to flip through the pages. "I liked it, but it wasn't my favorite class or anything. I mean, the Greek myths are as good as it gets, but *Bulfinch*? Kind of dry, don't you think?" His smile is dazzling in the sunlight. "Who's teaching it this semester?"

He says all this easily, as if they've already had a million conversations. As if they were friends.

She should sit down and talk to him. There's no real reason not to. That conversation in the stacks, that had been good before it turned. Why not talk about the *Bulfinch*, talk about school, and maybe some other stuff too?

But Willow's already decided that it's too dangerous to speak to him. She thinks back to the other day—how does she know that when she's done talking, when she's laid herself bare before him, that he won't turn to her and say something as clumsy, as blunt, and as painful as that girl in the lab?

No. There will be no talking. Not about *Bulfinch* and not about anything else either.

She has other things to do.

"Sorry, I . . . I can't really talk. . . . I'm kind of in a hurry," Willow says as she reaches to pick up her bag.

"Oh, c'mon, stay. If you go I'll have to get to work, and I feel like wasting time. Look." Guy sits up, propping himself on one elbow. "If you stay and talk to me I'll buy you a cappuccino at that place I told you about." He grabs one of the straps on her backpack and tries to pull her down.

"I can't!" Willow says somewhat wildly. She pulls in the opposite direction, but Guy is stronger and she stumbles against him.

"Hey, watch it." Guy lets go of the bag and reaches out to steady her. His grip is stronger than he knows, and Willow can't stop herself from wincing as his wrists close around her fresh scars.

"Is something wrong?" Guy frowns.

"No." Willow pulls her arms away, but the damage is done. He's disturbed the cuts before they had time to scab over. She can see the blood seeping through her shirt. Willow doesn't look at him. She just starts moving as quickly as possible. She doesn't even care which direction.

"Hey." Guy stands up. This time his hand is on her shoulder as he turns her around to face him. "You're bleeding!"

Willow doesn't know what to say. She's frozen to the spot.

"That looks bad." Guy stares at the blood drenching her sleeve, staining her white blouse crimson.

He hasn't figured it out, Willow thinks, relieved. Is it possible that he doesn't make any connection between the blood that's dripping down her arm today, and the blood that was dripping down her leg in the lab yesterday?

If only she could think of some plausible story. If only the cuts weren't in such a telling place. It had been simple with her leg. Of course, she wishes that she had claimed some kind of fall, an accident, anything but shaving, but still . . . Legs were easy . . . but her *forearms*?

Guy seems more and more bewildered as he looks at the blood. He glances up at Willow, a question in his eyes.

Well, too bad, Willow thinks. She's not going to answer it. She yanks her hand away, mindless of the pain. Unfortunately, as she does so, her bag slips down her arm and the contents spill out onto the lawn.

"No!" Willow yells as Guy bends down to pick up her things. Why does he have to be so polite? She considers shoving him, pushing him, even doing something as outrageous, as crazy, as kicking him in the shins, *anything,* just so she can get him off her case, just so she can make sure that he stays away from her cargo.

Willow lunges for her stash, but it's too late. Guy is there first. His hand closes around her supplies. He stands up and starts to give them to her, along with a couple of pens, some gum, and the rest of her belongings.

Willow can't believe it. He's found her stuff and he *doesn't get it.* He doesn't make the connection between the blood spurting from her arm and the soiled razor that he's about to pass to her.

She's so relieved that she can't stop herself, she bursts into laughter. Guy looks confused for a moment—after all, there's nothing so funny about her dropping her bag. But he's a good sport. His face creases into a smile and he starts laughing with her. Willow thinks of how they must look: like a young couple in love. *That* makes her laugh even harder. Who watching them would know that she's laughing because he doesn't realize the meaning of what he's holding?

"Hey," Guy says suddenly. "I use this brand." He's looking at the blade, his laughter stops, and Willow realizes that she should have run, that she misjudged him, that he does, after all, *get it*.

"Hey!" His voice is panicked. Willow knows she should get out of there, but she's rooted to the spot. Her mind is racing furiously. But she can't think of anything to say, she can't think of any way to guarantee his silence.

"Hey!" Guy says once again. He rips up her sleeve and stares at her arm. Willow turns beet red. She couldn't feel more exposed if she were standing naked and he was staring at her breasts. She can feel his eyes as they drink in the terrible sight, the old scars and the fresh scabs, the bleeding flesh and the puckered ugly wounds.

He raises his head and looks her in the eye, his expression equal parts shock and revulsion. Willow stares back. Guy is as quiet as she is, and no wonder. There's simply nothing to say. Willow drops her arm. The worst is over. Maybe now she can just leave. After all, what can he really do? But as Willow watches him slowly back away from her, as she sees the look of horror on his face change to one of determination, she realizes that there is in fact something he can do, something that he is clearly intent on doing, something so awful that her knees nearly give way at the thought.

He can tell David.

Guy turns suddenly and begins running across the lawn. Willow doesn't hesitate, she takes off after him. But he's *fast,* faster then she'll ever be. He's crossing college walk, running up the stairs, in a second he'll be at the anthropology building, and she still hasn't caught up.

Willow wants to yell at him to stop, but she's afraid of attracting any more attention. Already people are turning to look at them. In any case, she is too breathless to get the words out, and what good would they do? Sweat is pouring down her back, her heart is pounding so hard, she's actually afraid it will burst, but that's nothing, *nothing* compared to the despair she feels at what is about to happen. She can't let Guy destroy her secret. She can't let him take away the only thing that gives her any comfort.

A group of students come out of the anthropology building just as he reaches the door. They're talking and laughing, blocking the entrance. Willow can't believe her luck. They stop him cold, there's nothing for him to do but stand there and wait until they move on.

She manages to catch up just as they finally clear out. Guy flings open the door, but she's on his heels now. He takes the stairs two at a time. Willow hurls herself after him, frantically reaching her arms out, determined to grab on to him, to halt his progress in some way, to prevent him from accomplishing his mission.

Willow catches hold of his shirt. She pulls on it, but he's stronger, and she lets go, afraid that if she doesn't she'll tear the fabric. He spins around then. Maybe he's surprised at how easily she's given up, or maybe he's surprised at the absurdity, the *insanity* of her unwillingness to destroy his shirt when she has no such hesitation destroying her own flesh. They stand there on the stairs, both of them with chests heaving, saying nothing, taking each other's measure. Then Guy turns again. This time as Willow lunges after him she is able to reach his hand, but even though she pulls on it with her full weight, he keeps on going. She grasps the banister with her other hand, drags her feet as if they're made of lead, but to no avail: He is relentless, and the only thing she can do is go along with him.

They arrive at the fourth floor, still holding hands. Guy pauses briefly in front of the door to David's office. He looks at Willow for a second but doesn't say anything.

"Please don't tell him," Willow begs, encouraged by his hesitation. "Please."

But she doesn't have time for any further entreaties. Because before Guy even has a chance to knock, the door opens and David appears, ushering the head of the department out.

"Well, hello there." David smiles widely as he looks at the two of them, both slightly flushed, both panting as they stand hand in hand.

It's clear from the expression on his face that he's completely misunderstood the situation. "I can't talk with you right now," he says after a moment. "I have to return a couple of phone calls, if you don't mind waiting. . . ." But he makes no move to go. He's practically beaming as he stares at their clasped hands.

Willow can hardly breathe; she feels as if she might collapse. She's not just frightened for herself either. The thought of having her fix taken away is bad enough. But the thought of Guy telling David, of seeing that smile disappear, is even worse. Her brother hasn't looked this happy in months.

And then it hits Willow. She knows how she can save herself; the relief that surges through her leaves her weak.

"I'll just be a second," David says finally. He shuts his office door, leaving Guy and Willow alone.

Guy sinks down onto the floor. His hand is still linked with Willow's and he pulls her down with him. Only now she's the one who's in control. Now she knows what to do.

"Did you see how happy he looked?" Willow hisses in Guy's ear. "He thinks that we were, you know, *together*."

"So?" Guy says roughly.

"Don't you get it?" Willow continues. "He thinks we're together. He thinks I'm getting better. I haven't seen him look that happy since, well, probably since the accident. Do you want to wipe that smile off his face?" She is relentless. "What do you think this will do to him? Do you think it will do him any good? This will *kill* him."

She wonders for a second if this is indeed accurate. Willow is sure that she has lost her brother's love, but that does not mean that he will not do everything in his power to take care of her. That does not mean that he isn't reassured by the sight of her and Guy, by the thought that she is getting on with her life. And that *most especially* does not mean that learning something new and dreadful about her could not still shatter his world even further. She simply will not allow Guy to do that to him.

But Guy looks less certain than he did a minute ago. He glances at Willow, then away.

"This will *kill* him," Willow repeats forcefully.

"But it might do you some good. You're going to . . ." Guy trails off. It's obvious that he can't bring himself to say the words.

"Kill myself?" Willow finishes the sentence for him. "That isn't my game at all."

"Fine." Guy looks at her in disgust. "You're just going to mutilate yourself. Hey, you're right, that's loads better."

"Better or not, what on earth makes you think that telling my brother will be the thing that gets me to stop?"

"Won't it?"

"Not even close." Willow's voice is like a whiplash. "Not even *close*," she says again. "The only thing you'll do is mess with his head so badly that . . . Well, I don't know what would happen, I just don't know, but something terrible, believe me. He's been through too much. How much more can he possibly take? And what good would it all do anyway? I mean it. Telling him *won't* get me to stop."

"What am I supposed to do then?" Guy looks at her angrily.

"I don't care what you do. But you can't tell him." Willow hears the door to David's office open. She leans back against the wall and attempts to compose herself.

"So what do you want to see me about?" David asks.

Guy gets to his feet. He's a little unsteady, and he holds Willow tighter than he realizes.

Willow stands absolutely still. She's done her best. Now it's up to Guy.

"I was . . ." Guy stops mid-sentence and looks back and forth between Willow and David. "I was just wondering if you already had your syllabus worked out for next semester," he finally mumbles.

Not bad.

Willow looks at Guy with some respect. Not that she really cares one way or the other what he tells David, as long as he doesn't give her up, but still, she's not sure that she could have come up with something that plausible on the spur of the moment.

Then the impact of his words hits her.

He hasn't given her up.

The relief is so overwhelming that she feels her knees give

way beneath her. If Guy weren't holding on to her so tightly, she'd fall down to the floor.

"Well, I've got to say, you have a pretty inaccurate impression of me if you think I have *next* semester together." David laughs. "I'm barely on top of this one. But c'mon in and I'll tell you what I'm thinking of, and maybe I can give you some ideas for a few other classes that you should take. My sister tells me that you want to major in anthropology next year."

Willow stares up at the ceiling and whistles a little tune under her breath.

But Guy doesn't seem to take in what David's saying. Clearly he's still quite rattled by everything that's just happened.

"I think that's great," David continues after a second. He sits down at his desk and gestures for them to take the couch. "But even if you do want that to be your major, maybe you should think about taking something in another department." He pauses and leafs through some of the papers on his desk.

Willow sits next to Guy on the couch. She's never been so uncomfortable in her life and she can't wait for their impromptu get-together to end.

"Oh, uh, yeah, I guess that's a point." Guy makes a visible effort to pull himself together. "But you know, last year I took two classes up here—yours, which I really liked, and then this really basic course in composition. I feel bad saying this, but it was a total waste of time. I only did it because my school sort of requires that most juniors taking classes here start with that . . ." He turns to Willow. "If you decide to take anything up here next semester, you'll probably have to—"

"Yes. Well, I don't think that kind of thing is appropriate for Willow right now," David interrupts, his tone abrupt.

Willow feels a little like she's been slapped. Not that she has any desire whatsoever to take any extra classes, but it's painful to hear her brother talk about her as if she's not even there. She's not sure that she likes the sound of *appropriate* either; clearly it's much easier for him to talk about Guy's prospects.

Maybe she's above letting herself be jealous of her six-month-old niece, but Guy is not exempt from her pettiness. She looks at him resentfully.

"You know what?" David goes on. "I thought I at least had some notes up here, but I must have left them at home. Why don't you give me your e-mail address, and as soon as I have my stuff together, I'll send you what I have."

"Great, thanks. I . . . um, well, I guess I'll see you next semester. . . ." Guy gets up from the couch, Willow follows him silently out of David's office and down the stairs.

"Fuck, Fuck, Fuck," Guy mutters under his breath. He gives the double doors to the building a savage kick.

The afternoon has turned into evening. There's a slight breeze that ruffles Willow's hair as they walk slowly across the campus. It's soothing after the turmoil that she's been through, and Willow is content to do nothing more than enjoy the sensation. She's too drained to talk, too drained to even think.

Guy, however, has no such problems.

"What am I doing?" he repeats over and over again. "I can't believe that whole charade just now! I must be as crazy as you are." Guy stops and looks at her, his expression a combination of disgust and disbelief.

"It was the right thing to do," Willow insists tiredly.

"At least let me take you to student health services," Guy says. "It's completely confidential. . . ."

"No."

"But I can't leave you like this! You can't put me in this position!"

"I haven't put you in any position," Willow says coldly. She quickens her steps. They've almost reached the park now.

"Yes you have," Guy says stubbornly. "I can't just forget about this. What if you—"

"I told you I'm not going to kill myself."

"Is that supposed to make it all right?" Guy sits them both down on a bench. "Slicing yourself up with a razor is cool as long as you don't die?"

"I guess what I mean is that you don't have to concern yourself, you don't have to—"

"Right!" Guy cuts her off mid-sentence. "I don't have to *concern* myself!

"I don't need this," he continues after a moment. "If I don't tell your brother, then what? Am I supposed to watch out for you? I can't do that! I'm taking some classes up here, I was going to start looking for a job. Goddammit! I have other things. Now I'm stuck with you!"

Willow stiffens at the thought. "No you're not! I just told you that!"

"I'm not?" He looks at her angrily. "Okay, let's get this straight. You don't want me telling your brother. . . ."

Willow nods fervently.

"So, fine, you make me promise that, and then you expect me to just walk away? Are you kidding me? I may have better things to do with my time, but that doesn't mean I need you on my conscience."

Willow has a sudden inspiration. "If I sleep with you," she says, "will you leave me alone then?"

Guy is silent for a few seconds, then he looks at her. He seems perfectly calm. Maybe the past hour has been so unsettling that he's immune to further shocks. He studies her carefully and Willow has the horrible feeling that he's deciding whether or not she's good enough for him to accept the offer.

And what will she do if he does?

Willow herself feels far from calm. Her heart is hammering as painfully as it did when she raced across the campus after him. She can't believe what she's just done. Would she actually be willing to sacrifice . . .

But after all, would doing that really be any different than the razor?

"Can I ask you something?" he says finally.

"Okay." Willow nods. She's sure that he's going to ask her if she's a virgin, or if she has any—

"Are you out of your mind?"

Yes.

"No. I mean it," he continues without waiting for an answer. "Are you out of your mind? Besides," he says as he kicks a stone out of the way. "Who says I feel that way about you?"

Willow is almost as humiliated as she is relieved. It never occurred to her that he would have to *feel* a certain way about her in order to sleep with her.

"Well, I just thought that, you know, you're a—"

"Stop talking," he interrupts her. "Now."

They are both silent for a while. He looks away from her and stares straight ahead. Willow isn't sure what to do next. Maybe she should just get up and go home, but even as she's considering this, Guy turns back to her with a question.

"Why do you do it?" he asks. "Can you at least explain that to me? Why you do it?"

"What makes you think I'd want to talk about that with you? What makes you think I feel that way about you?" Willow says, mimicking his words. She tries to inject as much venom into her voice as possible. She's smarting with embarrassment and shame, both by her crazy offer and his easy rejection.

"Right! You'd just be willing to have sex with me!" He shakes his head at the absurdity of the thing. For the first time Willow notices that he's still holding her hand. And, even though he's just humiliated her, even though he's just made her feel like an idiot, she's reluctant to relinquish the contact.

"What am I supposed to do with you?" Guy says the words out loud, but it's clear that he's not really talking to her. "I was going to have a great semester too. I can't spend my time . . . Jesus I don't *want* this!" he mutters angrily.

Willow can't help laughing. Does he think that she does?

"What's so funny?" He turns to her. "You think this is funny?"

Willow shrugs. "Oh sure, both of my parents dying, that was *hilarious*."

Guy looks embarrassed for a moment. "How . . . Do you mind telling me . . . How did it happen exactly? When did it happen?"

This isn't the first time that someone has asked. The answer never gets easier, but Willow appreciates the tentative way that Guy has framed the question.

"It was . . . I was . . . I was driving. And it was about seven months ago." She states the facts baldly.

"Did you even have your license yet?" Guy frowns.

"Huh?" Willow frowns in return. That was not the response she expected. "No. A permit. What does that matter?"

"Well, it—"

"Look," Willow interrupts. "I really don't want to talk about it, okay? It's hard for me." She shakes her head over how ridiculously inadequate that sounds, how mild.

"Yeah, I get that." He picks up her wrist and stares at the blood that's starting to dry. "I get that it's hard, but that doesn't mean that this is the way to go."

"When you're where I am, then you can tell me what to do." Willow jerks her arm away from him. She pulls so hard, the blood starts flowing again.

"Be careful, will you?" Guy snaps. He starts to rummage around in his backpack. "Here." He tosses some Band-Aids, a small bottle of hydrogen peroxide, and a box of sterile cotton into her lap.

Willow looks at him, a question in her eyes. It's one thing for *her* to carry stuff like this around . . .

"I'm on the crew team," Guy explains. "We're out on the river three mornings a week. Anyway, you get a lot of blisters rowing, and the last thing you want is polluted water getting into an open cut."

Willow nods. Should she clean herself up in front of him? Prolong this encounter, which has been nothing less than harrowing? The smartest thing to do would be to get up and run. Quit her job at the library, avoid him in the halls, *never see him again.*

"Well, go ahead," he says after a moment, gesturing toward the bandages.

Somehow the idea of taking care of herself in front of him seems embarrassing, as private, as intimate as cutting would be. *Right!* Unconsciously she echoes Guy's words. *You'd just be willing to have sex with him!*

With a sigh she unscrews the top of the hydrogen peroxide and pours some onto the sterile cotton. Willow should be a pro at this kind of thing by now, but she's having a little difficulty. For one thing, she's right-handed, and this particular slash is too inconveniently placed on that arm for her to be able to reach it easily with her left hand, and for another . . . The events of the afternoon have finally caught up with her. She's just completely worn out. She dabs ineffectually at the cut for a few moments before dropping the cotton in her lap, closing her eyes, and giving up. She is much too tired to care.

Willow is leaning back against the bench, thinking about whether she should just go to sleep there, trying hard to forget the last hour, when she feels Guy's hand on her arm.

What now?

She opens her eyes, wondering what he's up to. Is another confrontation in the offing? Maybe a lecture about her lack of hygiene? But it seems as if Guy has moved beyond arguments. He is completely focused on her arm as he examines the damage she has done to herself. She watches him through half-closed lids as he picks up the cotton and tenderly swabs the cut. His hands are beautiful, large and gentle. Willow can't remember the last time she was touched this way. He's actually much more careful than she herself ever is as he disinfects several of the more recent wounds, then deftly bandages her up and pulls down her shirtsleeve.

They have both been silent throughout. And now, although Willow feels she should thank him, not only for what he's just done, but also for keeping her secret, she can't find the words to speak. Guy too looks like he wants to say something, but doesn't quite know how or what. So they just sit there, regarding each other steadily, the dusk growing and deepening around them.

CHAPTER SIX

Willow glances at her brother as she eats her cereal. He has a cup of coffee in one hand and a scholarly journal in the other. He seems totally absorbed in what he's reading, but she can see he's almost at the end of the article, and she's dreading what will happen when he finishes.

She knows that he's going to bring up yesterday. He'll ask her all sorts of questions about Guy. He'll want to know if there's anything going on between them.

Willow hasn't seen her brother since she and Guy showed up at his office yesterday. David had some conference to go to and hadn't come home until after she was asleep. "Good morning" and "The coffee's hot" are about the only words they've exchanged, but she knows that sooner or later he's bound to bring up that little scene in his office yesterday.

Sure enough, David puts the journal down and turns to her with a serious expression on his face.

"So what's going on with you and Guy? Are you seeing a

lot of him? From what I remember he's very nice, very responsible too. . . ."

It's as if her life has become something out of a nineteenth-century English novel. She's an orphan. She's living in the maid's room in the attic. And now her brother's an inch away from asking her whether Guy's intentions are honorable. . . .

What's next, the workhouse?

Willow knows that he's waiting for an answer. Maybe she should just tell him what he wants to hear. After all, isn't this just the kind of thing she was searching for at the dinner table the other night, something that would make him happy? Why not go along with it? Spin some tale? She's done it before. After all, did Guy really say that he wanted to go into anthropology because of David? But this time it's too hard;the disconnect between why she and Guy were together and why David *thinks* they were together is too great. She can't lie about it, she just can't, not even for her brother.

"No. I haven't been seeing that much of Guy," she says after a few moments. "He hangs around campus a lot because of those courses that he's taking, and I've run into him once or twice up there. That's really all there is to it. I mean, don't get too excited, okay?"

"I see," David says slowly.

That came out more sharply than she intended. The last thing she wanted to do was upset him more than she already has. Her only intention was to stop him from prying. Willow avoids his gaze as she buries her face in her cereal bowl, but she can feel David's eyes on her before he too turns back to his breakfast.

Willow feels terrible, but what can she do? Thankfully there's a distraction at hand as Cathy comes in, dressed for work, carrying Isabelle, who is dressed for day care.

"We're off," she says, kissing David on the cheek.

"Oh hey, Cath." David looks up. "Have you seen my old issues of *American Anthropology*? I can't find them anywhere. Do you have any idea where I might have put them?"

"Well sure, didn't they used to be in your study?"

There is an uncomfortable silence while they all think about the fact that David doesn't have a study anymore.

"Yes, yes they did," David says after a moment.

"Well then, we packed them up when we were clearing the bookshelves for Willow. Remember, we shoved all the boxes under her bed?"

Cathy buries her head in Isabelle's hair and gives her a kiss. It's a natural gesture, but Willow wonders if she's doing it just to avoid looking at her.

"That's right, I forgot." David gets up, his journal tucked under his arm. "I guess I'll go look for them."

Cathy blows him a kiss as she heads for the door. "See you later, Willow," she calls over her shoulder.

"See you later," Willow calls back.

She can hear David rooting around upstairs, dragging boxes out from under the bed. She has nothing to worry about, not really. Under the bed is fair game.

But what if David doesn't confine his searching to that area?

Willow breaks out in a cold sweat. Maybe she hasn't hidden anything under the bed, but that doesn't mean that she hasn't hidden anything under the *mattress*. In time-honored fashion, she's done what countless other girls have done before her, only it isn't love letters that she's stuffed in there.

She imagines the look on David's face if he finds her stash. There's not much really. Some old blades, not very clean, along with some rags that she's used to staunch the blood, but their meaning would be horribly obvious to anyone.

Of course she should go up there after him, make sure that he doesn't find anything. But she doesn't seem to have the energy, the will, to get up from the table. For just a second she thinks about staying downstairs, letting fate decide the thing for her. Maybe it's better this way. After all, it's probably just a matter of time. Can she really trust Guy to keep her secret?

Willow considers life without the razors, thinks about her brother's reaction to the find. Those thoughts are more than enough to propel her out of her chair. She races up the stairs, two at a time, and pauses at the entrance to her borrowed bedroom, slightly out of breath. She watches her brother as he hauls carton after dirty carton out from under her bed.

So far things are okay. He's busy sorting through the various books and scholarly journals, totally absorbed in the boxes. He clearly has no interest in searching under the mattress.

Willow wanders over to the mirror and watches David in the reflection. She notices that he's placed the journal that he'd been reading earlier on top of the dresser, and starts idly leafing through it: some tome on the funerary rites of the ancient Greeks. Willow is about to put it down again, when she glimpses a piece of paper folded in between the pages. Her school's letterhead jumps out at her in bold black writing.

It can only mean one thing. It must be a summons. Someone must have found out about her. Her fingers tremble as with one eye on the mirror she unfolds the paper and starts to read.

But it's not that at all. It's nothing more than a generic letter addressed to the parents of students in the junior class. Each parent or guardian should make an appointment to come in and discuss PSATs, SAT prep courses that the school offers . . . Blah, blah, blah . . .

The same junk that Claudia and company were talking about. Nothing important.

Willow is so relieved that it takes her a second to realize all the implications of the letter. Sure it means nothing to *her*. She couldn't care less if David has to sit through some boring meet and greet with the teachers.

But what about *David*? This wasn't part of his game plan. He should be doing this kind of thing for Isabelle, for his *daughter*. He doesn't need a dress rehearsal. She's sure he resents her terribly for this added burden. If he didn't, wouldn't he simply have mentioned it? After all, school is the one thing that he seems able to talk to her about. Willow places the letter back in the journal, ashamed that her first thoughts had been for herself.

"David, I'm sorry." Willow turns away from the mirror.

"Sorry?" He frowns as he continues ferreting among the boxes. "What for?"

"Well, for . . ." Willow trails off. What can she say? Sorry for ruining his life? Sorry that she was driving that night? What can she say to him that would possibly express what she feels?

Maybe I should just go ahead and ask him if he has a kitten!

She could say that she's sorry for the fact that he has to

attend a parent-teacher conference fifteen years ahead of schedule. That *might* be something she could apologize for without sounding overly melodramatic, except clearly it's something she's not supposed to know about.

Talking to her brother has become like walking through a minefield. She has to step carefully to avoid setting foot in one of the traps.

"Hey, look at this," David exclaims as he reaches into one of the cartons and pulls out a small blue volume. "I forgot about this," he murmurs, blowing some dust off the spine. Willow can see that it's one of their father's. David puts it down on the floor, and shoves the cartons back under the bed. "So." He stands up. "You were saying?"

"Nothing," Willow says sadly. She grabs her sweater and her backpack from the chair. It's time to get going or she'll be late for school. She pauses in the doorway and looks back at David. "I have nothing to say."

And that, at least, is the truth.

❋

Willow knows that to the outside observer she must look like a model student. Her hand races across the page as she takes down every word the teacher says. She's perfected the art of looking like she's listening when her mind is a million miles away. Not only that, but she knows when to nod along to show that she's really interested. . . .

The fact is she hasn't heard a thing. Not one thing all day. She might as well be on another planet.

Willow can't be bothered with irregular verbs or Greek mythology. Her mind is elsewhere. She keeps bouncing back and forth between relief that David didn't find her stash, and terror that Guy will out her anyway.

She hasn't seen him anywhere. Well, that's not so surprising since they don't have any classes together, but still . . . She needs to talk to him. She needs to figure out what the future holds. She still hasn't fully metabolized the fact that *someone else is in on her secret.*

If she had to pick someone to find out about her, she supposes that Guy is better than, say, Claudia, from history class. But that doesn't stop her stomach from turning over as the realization that he *knows* about her hits her once again.

Willow looks up as everyone around her stands and gathers their books. The bell must have rung.

Bonus points! Willow can't help smirking. She knows that she must look extra-conscientious, sitting there, scribbling away . . .

Fine. Enough of that. She slams her notebook shut and shoves it into her backpack. She's managed to get through a school day without embarrassing herself.

Well, that's something.

Willow heads toward the double doors along with everyone else. Time for her stint at the library. In her hurry to leave she collides with another girl, who's headed in the opposite direction.

"I'm sorry," Willow apologizes as they both attempt to untangle themselves.

"Yeah, don't worry about it. Listen, can I ask you something?"

Willow looks at her warily. What could this girl, this complete stranger, possibly want to ask her?

Maybe she just wants to know the easiest way to kill your parents, or else she's looking for the best price on kittens.

"I just need . . . If you could help me out . . ." the girl continues, somewhat impatiently. "I'm—"

"Excuse me?" Willow interrupts, completely startled by the request. The idea that anyone would look to her for help is so novel, so alluring, that it stops her cold.

"I'm kind of lost. I'm new here, and I'm supposed to meet . . . Look, you know your way around. Could you tell me where the library is?"

I know my way around?

Well, I do know where the library is. . . .

Should she just take her there? It might be uncomfortable, but wouldn't it be more uncomfortable to point her in the right direction and then walk five yards ahead of her the whole way?

Maybe going up together would be okay. After all, this girl doesn't know anything about her, not even that she's new too. And more than that, she has invested Willow with an aura of competence that is irresistible.

"Yeah, I'm actually headed that way myself. C'mon," Willow says after a few moments. She starts moving toward the exit again, the other girl in tow.

Maybe I should ask her what she's going up there for, we could—

"The library's in another *building*?"

"Huh?"

"How come we're outside? Where's the library?" The girl sounds highly irritated, and the expression on her face is distinctly less friendly than it was a minute ago.

"You looking for the library?" A really cute guy ambles over, clearly interested in Willow's companion. "It's back in there," he says, nodding at the building.

"Thanks. I didn't think it could be outside." The two of them stare at Willow.

Oh my God! Of course! She didn't mean that *library!*

Willow can't believe that she made such a stupid mistake. When she heard *library,* she just assumed . . .

"I . . . Look, I thought you meant the one . . . I work at the university library, and I just . . ."

"You're a *librarian*?" the guy asks. It's obvious that he doesn't mean this as a compliment, and the girl giggles a little. "C'mon, I'll show you," he says to her. Willow watches as the guy holds the door open.

So much for getting through the day without embarrassing myself!

"Hey, Willow!"

What now?

She turns and sees Guy standing near where the bikes are chained, Laurie by his side.

Willow nods cautiously. She's a little unsettled by what just happened, and she fervently hopes that Guy and Laurie didn't catch what was going on. She wonders if that's why he's calling her over. And what's he doing with Laurie? She shouldn't be so surprised that they know each other—they're both seniors and it's a small school. But it makes her nervous. Maybe the two of them are having a little talk about her kitten fetish, maybe they're talking about something worse. Is Laurie his girlfriend or something?

Not that Willow cares about *that.*

"Are you going to the library?" Guy calls out.

Is this some kind of joke?

"Which one?" Willow asks as she makes her way over to them.

"The university one," Guy says easily. "Walk you there? Laurie's headed that way too. You guys know each other, right?"

"Sure." Laurie nods.

Willow gives her a sideways glance. The other girl looks friendly, a little bored maybe, but nothing beyond that.

Still, are things as innocent as they seem? How does she know that the two of them haven't pooled information, shared stories maybe?

Willow feels terribly tense. She doesn't know why Guy wants to walk her to campus. Sure, she was hoping to talk to him again, but she's not going to do it now. Not with an audience.

"All right," she says after a few moments. She looks at the bike rack, once again wishing that she still had her own. If it were chained up there, it would give her the perfect excuse not to join them, but as it is, she can't see any way of getting out of going with them. Sweat trickles down her back.

"I didn't know you worked up at the library," Laurie says as they fall into step together. She fishes in her backpack for a pair of sunglasses. "That's a great gig, how did you get it? I thought you had to be in the college. I mean, you must have some pull or something to get special treatment like that. . . ."

Pull? Not quite. After I killed my parents the school relaxed the rules a little. Kind of like a consolation prize.

"Oh hey, I almost forgot," Guy interrupts her—he's smooth,

but it's still a little jarring, and Laurie looks surprised. "I'm not going to be in history tomorrow," he continues. "Could you get the notes for me?"

"Yeah, no problem." Laurie shrugs.

"Thanks," Guy says. "I really appreciate it."

Willow isn't sure what just happened. Did she imagine it or did Guy just come to her rescue? Did he stop Laurie from asking painful questions?

"So." Willow clears her throat. "How come you guys are going uptown?" She's pleased at how that sounds. A little on the dull side, sure, but a real improvement over kittens.

"I'm trying to find out about an internship," Laurie says as they cross the street and head into the park. "I'd rather get a regular job or something, for the money. But an internship at a college? It's like the finishing touch that I need on my record."

"I have to do some research in the library," Guy says. "Plus I need to return *Tristes*."

"Oh, God, are you still hung up on that moldy old book?" Laurie shakes her head. "You're obsessed!"

"But it's a great book!" Willow exclaims. She's a little surprised by the intensity of her outburst, and judging by the look on her face, Laurie is too, but Guy smiles.

"Oh, you know it?" Laurie adjusts her sunglasses. "I didn't think it was that famous. I mean, Guy's into all these obscure books that no one else has ever heard of. Like, why? But I guess you're into all that stuff too, huh? What is it again, anthropology?"

"I . . . Yes," Willow says faintly. She's glad to see that there are only a few blocks left until they get to campus. Things aren't going as badly as they did the other day, but trying to keep up without saying or doing anything stupid, well, it's a strain.

"Those are the kind of things that really make you stand out on your transcripts though," Laurie continues thoughtfully. "You know, reading all that stuff that isn't required."

Willow can't help finding this a little funny. She's sure that to Laurie, anthropology is nothing more than a way to spice up your resume.

"I mean classes in anthropology," Laurie goes on as if she can read Willow's mind. "That's pretty inventive."

Willow wonders what her father would have made of such a remark.

She wants to change the subject, but how? She can't think of anything that would be either appropriate or interesting. Maybe she should just say something nasty. Tell the other girl she finds her boring. Or better yet, frighten her with stories of people with perfect SATs who didn't even get into their *safety* schools. . . .

That would do the trick.

But Willow doesn't want to be mean. She only wants Laurie to talk about something different.

"What made you even think of taking it up?" Laurie asks, glancing over at Willow. "I mean, how did you even get interested in the subject?" If she notices that Willow is looking somewhat desperate, it fails to register. "Did someone tell—"

But Guy interrupts suddenly. Even more abruptly than the last time.

"Oh who cares?" He sounds bored. "Let's talk about something else. So what's this internship about anyway?" he asks as they leave the park.

Willow is impressed by how deftly Guy manages to change the subject. At how easily he saves her from saying something she would regret. It's the second time that he's come to her rescue just as things were starting to get uncomfortable.

He couldn't possibly be that considerate, could he? That kind? After all, she's nothing but a burden to him, she's just someone who's gotten in the way of his having a great semester.

Willow remembers the way that he bandaged her arm.

Without thinking she reaches out and touches his sleeve—just barely. He'd miss it he weren't looking directly at her. Guy seems confused for a moment. It's clear that he doesn't know what to make of the gesture, but after a second he gives her a small smile. Willow notices that Laurie is watching them and quickly drops her hand.

"Well, there are two different internships." If Laurie thinks it's strange that Willow touched Guy, she's not letting on. "One's helping out at the women's health center, which I'm sort of into, and the other is doing some pretty simple research for this comp lit professor. It's really basic stuff, he'd never give the job to someone in high school otherwise. He might be able to give me a good recommendation, though, and that's something, you know?"

"Well, sure." Willow tries to focus on what Laurie is saying. So maybe she asks a lot of awkward questions, but still, Willow is grateful to the other girl for not mentioning the episode in the garden the other day. The least she can do in return is to pay attention to what she's saying.

"That makes total sense," Willow continues. "Because I know that—"

"Hey!" This time Laurie is the one doing the interrupting. "Look at that!" She grabs Willow's arm, really *grabs* her—right where the bandage is—and drags her over to a drugstore window display.

"That's exactly what I'm talking about!" Laurie presses her face against the window. "That's the color I'm thinking of. Isn't it fabulous?" She takes off her sunglasses and waves them at a pyramid made out of boxes and boxes of hair color.

"Sure is," Willow murmurs. Her attention is riveted too. But not by the boxes of Auburn Flame. Willow is far more interested in the sign just off to the left. The one announcing a sale on stationery supplies.

That's a great price on razor blades.

Is it her imagination, or is Guy looking at her strangely?

Willow shifts her focus to the boxes of Auburn Flame. "I think you'd look amazing in that color," she says with perfect sincerity.

"Thanks." Laurie looks pleased by the compliment.

"Adrian wants you to be a redhead?" Guy asks.

"The only thing he really cares about is that we both get into the same school," Laurie says, putting her glasses back on. "I mean, he's so focused on other things right now, he probably won't even notice if I go red." She steps away from the window.

"Adrian?" Willow asks casually as they walk through the campus gates.

"My boyfriend." Laurie smiles.

"You met him, Willow," Guy interjects. "Remember, with me, up on campus?"

"Oh, that was your boyfriend?" Willow thinks about this

for a moment. "Well, this is where I get off," she says as they pass the marble steps leading to the library.

"Yeah, me too." Guy stops walking. "So Laurie, listen, thanks for covering me in history. I'll catch up with you after tomorrow, okay?"

"Great." Laurie nods to both of them and walks off, leaving them alone.

"Good luck with the internships," Willow calls after her. "I'd better hurry," she says, turning to face Guy. Her eyes don't quite meet his. She's feeling somewhat conflicted: The way Guy seemed to be looking out for her has confused her. She's grateful, but . . .

She'd have to be made of stone not to be touched by his concern, and yet—and yet—he has complete power over her. He could smash her world to smithereens if he chose, and that frightens her. "I'll be late for work." She starts up the steps.

"I called your brother."

Willow freezes. She turns back to Guy, a look of pure terror on her face.

"Relax," Guy says. He leans against the balustrade, his arms crossed in front of him. *He* certainly looks calm. "I kept my promise. I didn't tell him anything, I just asked when you'd be working. I wanted to make sure I saw you today. You and I, we have some things to talk over."

So *that's* why he wanted to walk with her. She should have figured that he would want to talk to her too. It can't be every day that he finds himself in a situation like this. Still, Willow can't help feeling nervous at the thought of what he might have to say to her. Her heart is beating nineteen to the dozen as she sinks down on the steps, oblivious to the students rushing past them.

"You okay?" Guy asks. He looks worried suddenly. He looks like he did when he saw her cuts, and now that she studies him more closely, Willow can see that his carefree demeanor is just an act. There are dark circles under his eyes, and his hair is disheveled. Odd that she didn't notice any of this on the walk. All in all he looks a lot less together than she realized.

"Stupid question." He laughs as he moves closer. "The last thing you are is okay."

Willow doesn't say anything, but she notices that in spite of his unkempt appearance his breath is sweet, like apples.

"Why . . . Well . . . I mean—why *didn't* you tell him?" she manages to stammer.

"Because I promised you that I wouldn't tell," Guy says simply. "But that doesn't mean that I still don't think I should. Or even that I won't. We have to talk, figure out some ground rules." He reaches out a hand and hauls her to her feet. "C'mon, tell the Hamilton witch I need help in the stacks. We can have privacy there." He propels her into the building, past the security guard.

Willow smiles a little at his description of Miss Hamilton, but, as it turns out, she isn't at the desk. Willow signs in and says hello to the clerk on duty before turning back to Guy.

"Now what?" She sighs. She knows what he wants to talk about, it's the last thing she feels like doing, but she doesn't see any way of getting out of it. After all, he holds all the cards.

"The stacks," Guy says decisively. "In fact, you can actually help me out." He shows her a piece of paper scrawled all over with call numbers. "I have some research I need to do."

Willow glances at the call numbers. Even if she hadn't been working in the library for the past few weeks she would have known which floor to go to. She hadn't spent all those hundreds of afternoons rooting through the stacks with her father for nothing. She knows that the books Guy wants are all going to be anthropology texts, and she knows what she's going to find when she goes up there.

"Okay," she says after a long moment. They head back toward the elevator. "This stuff is on the top floor."

"So," Guy says as they walk into the dimly lit stacks. "Why don't we get my stuff first, then we can talk about . . . well . . . you know . . ." He stops speaking for a second, and Willow can see that he's just as uncomfortable as she is. "We can talk about what's going on with you," he continues. "What we can do about it."

Oh, please.

Willow thinks that he sounds like one of those people you hear interviewed on afternoon television. The kind that come out with books promising self-esteem in ten easy steps.

"*We* don't have to do anything about it," she says.

"Oh yeah?" Guy raises his eyebrows as he follows her down the narrow aisles. "Sorry, but that wasn't the deal. If I'm not going to tell your brother, then you're going to have to promise me some things. You don't just get to waltz across my path, totally screw with my head, and have everything your way. It doesn't work like that."

"All right." She shrugs. She really doesn't have a choice. "Let's just get your books first, okay?" Willow stops in front of a dusty shelving unit, pulls some volumes out, and hands them to Guy.

She pauses for a second before reaching for the next one on his list. She feels dizzy. All of a sudden it's too warm. Her skin is starting to itch, but there's nothing she can do about that. Willow takes a few deep breaths, anything to calm herself, but it's useless, why is she even bothering? *Forget it,* she thinks as she holds on to the edge of the shelf to steady herself. *Just hand him the stupid thing already.*

"Here," she says in a brusque voice. She grabs the book, a monograph her father had written about five years ago. Willow remembers it well. The whole family had gone to Guatemala, where her father had done fieldwork. "Here," she repeats as she holds it out to Guy. But Guy is busy juggling the other books she's handed him and he doesn't accept it right away. "Will you just take it?" Willow is angry suddenly and she throws the slim volume at him, not caring whether she hits him or not.

"Hey, watch what you're doing." Guy tries to catch the book, but instead ends up dropping everything else. "What's up with you anyway?" he mutters as he bends down.

"Look, you practically broke the spine on this one." He's obviously upset. Willow watches him as he carefully turns the book over in his hands. Once again she thinks of the way his hands felt as they bandaged her the day before. He handles the book in the same gentle way. It's clear that he doesn't like destruction of any kind, flesh or paper.

"You shouldn't treat books that way," Guy lectures, but she can't hold it against him. She knows her father would have been appalled if he'd seen what she'd done. "I mean, this is a first edition," Guy continues. "Why would you want to . . ." His voice trails off as he picks up her father's book. He doesn't say anything for a long moment.

"Are we done here?" Willow asks roughly.

"Well, done with the books anyway," Guy says. He sounds subdued. "Look, why don't we sit down for a while." He tucks the monograph under his arm. Willow notices that he deliberately turns her father's picture away from her. His thoughtfulness irritates her, it seems staged somehow.

"You didn't plan this little jaunt as some kind of test, did you?" she bursts out. "Just to see how far you could push me or something?" Maybe she's wrong about him. Maybe she misinterpreted his behavior on the walk. Maybe he kept changing the subject out of boredom, not consideration for her feelings. She crosses her arms over her chest defensively and glares at him.

"Of course not," Guy says. "I really needed this book. I honestly forgot for a moment what it was. I mean, who wrote it. I guess I should have found it on my own."

He looks stricken, and Willow knows, deep inside, that she hadn't been wrong about him. He *is* that considerate.

"I'm sorry," she says after a few moments, embarrassed that she could repay such kindness with hostility. She drops her arms and attempts a smile. "You'll like the book. It's good."

"How could it not be?" Guy is quick to agree. "You know . . ." He hesitates. "I heard your father give a lecture once."

"Really?" Willow is intrigued. "Where? When? Do you know if my mother was there too?" The questions tumble out of her. "What was it about?"

"It was about this," Guy says, gesturing with the book. "About the trip they took to Guatemala. And yes, your mother was there. It was at the museum, late last winter."

"Oh my God." Willow claps a hand over her mouth. She's

going to lose it, she's really going to lose it right here in the stacks. She is shocked by the sudden rush of bile that fills her mouth. But she supposes in a way that it makes sense. She has so conditioned herself to transmute emotional pain into the physical realm, that without the razor to blunt her feelings, her body is responding the best way it possibly can. She is literally making herself sick.

She knows exactly what lecture series Guy is talking about. She hadn't bothered to go, because why should she? She'd heard her parents speak a million times before, and she'd hear them a million times again. Except that late last winter was the last time they ever gave a lecture. Because it was only a few weeks after that that Willow decided to take them for a drive.

"Oh my God, oh my God! I'm going to throw up!"

The lights click off at just that moment. Guy hits the timer with his fist.

"Willow!" He places the books down on the floor and grabs her by the shoulders. "Do you need me to hold your hair back? Should I see if there's a garbage can around? Will you be okay if I leave you for a second and go and look for one?"

"No, no," Willow manages to gasp. "I'll be fine, really. I'm just a little . . ." She presses her hand against her stomach. "Give me a second."

"Of course. Here, let me . . ." Guy positions her so that she's resting with her back against the stacks. "Is that any better?"

"Uh-huh." Willow nods; she's grateful for the support. "Thank you," she says when she finally catches her breath. "Thank you. Really. I'm sorry about what just happened. I just . . . I was sort of overcome. I *can't* believe that you'd be willing to hold my hair back!" she exclaims as the absurdity of the situation hits her.

"No? Haven't you ever had someone do that for you before?"

"Well, sure. Who hasn't done Jell-O shots with their best friend? But c'mon, you've got to admit, it's kind of hard-core with someone you're just . . . Well, someone you're just getting to know."

"Hey, I'm not saying I was going to enjoy the experience." Guy starts to laugh. "But at least getting sick is a reaction that I can understand." He stops talking and looks at her closely. "Willow, I'm sorry." He's no longer laughing. "I should never have brought any of that up." He lets go of her shoulders.

"No!" Willow is quick to reassure him. "I'm glad you did. Really! And I want to hear more. I was just thrown for a little bit, that's all."

"You want to hear more?" Guy asks dubiously.

"Yes." Willow is insistent. "Maybe that's hard for you to believe, but I do! David *never* talks about them with me. Cathy either. That's his wife. It's like my parents never even existed." Willow pauses and tries to think of how to make Guy understand. "You know, so much of what my parents were about was preserving other civilizations, keeping lost memories alive. It's just so ironic that David doesn't mention them. It only makes it so much worse."

"All right," Guy says slowly. "But if it gets to be too much, let me know—promise?"

"Promise." Willow nods.

"First of all, let's move. C'mon, this has to be the least comfortable part of the stacks." Guy picks up the books and leads them over to a far corner. He sits down cross-legged in a small patch of sunlight that filters down from the high mullioned windows and motions for her to do the same.

"We don't have to keep worrying about the lights here either," he explains.

Willow sits down next to him and picks her father's book up off the floor. It's a small volume, bound in light blue linen. She has always loved the feel of her parents' books—textured, rough almost, so different from the glossy hardcovers for sale in the bookstores. She turns each page by its top corner carefully, the way her parents taught her. Willow examines them slowly, looks without flinching, pausing to read certain descriptions. Guy is silent while she does so. After a moment she puts the book down and looks at him.

"Will you please tell me about the lecture?"

"What do you want to know?" Guy says. He picks up the book and begins leafing through it. Willow is struck by how he handles it, even more respectfully, if possible, than she herself did.

"Well, everything, really. What were your impressions of them?"

"Hmm." Guy puts his head on one side and considers this carefully. "About your father? Brilliant, of course."

"Okay." Willow nods encouragingly. "But don't just tell me what you think I want to hear."

"Umm . . . All right. Well then, he tells really bad jokes."

"The worst! I know. David and I always used to make fun of him. I mean, he had a good sense of humor, he'd laugh at funny stuff, but his jokes . . . forget it."

"Seriously, I mean he needed to get out of the ivory tower and into the real world once in a while. I distinctly got the feeling that he hadn't done too many Jell-O shots in his time."

"Absolutely right."

"But he was just so compelling." Guy sounds admiring. "He really got excited about what he was talking about. He *loved* his subject."

"And my mom? What did you think of her?"

"Not so exuberant about the topic maybe, but more in touch with the audience if you know what I mean."

"I know what you mean." Willow closes her eyes for a second.

"They talked a lot about the trip. The one to Guatemala. I have to say, they made fieldwork sound like the most amazing thing in the world."

"Right!" Willow snorts.

"It isn't?" Guy looks at her in disbelief.

"Maybe for some people." She shrugs. "But what always stood out the most to me were the mosquitoes. There were *always* mosquitoes, didn't matter where we went, and *really* bad showers."

"You're killing me!" Guy truly does look crushed. "I don't think I can handle that kind of thing."

"Oh, you'd love it," Willow reassures him. "You're the type who would be really good in that kind of situation. And I'm not just saying that either." She holds up her hands as if to ward off his protests. "David said that you were really smart. Hardworking too. Believe me, he doesn't say that about many people." Willow pauses for a second as she considers her own impressions of him. "You're careful about things, I can tell, and you're thoughtful. . . . That's the way you need to be if you're going to do this kind of stuff. . . . You probably think that I'm just spoiled," she concludes after a moment.

"Spoiled is about the last way I would describe you," Guy

says slowly. "And don't be so sure about me either. I have to say, I like my showers."

How would you describe me?

Willow has to bite her lip to keep from asking the question out loud. She's shocked that she even thought it, that she actually cares, quite a bit, what he thinks about her.

"But I have to say, I'm surprised," Guy continues. "I would have thought you'd want to go into the family business."

"Oh no, that's David's thing, not mine at all."

"You really didn't like fieldwork? I mean, all that traveling around and everything?"

"Traveling around can be fun, especially if you're just taking a vacation, but if you're asking me why I'm not interested in doing the kind of work my parents did, then I'll tell you something. I much prefer the kind of places that you can only visit in your imagination."

Willow shrugs her shoulders, a little embarrassed. She glances at Guy, half expecting him to be laughing at her or looking bored, but in fact, he seems anything but that. He looks . . . well, maybe *fascinated* is too strong a word, but . . .

"Tell me about an imaginary place," he says, leaning closer. "I don't know any."

"Okay," she says slowly. "I'll tell you about an actual place, but even though it existed, *I* think that you can only really know it in your mind."

"Go on."

"It's called Çatal Hüyük."

"Whosit whatsit?"

"Çatal Hüyük." Willow laughs. "It's in Turkey, or *was* in Turkey. I've never been there. Well, the whole culture was wiped out about seven thousand years ago. I mean, I've never been to the site, but my mother wrote her dissertation on it. You want to know what they had that makes it so interesting to me?"

"Yes."

"They were the first people to have mirrors. They were made out of polished black obsidian. That's what my mother wrote about. That's what a lot of people write about. They want to know *how* they made them, what tools they used to polish the stone, how long it took to make them. But don't they know that those aren't the interesting questions? I want to know *why* someone made the first mirror. Oh, I know that people must have seen themselves before, in water or whatever, but that's not really the same thing, is it? What did the first person who saw themselves in an actual mirror think? Were they embarrassed, or did they like what they saw? I want to know the things that you can never learn by carbon dating or digging around, I want to know the things you can only *imagine* the answers to."

"Those *are* amazing things to think about," Guy says thoughtfully. "And I'd really like to know what you think—sorry, what you *imagine* the answers might be."

"Oh, but I don't think about things like that anymore." Willow shakes her head. "Now I just think about the day in front of me, and if that's too much, I think about the hour."

And if that's too much, then I know just what to do.

She stops speaking. Guy too is silent; he appears to be mulling over what she told him. Willow is surprised at the turn the conversation has taken. She never thought when he told her that they had to talk, that she'd end up telling him about this kind of thing. She's never even talked to Markie about this stuff. She's surprised too by how peaceful she feels, and she realizes how frightened she'd been of having some big scene.

But Willow isn't prepared for what Guy does next.

"Don't you want to stop?!" he bursts out, shattering the calm. Willow doesn't need to ask him what he's referring to.

"I mean, how can you do it to yourself? Listen to you! You're so . . ."

"I'm so what?" she can't help asking. "I'm so what?"

"Never mind." He looks away from her, clearly making an effort to compose himself.

They're both quiet for a few minutes. So quiet that she can hear him breathing. Somehow the sound is reassuring. She wishes that she could just sit there with him and do nothing but listen to him breathe and watch the small particles of dust that float by highlighted by the sun streaming through the windows.

"Don't you want to stop?" he says once again, only this time he isn't shouting.

Willow doesn't want to talk about her cutting, not with him, not with anyone. But it's an interesting question, and one that not everybody would think to ask. Most people would assume that if she wanted to stop she would. But Willow knows it's not nearly that simple, and apparently Guy does too.

She decides that after all he's done for her—not telling her brother, offering to hold her hair back—she owes him an answer.

"If things were different, and I don't mean if my parents were alive, but if things were different, then yes, I would want to stop."

"What would have to be different?"

"I can't tell you that part."

Guy doesn't say anything to this. He just stares at her, his expression inscrutable, but Willow can tell that he feels uncomfortable, nervous even. This isn't what she was expecting. A lecture maybe, or even him yelling at her, but not this steady gaze, this unwavering focus directed straight at her.

He never takes his eyes off hers as he reaches for her hand. She's moved by how tender he is, and just for a moment she allows herself to imagine that things are different. That he doesn't know she's a cutter. That she *isn't* a cutter.

What if the reason he'd bandaged her hand was because she'd fallen Rollerblading? How innocent that would have been! What if they were up here now because they wanted to be alone together, and not because they couldn't risk anyone overhearing their unwholesome pact? What if they could just keep talking and laughing like they had been and not have to deal with the gruesome and gritty?

Guy rolls up her sleeve and she thinks he wants to check to make sure that his bandage is holding, but instead he peels back the Band-Aid and stares at the cut.

"It's so ugly." His tone is matter-of-fact.

Willow jerks her hand away. She can't believe that he said that and she can't believe that she cares. She knows the cuts are ugly, and she's not interested in his opinion, but still, she's horribly insulted. Hurt and insulted. It's almost as if he said that her *face* was ugly.

Guy tears his eyes away from her cuts and looks up at her. He must see from her stricken expression that his words have had an impact, but he doesn't apologize. "Getting back to what I said before," he continues. "I really did call your brother. And not just about when you would be working either."

Willow is stunned. Did he tell David after all? What happened? She's at a loss for words, but Guy goes on unperturbed.

"I called him last night. After I left you. I did." He starts drumming his fingers on the floor. "The thing is, though, I had no idea what to say. I just hung up after a few seconds of heavy breathing." He sighs deeply. "I wanted to tell him, but . . . I kept thinking about what you said. I mean, that it would kill him. What if you're right? Look, there's no way you can make me believe that he'd totally fall apart, but what if me telling him caused some kind of . . . I don't know what. Also, what if my telling him made *you* fall apart? What if it made you cut yourself so badly that . . . well, worse than you ever have before?" He chooses his words delicately. "Besides, I did promise you." Guy reaches for her arm again. This time he keeps his eyes on her face as he fixes the Band-Aid and rolls down her sleeve. "And I just figured, and maybe I figured wrong, that you would be okay, that between when I last saw you and now you wouldn't be able to, to well, do it. I mean, I kept wondering. *When* would you be able to do it? Not at home with your brother and his wife around, not at school either."

An image of the girls' bathroom flashes through Willow's head, but she doesn't say anything.

"Still," Guy continues. "I kept going back and forth between thinking I should tell him and deciding against it. I couldn't sleep all night, just wondering what to do."

Now Willow knows why he has those circles under his eyes. He does look completely wiped out, and she feels terribly guilty. She never meant to give anyone *else* pain.

"Will you tell me something?" Guy has a guarded expression on his face, as if he's afraid of her reaction.

"I might," Willow says thoughtfully. It occurs to her that she doesn't have to hide in front of Guy anymore. This isn't like hanging out in the garden with Laurie and the other girls. She doesn't have to worry about saying the wrong thing, she doesn't have to pretend *anything*.

"Why do you do it? I'm not asking why you're so unhappy, I think I got that. I mean why go this route?"

Willow nods thoughtfully. She should have seen that one coming. After all, it's the first thing *she* would ask. "It's not something that I can just explain so easily."

"When we were walking here . . ." Guy starts, then trails off and looks away.

"Yes," Willow prods gently.

"I was worried that Laurie was going to say something that would set you off. Of course, it turned out that I was the one who set you off. I mean when I told you that I'd heard your parents' lecture. *I* was the one who said the wrong thing." He sounds unhappy with himself.

"There is no wrong thing," Willow says. She means it too, she can never tell what it is that will send her scrambling for the razor. "There is no right thing either."

Guy considers this for a moment. "Will you tell me something else? Can you tell me where you do it? I don't like thinking about it, but I can't stop, and I'm driving myself crazy."

"You mean where on my body, or where I am when I do it?"

"Well, both actually," Guy says. This time he's the one who looks as if he's going to throw up.

"Mostly on my arms," Willow says quickly, as if that makes it all right. "And you're wrong about school. I *do* do it there, at home too, if no one is around, but that's a little trickier."

"God," Guy whispers. "And I thought you were safe."

"I am," Willow assures him. "I told you that already. I'm very careful to keep the cuts clean. I never do too much at one time. . . ." She stops speaking. Guy's mood must be contagious, because all of a sudden she can't bring herself to say the words.

"Oh Willow, the last thing you are is safe."

Willow doesn't know how to respond to this. She feels lost in a way that she can't describe. The stacks seem darker suddenly; their little patch of sunlight is fading. She moves closer to Guy.

"Can I see your bag?" Guy asks suddenly.

Willow doesn't get why he's asking, but she gives a little shrug and passes him her backpack.

Guy flips it open and takes out her stash: a used razor and a spare, still in its wrappings, along with the Band-Aids he gave her and some bacitracin.

"Of course it wouldn't do any good to throw these out," he mutters, turning the razors over in his hands.

"No," Willow agrees. "It wouldn't."

"Promise me something," Guy says suddenly. "Okay? Will you promise me something?"

"It depends." Willow is cautious. "What do you want?"

"You have to call me before you do it the next time. I mean it. Just call me before you do it."

"So you can talk me down?" Willow asks. She isn't sure why there's such an edge to her voice. "I mean, what for?"

"Talk you down?" He shakes his head. "I wouldn't even know how." He puts the razors back in her bag reluctantly. "Here's what for. You've got me spooked about calling your brother. I'm sure you're wrong about him, but I don't know really, and I'm afraid to take the chance. At least with you, things are fairly . . ."

"Cut and dried?" Willow can't resist saying.

"That's one way of putting it." Guy gives her a look. "I was going to say that things are out in the open between us. Listen, if you call me, at least I'll know that you're, well . . . obviously not okay, but at least . . ." He doesn't finish the sentence.

"At least?" Willow prompts.

"At least I'll know that you aren't fucking bleeding to death!"

Willow doesn't have a comeback for this. His vehemence has shocked her, it seems so out of character. She watches silently as Guy tears a piece of paper out of one of her notebooks and scribbles something down.

"Here, these are all my numbers, okay?"

"Why are you doing this?" Willow finally bursts out. "You don't have to help me. You don't have to talk to me. You don't have to come up with any answers. So why are you doing this? You didn't have to bandage me yesterday either, but you did anyway. Why? You could just walk away. I'm not asking you to do this. I don't *want* you to do this. I probably won't even call you."

"I can't just walk away. And you know what? You couldn't either."

"Oh yes I could," Willow is quick to correct him. "I'd never even look back, I'd—"

"Right," Guy interrupts her. "Just like you did with Vicki."

It takes a second for Willow to even get what he's talking about. "You mean that girl in the physics lab?" She is incredulous.

"That's the one." Guy nods.

"You've got me all wrong," Willow tries to explain herself. "You think I'm nice? That I'm kind? That's not the way it was at all. I thought she was *pathetic*, I thought she was a loser!"

"I know. That's why what you did was so special."

Willow is silent.

"You helped her." Guy's voice is quiet. "You didn't have to, but you did anyway. So don't go giving me some bullshit line about how you'd walk away, because it just isn't true.

"Look, I have to get going." He stands up. "Call me, or maybe don't. Maybe figure out another way to deal with your problems instead of slicing and dicing." He looks like he wants to say something else. But after a few moments he just gives her a sort of half smile and heads for the elevator.

The doors close and Willow is left alone. She crumples the paper with his numbers into a little ball and throws it as far away as she can.

She's not going to let him control her like this. How does he know how she'd behave anyway? She *would* walk away. And she *will* walk away from Guy's good intentions.

Willow grabs her bag and hurries down the side stairs—she doesn't have time to wait for the elevator—right into Miss Hamilton's welcoming scowl.

"Where have you been?" she asks. It's clear that she's upset. "You need to hurry and start shelving, we're backed up and Carlos isn't here. I don't want you taking your break today. Even if you had been on time I wouldn't have let you take it, we're simply understaffed. By the way, you made a mistake on the interlibrary loan you requested last time and I had to apologize to that nice old man. Do I have to tell you . . ."

She yammers on relentlessly, her voice querulous and unpleasant. With her scraped-back hair and outmoded dress she's like a fugitive from a Dickens novel. Willow can hardly bear to listen to her. She doesn't know how she'll be able to make it through the next few hours under this woman's watchful eye. Unbidden an image of Guy flashes before her. His face. His hands. The way he held her father's book. The way he bandaged her.

"I'm sorry," she cuts off Miss Hamilton abruptly. "I'll do the shelving right away." Willow grabs a cart full of books and races with it into the elevator. She punches the button for the eleventh floor, not noticing or caring where the books belong.

C'mon, c'mon, hurry!

Willow flings the cart aside and runs over to where she and Guy had been sitting. The paper isn't there. For God's sake! She's only been gone a few minutes! Who else has been up here? Who would even take a crumpled-up piece of paper anyway? She drops to her knees and begins crawling around. How far could she have thrown it? Willow looks under the metal stacks. Nothing but dirt.

What's that?

She sees something small and white among the dust bunnies and scrabbles after it with her hand. Willow can barely reach it and she feels as if her shoulder is about to be dislocated as she stretches her arm as far as she can under the shelving unit.

Got it!

She uncrumples the paper and refolds it smoothly, but she's not sure what to do with it. She left her bag downstairs, and she's wearing a skirt today, so . . . no pockets. After a second Willow sticks the folded-up square in her bra.

She's not sure why she wants his numbers. She won't call. But really, what harm can it do to keep them? She likes the way the paper feels against her breasts. Scratchy, not painful like the razor, but not something she can just ignore either.

It stays there all day, until she gets undressed for bed.

She falls asleep easily. No problem, she's exhausted. But staying asleep—*that's* another matter.

Willow doesn't have nightmares, not exactly, at least not that she can remember, but something usually manages to wake her up at night, shivering and shaking. Maybe it's a car outside her window that reminds her of the accident, or maybe it's the sound of the rain pattering against the window.

She's not sure what it is tonight, some shadowy fragments of a dream come to her: the sound of broken glass, the *feel* of broken glass, is that what's making her tremble? It doesn't matter. Willow grabs her stash from under the mattress. She squeezes the blade convulsively.

She lies there, but she's not cutting, not yet. Suddenly she reaches out, knocking the phone off the bedside table. She roots around on the little nightstand until her hand closes over the piece of paper that she left there earlier. She never lets go of the razor, but she does take the paper and the phone back with her under the covers.

The phone's not a cordless, and the dial tone fractures the

silence. The noise is comforting, though, and so is the *idea* of calling Guy. She's not going to call him, she'd never do that. But her hand grasps the paper tightly, as if it were a lifeline, as she cradles the phone next to her chest, its insistent buzzing echoing the beating of her heart.

CHAPTER SEVEN

Willow hums a little tune as she roots around the various beauty products on offer at the drugstore. For once she's in a good mood. And why not? School had let out early today and she doesn't have to work at the library. She has almost a whole day to do whatever she wants.

She wants to buy more supplies.

So she'd gone back to the shop that she'd passed on her walk with Guy and Laurie. Buying razor blades wasn't always so easy. They were usually confined to art supply stores, but since she'd given up watercolors, she didn't like frequenting them, so finding a new source was particularly gratifying.

Of course any sharp edge could do in a pinch, and Willow has used them all: nail scissors, a steak knife, a man's razor—if he doesn't use safety blades—that's what she'd been carrying when Guy discovered her. But Willow is a purist. She likes to reserve her cutting implement for cutting herself alone. She just can't see hacking her flesh with the same razor she slices her dinner with.

Willow pauses near the boxes of Auburn Flame. Should she buy some? Not that she has any desire to color her hair, but she always gets a few things, just so she won't raise any eyebrows at the cash register.

She must have a dozen sketch pads at home. All with blank pages.

This time Willow grabs some shampoo—at least it's something she'll use—and hurries over to the cashier. Asking for the razors always makes her nervous. Why do they have to be behind the counter anyway? Her heart beats a little faster as she lays her things down. She tries to look as innocent as possible, but she can't help feeling like a criminal.

"Can I please have three boxes of the razor blades?"

"Three boxes? Why do you want *three* boxes?" The clerk gives her an odd look.

Twenty to a box, sixty razors! He has to know!

"I, well, I just . . ." Willow doesn't know what to say. Should she just get out of there? Make a run for it? Could he do anything anyway?

I mean, he's not going to call the police, is he?

"Because they're priced four for two dollars," he continues, unperturbed.

Oh.

"Right, I mean I knew that, I just . . . Sure. Four boxes, that would be great. Thanks." The worst is over. She feels almost light-headed with relief, she's back to humming to herself as she pays for her purchases and heads out the door.

Now what?

Willow stuffs her new provisions into her backpack as she starts walking down the street. She's not sure where she's headed yet. Maybe she should go up to campus to hang out on the lawn. Bad idea. She shakes her head as she recalls what happened the last time she did that. She could just go home and do some work, finish the *Bulfinch* and get started on that paper she's supposed to write for class.

That'll happen.

Of course she could always go to the park. That's a lot nicer than the campus lawn, and no bad associations either.

Funny how she thinks of Guy finding out as bad, but his bandaging her as . . . well, not something *bad,* anyway. Willow rubs the bandage absentmindedly. It's getting a little dirty, she should really change it. Somehow she hasn't had the time.

She heads in the direction of the park, but she's a little uncertain. Going to the park by herself . . . She's been so alone these last few months, and a lot of that by her own choice, but still. . . . Willow remembers the other day in the stacks with Guy. Even though much of their discussion was painful, there was a lot that was interesting. Certainly the pleasure of her own company is starting to wear thin.

That feeling is only intensified as she watches a group of girls from her school drift by and head their way into the park. Vicki is among them. Willow wonders what Vicki would do if she went up and tried to join them. Would she be nice, or would she just say something hurtful again?

Well, she has no desire to hang out with Vicki and her friends anyway.

Willow turns away from the park and walks back toward school. There are a lot of outdoor cafes scattered around the area, and maybe getting a drink at one of them wouldn't be such a bad idea.

She stops outside one with a pretty green and white striped awning and studies the menu. She doesn't have much money. She gives David and Cathy almost everything that she earns, but still, she has enough to get *something*.

"Willow!"

David?! What is he doing here?

Shouldn't her brother be teaching a class, or working at home? What is he doing sitting with an iced coffee at a sidewalk cafe in the middle of the day?

Willow's first thought, after she gets over the shock of seeing her brother at one of the tables, is that of course, *of course* she'd be likely to run into him. The reason that school had let out early was for those parent–guidance counselor conferences. The same ones that David had gotten a letter about.

Even as Willow thinks this, she notices other students walking by with their parents, stopping at other cafes.

"David," Willow says uncertainly as she goes over to where he's sitting.

How to play this? Should she let on that she knows why he's in the neighborhood? She's sure that he doesn't want her to know. If he did, he would have just told her about the whole thing. She would have been in the meeting with him.

"Don't you have a class or something like that now?" Willow asks. David removes his jacket and a stack of books from the other chair and she sits down next to him. "I mean, what are you doing over here?"

If he's not straight with her, then she'll know how to handle the conversation. She'll simply go on the way they have ever since the accident, speaking without saying anything.

"No, no class right now. . . ." David doesn't look at her as he says this. He fusses with his napkin, hands her a menu, does everything except meet her eyes. "I should be preparing a lecture, but I needed a break. So I just sort of wandered down here . . ." He trails off. Willow nods understandingly as if she totally buys into his explanation. Sighing deeply, she opens the menu.

"So, how are your classes going?" she says, after ordering an iced cappuccino.

Great, now you sound like you're trying to be the parent!

"Fine." David shrugs.

And a fabulously witty comeback from David in the right-hand corner!

"What are you teaching this year anyway?"

"Oh, you know, same old, same old."

How the hell would I know?! You never tell me anything anymore! And how same old *could it be? You haven't even been teaching that long!*

"Right." The waiter places her drink in front of her and Willow takes a long time adding sweetener, stirring it, trying to come up with something to say. But she doesn't have to worry, because David is ever ready with his topic of choice.

"How was school today?" he asks. "What happened with that French test? You must have gotten it back by now. Any problems, or did it go well? And what's going on with that paper you mentioned? The one on the *Bulfinch*?"

Why don't you tell me how school was today, seeing as how you were there too!

Willow has to bite her lip to keep from saying the words out loud. Why is he sitting there pretending to enjoy his drink, pretending that the only reason he came downtown was because he needed a break?

She knows why he doesn't want to talk about it. Maybe he's equipped to deal with all the stupid details of her education like papers and quizzes, but to have to sit through some parent-teacher conference, to have his face rubbed in the fact, that yes, he is the parent now . . .

Willow gets it. She gets it totally. But still . . .

Yell at me! Hit me! Do anything! But stop being like this!! Stop acting like nothing's happened! Stop acting like you're okay with it all!!

"So, did you get your test back?" David looks at her expectantly.

Willow doesn't even bother to answer. She's not going to sit there and continue this farce, and if she can't talk about what's really going on, then she'll at least talk about something more interesting. She casts about for something to say, she doesn't care what, as long as it isn't this meaningless chatter between two strangers.

She glances at the stack of books next to his elbow, hoping for some inspiration. "What are you reading these days?" Willow asks, and for the first time in the entire conversation her voice is natural. This is safe. Better than safe. This is *familiar*. This is the talk around the dinner table throughout her entire childhood. Why has she never thought of this before?

"Well, you know." David's face lights up for a second, looks, just for a moment, like it used to. "I've been doing some digging, going back and questioning some theories. Remember that journal I was looking for the other day? I wanted it because I'm fairly certain that some new finds completely contradict the accepted view regarding burial rites." He's more animated than she's seen him in ages, so interested in his subject that he doesn't even notice that she didn't answer his question.

Willow can't help laughing. She knows that if any of her old friends were with her, they'd be squirming in their seats, dying to get out of there. All of them used to beg to come into the city with her and do something with David. They all had a crush on him because he was so cute, and well, older. But once they got there they were inevitably bored by her eccentric, brilliant brother.

Willow isn't bored at all. Maybe burial rites aren't her first choice of topic, but who cares? He's talking, talking about something real to him, and she's happy about that.

"That's so funny." Willow leans forward. "Because you know what I've been thinking of reading again? *Tristes Tropiques*. I haven't looked at it since . . . in years." She carefully avoids any mention of their father. "But the other day I thought that I should read it again. It's such a beautiful book."

"Amazing," David agrees. "What's so extraordinary about it is that it reads as so much more than an anthropological text because . . . Wait a minute. . . ." His smiles fades as abruptly as a light being switched off. "Willow. I don't think you have that kind of time right now. Are you totally caught up in your classes? You're not falling behind, are you? And you didn't answer me about your paper. Do you have a rough draft already? Why are you even thinking of reading *Tristes Tropiques*?"

It's as if that brief, pleasant interlude never even happened.

"Right, you're right," Willow says, too dispirited to even argue. "I should be getting on with my school stuff. Here," she says, digging into her bag. "I cashed my paycheck yesterday and I forgot to give Cathy the housekeeping money before I left for school this morning."

She shoves a handful of bills across the table. David looks at them as if they were poisoned, then, reluctantly, puts them into his wallet.

"Thank you," he mumbles.

"You're welcome." Willow is just as stiff. She hates it when he thanks her for her pitiful contribution. Hates it.

"Hey." David is staring at her arm, his now familiar frown in place. "Did you cut yourself?"

Willow is startled for a moment. Then she glances down at her arm. She tries to see Guy's bandage the way that David might be seeing it. Dirty for sure, but not much more than that. A single bandage is a pretty innocent thing.

"Yes, David." She looks straight at him. "I cut myself."

The irony of this is overwhelming. The whole experience of sitting there with him is overwhelming. She can't stay there with him anymore, and talk without saying anything. She has to leave, but how? Willow is diverted suddenly by a group of people laughing and talking especially loudly on the other side of the street.

Guy.

Laurie's there too, and so is Adrian—at least Willow thinks she recognizes the guy whose arm is around Laurie's waist. Willow isn't familiar with any of the other people that are with them.

"I have to go." Willow looks back at her brother. "I'm meeting my friends." She barely winces at the lie. They're certainly not expecting her. And they're certainly not her friends. Well, Guy is something more than a *friend*, although just what he is exactly isn't clear. But they're a believable excuse, they're giving her a way out.

Willow hurries across the street. She's sure that her brother is watching her and she hopes that if she won't be greeted with open arms, she at least will be allowed to join their little group.

She's worried that Guy won't want to see her. Why should he, after all? She's nothing but trouble to him. Their pact didn't extend beyond cutting and calling.

Willow is a few steps behind them now. They haven't seen her, and in spite of the fact that she's feeling lonely, she knows that if her brother weren't looking she would walk away as fast as she could in the other direction.

Willow takes a deep breath.

Out of the frying pan . . .

"Hi," she says, touching Guy's sleeve.

Guy turns around, as does everyone else. It takes all of her courage to stand there and hold her ground, but she's rewarded for it, because Guy smiles at her, and Laurie acts as if her joining them is the most natural thing in the world.

"Hey, Willow, wanna hang in the park with us? You can help me convince Adrian that I should color my hair."

Willow doesn't care that Laurie's range of interests is limited, to say the least. She's too relieved by her casual acceptance to be critical.

"Hi." Guy isn't quite as forthcoming, but he takes the time to introduce her around. "You remember Adrian? This is

Chloe, and Andy." He gestures toward the rest of the group. "You guys know Willow yet?"

"Oh yeah, I've seen you around school." Andy nods. Chloe doesn't really pay her any attention. She's too busy scrounging in her bag for something. "Can anyone lend me some money?"

"What for?" Andy reaches into his pocket.

"Ice cream." Chloe nods toward the small truck at the entrance to the park.

"Get me one too." Andy gives her a fistful of change.

"You want some?" Guy asks Willow.

"Oh, no. . . ." Willow shakes her head. She wonders if Guy thinks it's strange that she's joined them. She looks at him sideways. He seems to be taking her appearance in stride.

"Where to?" Andy asks as Chloe returns with the ice cream.

"I can't believe you eat that stuff." Laurie shakes her head at Chloe.

"Why not? No carbs." Chloe waves her fuchsia-colored Popsicle at Laurie.

"Try no *fat*. All carbs," Laurie says, but Chloe just shrugs.

"How about by the river." Andy looks at Guy. "I want to check out the boats."

"No river," Adrian says firmly. "I need to lie down. You know, *grass*."

"Haven't you guys had enough of the river anyway?" Chloe asks as she makes quick work of her Popsicle.

"You have a point." Guy looks at Willow. "Andy is on the crew team with me. I think I told you that we row three mornings a week."

"Yeah, this morning was pretty bad, though." Andy frowns. "I really want to shave, I don't know, about ten seconds off of our time."

"Then you're going to have to do some extra cardio," Guy says. "I'm telling you that's what's stopping us. But I've got news for you, I am *not* interested in spending more time at the gym."

"No rowing talk!" Chloe insists. "It's beyond boring."

"It's perfect right over here," Laurie says, gesturing to a clearing under some cherry trees. She flops down on the grass before anyone can object.

"Did you bring nail stuff?" She looks over at Chloe as she takes a file out of her bag and gets to work.

"I did." Chloe begins unloading her bag. "But I'm totally out of that color you like."

"Are you comfortable?" Guy asks Willow as she tries to arrange her backpack like a pillow.

"Not quite." She takes the *Bulfinch* out of her bag to see if that will make it any more yielding.

"My hands are all sticky now." Andy makes a face.

"Yeah, mine too." Chloe looks put out.

"Here, try this." Guy hands Willow a rolled-up sweatshirt out of his own bag.

"Thank you." Willow places it carefully on the ground, then turns toward Andy. "I have some of those wipey things," she offers. She carries them with her everywhere, they're perfect for cleanup after a little razor work.

"Great." Andy catches the little foil packets.

"Are you giving her your dirty old sweatshirt?" Adrian laughs.

"It hasn't been cold enough to wear it yet." Guy gives him a look.

Willow leans back on the rolled-up sweatshirt. It makes a perfect pillow, and it certainly doesn't smell bad either.

"Would you pass me the remover?" Laurie puts her nail file down and reaches out her hand.

"Here, give this to her." Chloe nudges Andy with her elbow. "How about you, Willow?" She makes a gesture with a bottle of nail polish.

"No, I'm good." Willow turns her hands palm side up to hide her nails, which are bitten to the quick.

"Aren't we going to a movie?" Adrian stretches out his legs and rests his booted feet on Laurie's lap.

"That's not until later." She gives him a shove. "Get off! You're way too heavy."

"Are you up for a movie?" Guy's voice is too quiet for anyone else to hear.

"Maybe," Willow is surprised to hear herself saying.

"Who's reading the *Bulfinch*?" Chloe asks. She waves her hands in the air to dry her nails.

"Myths and Heroes!" Laurie picks up the book and riffles through it. "I loved that class!"

"They should change the name to Gods and Goddesses," Chloe remarks.

"You're right," Guy agrees. "That's what the class is really about."

"You like Greek myths?" Willow looks at Laurie.

"Oh, you know, they're okay. It's more that it's such an easy class to do well in. I *love* easy A's. If only I had some classes like that this year." She puts the book down and reaches for the bottle of polish. "This semester is so key. It's like schools want to see that you're still really committed—"

"No! No!" Andy sits up and claps his hands over his ears. "Stop her, Adrian! I can't listen to her go on about this stuff one more time! She's obsessed! God, and you guys think *rowing* is boring!"

Laurie makes a face at him, but Adrian just laughs and turns toward Willow. "So what about you?" he asks. "Do you like the class?"

"I *should,*" Willow says with a wry smile. "Because I do love the classics, but actually, I'm having a hard time with it."

"Really?" Guy seems surprised. "C'mon, you must have been raised on this stuff. I can't believe you'd find it difficult."

"Raised on it?" Chloe looks confused. "What do you mean?" She looks at Willow expectantly.

"Well, I . . ." Willow pauses. "My parents were both professors." It comes out in a rush. But there. She's done. They can all go back to talking about Myths and Heroes.

"What kind?" Adrian says.

"Were?" Andy says.

No. She's not done. There's no getting away from it. She will be pursued by this kind of question until the day that she herself dies. Out of the corner of her eye, Willow can see Guy getting ready to say something. She has a feeling that he's going to change the subject. Take the heat off, just the way he did with Laurie the other day.

But this time she won't let him. She deserves this question, this *punishment.*

"They're dead," she says flatly.

"That's pretty harsh, huh?" Andy shakes his head. "You know, I thought that I heard something like that."

Pretty harsh? Pretty harsh? You idiot! Harsh is Laurie not getting into the school she wants. Harsh is you not being able to shave some time off your rowing! This *is not harsh!*

"I'm so sorry. I had no idea." Laurie's voice is hardly above a whisper as she reaches out and gives Willow's arm a brief squeeze.

Willow just nods, but she's touched. She would never have looked for any kind of support from Laurie.

The rest of the group is silent. Willow is glad that she's not on the receiving end of the look that Guy is giving Andy.

"So." Adrian clears his throat. "Maybe we should check on the movie times now."

"Yeah, good idea." Chloe nods. She rifles through her bag for her cell phone and punches in a number. "I need a pen." She frowns.

"One sec." Andy looks in his backpack, but he doesn't find anything, and his gaze falls on Willow's, which is lying half-open, spilling her belongings onto the grass.

"You mind?" He reaches across for a pen.

"Excuse me?" Willow is startled. She had no idea that most of her things were on display.

"Here, let me get one for you . . ." She tries to head him off at the pass, give him the pen instead of having him root around in her stuff for it. In the process she manages to spill the boxes of razors out onto the lawn. The boxes themselves are plain brown, but the bright red lettering emblazoned on the sides looks like blood against the grass.

Andy raises an eyebrow, but it's Guy who says something.

"Thanks for picking these up for me. What do I owe you?"

Willow is surprised, but she plays along. "Oh, don't worry about it, they hardly cost anything." She's sure that nothing too terrible would have happened if Guy hadn't copped to the blades. The brand-new boxes of razors are a lot less suspicious-looking than the single bloody razor that she'd spilled in front of him. Not only that, but she suspects that Andy isn't that perceptive. He'd *never* figure anything out.

But she's glad that she doesn't have to worry about the possibility. She's glad that Guy made sure that she wouldn't have to. For a second she feels like she and Guy are in a conspiracy against everyone else.

"What do you need with all those razor blades?" Laurie looks at Guy.

"Just something I'm working on." He brushes off the question.

"An extra credit project?" She looks interested.

"Okay." Chloe closes her cell phone with a snap. "There's a show in like twenty minutes. We can make it if we hurry." She jumps to her feet and starts gathering her things.

So does everyone else, except for Willow, who is silent, still thinking about the way Guy just covered for her, and Guy, who is watching her.

"You coming?" Adrian looks at Willow.

"You want to just stay in the park?" Guy puts the boxes of blades in his backpack.

Willow isn't sure if he's just continuing the charade, or if his goal really is to confiscate the razors. But would he do that? She did tell him, the other day in the library, that getting rid of her blades would be futile.

Well, now she has to stay with him. Just to get the blades back.

Is that why he did it? So that I would stay with him?

"Are you staying?" she asks.

"If you are."

"I'm staying," she says after a moment.

"I think we're going to forget the movie." Guy leans back on his elbows.

"Sure." Adrian doesn't seem to care one way or the other. Chloe is busy dusting the grass off of her jeans, and Andy and Laurie are already on their way out of the park.

"You didn't have to do that." Willow turns to Guy as soon as everyone is out of earshot. "I mean, about the razor blades. He would never have figured it out. I can tell." She blushes a little as she realizes how ungrateful she sounds. "Thank you though. For doing it anyway."

"I did have to do it." Guy shakes his head. "Oh, you're right, he would never have figured it out, but I was angry at myself. I put you in the position of having to tell everyone about your parents." He pauses for a second. "I can see how hard that is for you." His tone is particularly gentle as he says this.

But Willow is stung by the sympathy in his voice.

"Wouldn't it just be easier for you if he found out anyway?" She says this so loudly that a couple walking by turn and stare. She knows he's being kind, sensitive, unlike that clod Andy, but she *hates* being the object of anyone's pity. "Wouldn't that be better? Then you wouldn't have to worry about keeping my secret. Someone else could tell my brother."

"Yeah, well, maybe you're right," Guy snaps back. "It *would* be easier for me. But something tells me that Andy isn't exactly the best person to be in on this."

"I'm sorry," Willow says after a few moments.

"It's okay." Guy sits up abruptly. He picks up a twig and starts drawing in the dirt.

"You're the one who's right," Willow goes on. "He'd be the worst person. He's so crass, how do you two even know each other?"

"I don't know him that well—I mean, we row together and sometimes we hang out, but we never really talk. He makes fun of Laurie, but he's the same way. Only with him, instead of SATs and recommendations, it's all about rowing and what frat he's going to join."

"Laurie isn't so bad," Willow says thoughtfully, remembering the other girl's sympathetic gesture. She turns over on her stomach and props her chin on her fists; her elbows rest on the rolled up sweatshirt.

"Yeah, she's okay, a little obsessive maybe. . . ."

"You think?" Willow laughs. "How do you know her? *She's* not on the crew team, is she?"

"No. I really know her through Adrian." Guy tosses the twig away and lies back down. "We've been friends forever. I used to see Laurie around the halls, but I never really talked to her until they started going out, sophomore year. Same with Chloe, I know her through Laurie. I think Andy's kind of interested in her, and he figured that since we're on the same team, that was as good an excuse as any to hang out with us." He shrugs.

"Laurie didn't tell you anything about me, did she?" Willow asks as she fiddles with a dandelion.

"Like what? Does she know about your cutting?" Guy is taken aback.

"No! No. I just got to talking to her and some other girls in school a couple of days ago. And, well, as usual the whole thing fell apart. I said some really stupid stuff. I thought she might have repeated it."

"You know, Willow, I don't think people are really talking about you. At least not the way you mean. I certainly haven't heard anyone say anything." Guy takes the dandelion, which is now mangled, out of Willow's hands. "I think maybe it's all in your head."

"Andy seemed to know all about me," Willow mutters. She starts to bite her nails, then shifts her position so she can shove her hands into her pockets. "That girl in the physics lab, what's her name? Vicki? She said something too."

"Okay, I'll give you Andy, and Vicki too, and maybe there *are* some other people saying stuff, but really, I would think that's the least of what you have to deal with. I mean seriously, even though Andy was a complete idiot, was it so bad today? Wasn't it okay being with the rest of us?" Guy picks another dandelion. "Here, take this one." He tugs her hand out of her pocket and wraps it around the stem of the dandelion.

"Are you kidding?" Willow snorts. She starts shredding the flower. "Okay, so after I tell everyone *that my parents are dead,* and after Andy is so *sympathetic,* everyone runs out of here like I'm contagious! *Their* parents aren't going to die because they've talked to me!"

"I don't think that's what was going on," Guy says thoughtfully. "I *know* that wasn't what was going on with Adrian. He was trying to be helpful, change the subject, take the spotlight off of you."

"Oh." Willow thinks about this for a minute. She's not sure that she believes Guy, but she'd like to, and she has to admit that he has a point, with all the things that she has going on right now, suddenly whether or not people are gossiping about her doesn't seem to matter that much.

"So what did you say to Laurie anyway? Somehow I can't imagine you ever doing anything very stupid."

"Try me." Willow sighs deeply. "It's a long story, I just . . . Well, something I said about kittens."

"Kittens?" Guy starts to laugh. "That isn't at all what I was expecting. Is this because Laurie's sister works in some pet shelter or something?"

"I'm not going to go through it again!" Willow swats Guy with her hand, but she's laughing too.

"I'm just wondering because you don't look like the cat type to me."

"Yeah well, I'm not. But what do you mean anyway?" Willow says curiously.

"Well, you know . . . There's the kind of people who like cats . . ." Guy pauses and gives her a look. Willow shakes her head vehemently. "And then there are people like you. And me. People who like dogs."

"I got it." Willow nods. "You mean like there are the chocolate ice cream types, and the vanilla ice cream types . . . Of course, there are *some* people who like Day-Glo Popsicles." She studies him closely. "Coffee, right?"

"Good call." Guy laces his hands behind his head. "But too easy."

"Get out of here! How could I know?"

"Yeah, yeah, I gave you the heads-up when I invited you for cappuccino."

"Fine." Willow rolls her eyes. "But if you're going to divide the world into two types, can't you come up with some more interesting categories?"

"*Odyssey* or *Iliad*," he says promptly.

"Please! The *Iliad*!"

"Totally." Guy is approving.

"Okay, look, like you said, I was raised on this stuff, but what's *your* excuse?"

"You have a leaf in your hair." Guy reaches out and brushes it away. They are silent for a moment.

"C'mon." Willow pulls on his sleeve. "Tell me."

"All right." Guy drops his hand. He sits up and stretches his legs out in front of him. "My parents aren't profs. My dad's a banker and we traveled a lot when I was a kid. I mean to some really far-flung places." He pauses.

"Go on." Willow nods encouragement. She shifts around. Her leg has fallen asleep and she's uncomfortable. After a second she lies down again with her face pillowed on Guy's sweatshirt and looks at him sideways.

"Two things happened," Guy continues. "One, there wasn't any good television, but I could always order books. And two, just so I'd be ahead of the game, 'cause the schools weren't always fabulous, my parents set me up with this really old-world tutor. I mean, we're talking a waistcoat and a gold watch on a chain, right? He had to be about a hundred and fifty. He was from

England, I think he'd been a banker too, but he'd been retired for years. He'd been to Oxford and Cambridge . . ."

"People don't usually go to both!" Willow protests with a laugh.

"Yeah, trust me, he did. Or maybe he went to one and taught at the other. Who knows. Anyway, he got me into books."

"What did you read?" Willow is intrigued.

"Anything. Everything. He could just as easily give me science fiction as Milton."

"Science fiction?" Willow makes a face.

"What's wrong with science fiction?"

"Try everything. And Milton? Why not Shakespeare?"

"Read him too. Now *that's* a good category." Guy looks thoughtful. "People who like Shakespeare and people who like Milton."

"Except people who like Milton more than Shakespeare are crazy!" Willow is indignant.

"That's true—well, my tutor liked Milton better, actually."

"Yeah, and he also gave you science fiction! What's *your* favorite Shakespeare?" Willow wonders if it's the same as hers.

"Umm, probably *Macbeth*."

"Oh, please! That's just because you're a guy!"

"You don't like it?" Guy looks at her like she's crazy.

"Well, sure, but it's got nothing on something like *The Tempest*. Who needs some drafty old castle in Scotland when you could be stranded on an enchanted island?"

"Never read it."

"Oh, but it's the best one! It's got this great relationship between Ferdinand and Miranda! It's so much more romantic than *Romeo and Juliet*—" Willow stops abruptly. She can't help blushing a little.

"I'm guessing this enchanted island is one of those imaginary places that you like so much?"

"That's right." Willow nods. "So, anyway, talking about different places, where were you living when you were doing all this reading?"

"The Far East. Singapore. Kuala Lumpur."

"Do you speak any . . ." Willow searches for the right word. "Kuala Lumpurish?"

"Malay." Guy laughs. "No. I wish I did."

"Look good on your transcript, huh?" Willow nudges him.

"Exactly! I guess I speak it well enough to ask for coffee ice cream. But seriously, everyone there speaks English."

"Do you have any brothers and sisters?"

"What is this? Twenty questions? Yes, a sister. Rebecca, six years younger. Okay? C'mon, you come up with a category now."

"Ummm." Willow thinks for a minute. "Let's see. . . ." *How about people who'd rather live in the city, and people who'd rather live in the country. . . . Talk about boring. People who umm. . . . vote Republican and . . . Forget that one. . . . People who are like Andy and people who are like Guy. Yeah right, who else is like Guy? People who kill their parents and people who don't. . . . People who cut and people who cover for them. . . .*

But Willow doesn't want to dwell on that right now. She's having—can it possibly be—a good time, so she racks her brain to come up with an interesting category.

"I've got it." She looks at him triumphantly. "People who like Sherlock Holmes stories . . ."

"Yeah." Guy leans forward.

"With Watson—and people who like them without."

"Nobody likes the stories without Watson!" Guy is incredulous.

"How do you know?" Willow sits up on her knees.

"Okay, have you ever met anyone who did?" Guy asks.

"No, but that doesn't mean they don't exist! Besides, I don't even know that many people who've read them to begin with!"

"Yeah, well, anyone who likes the stories without Watson . . ." Guy makes a face. "Wait a second, you aren't one of—"

"No!" Willow exclaims. "Total Watson fan. I can't even read the other ones."

"Well, that's a relief." Guy collapses back on his elbows.

"Okay, now tell me more about Kuala Lumpur."

"Ummm, the weather's really bad."

"Is that the only thing you can come up with?" Willow laughs. "Okay, tell me more about your sister then. Are you guys close?"

"Well, we can be. We have been. But right now? She's twelve, so you know, we have different stuff going on."

"I get it completely." Willow nods. "David and I used to be like that, but when I got older things got better. Only now they're worse. Much worse."

"I'm sorry," Guy says, and he sounds it too.

"I . . . I was sitting at this cafe with him when I saw you and Laurie go by." Willow is talking very quickly and the words come out in a rush. "And, well, I just couldn't sit with him anymore, it was just too hard. So I told him I was meeting you.

I hope you don't mind. That I joined you, I mean." Willow looks away from him.

"Hmm. Well, let's think for a sec." Guy makes a show of considering the problem. "What's more fun to talk about? Rowing? Nail polish? Or Sherlock Holmes? Tough call, right?"

"Okay." Willow smiles a little.

"What was going on with you two anyway?"

"We weren't talking." Willow pauses. "We were sitting across from each other and saying things, but we weren't *talking*. It's just like everything else now." She lies back down on her side and faces Guy. "Things don't work."

"Like what exactly?"

"He was at school today. He had one of those guidance counselor meetings, you know where you discuss your whole life plan or something."

"Sure, I know the drill. My parents were there today too. I had to go with them." Guy stops suddenly. "Go on," he says quietly.

"He pretended like he never went." Willow is unable to keep the bitterness from her voice. "He couldn't talk to me about it. Why can't he just tell me what a pain in the ass it is for him to have to deal with stuff like that?"

"Maybe he didn't tell you for some other reason. Maybe he feels bad for you. If it were me with Rebecca ten years from now, I'd just feel sorry for her. I'd be sad that my parents were around to help me grow up, but not her."

"Maybe." Willow is unconvinced. "But that's not the only thing. What about this one? I give David, well, David and

Cathy, most of the money I make. It's not as if it's even that much, it probably only pays for the light bill and one package of diapers or something. I don't think Isabelle—my niece—was planned." She blushes once again. "And having me live with them for sure wasn't planned. I mean, it's just that there are all these extra expenses suddenly, and until my parents' life insurance comes through I really need to help out. But David is always so angry when he takes my money. Why can't he just tell me that it's not enough?"

"I think you're totally off base with that one." Guy shakes his head. "I bet it's something completely different, like that he feels guilty that he has to take your money."

"*He* feels guilty?" Willow is incredulous. "He's not the one who should be feeling guilty!"

"Is that what it's all about? I mean why you cut?" Guy looks at her. "Because you feel guilty?"

"That's not what it's about at all," Willow says. She doesn't like the direction the conversation has taken. She'd thought that they'd moved beyond his trying to analyze her.

"Is it—"

"Can I have my blades back?"

"Sure. Fine. Anything you say." Guy sits up abruptly. He reaches in his backpack for her things.

"I'm sorry, but it's not so easy to talk about. I can't just explain it to you, and I don't even—"

"Forget it," Guy interrupts. "I can't *believe* that I'm giving these back to you. Here!" He throws the boxes of razor blades at her.

Willow doesn't quite make the catch. She feels humiliated as she watches the boxes fall to the ground, breaking open as they hit, littering the grass with bright metal blades. But her desire for the razors is stronger than any embarrassment she could ever feel, so she scrabbles around in the dirt on her hands and knees until every last razor is safely in her hands.

"I shouldn't have done that," Guy says. "It's just—I don't get it, all right? I don't get it at all."

"I don't always get it either." Willow looks him straight in the face for a long moment. Then she turns away and busies herself with putting the blades into her bag, noting as she does so that she'll have to clean them off before she uses them.

"You didn't do it since I saw you in the library, did you? Well, what stopped you? Maybe you should try and figure out what sets you off. How did you manage to control yourself then?"

"How do you know what I have or haven't done?" Willow snaps. "And what makes you think that you can figure me out so easily?"

"Oh, I see." Guy's voice is even more biting. "I guess I was stupid. I just thought that since I gave you my word and didn't tell your brother, you'd keep your end of the bargain."

"I never promised you anything," Willow says angrily.

"Fine. You're right. No, really." Guy holds his hands up in front of him. "You think I was hanging out by the phone waiting to hear from you? Sorry, that isn't the way things are with me. I just figured that you were the type to keep *your* word, and I was really happy that you hadn't hurt yourself again." He pauses and takes a deep breath. "Look, this stuff is way beyond me. I can try and be your friend, but you're on your own with the rest of it."

"I haven't cut myself since I saw you." Willow is suddenly desperate to convince him of that fact, win his good opinion, have him smile at her again. She doesn't know how the conversation turned, but she knows that she doesn't like it at all.

"Good." But he sounds as if he really doesn't care. He stands up and starts gathering his things.

"Please don't go," Willow bursts out.

"Why?" He looks at her unflinchingly.

Why?

He has a point, doesn't he? Doesn't she want to be alone? Wasn't her first impulse on meeting him to push him away? Wasn't she bound and determined not to feel anything?

Except the only times that she's laughed in the past seven months have been in his company. When he's with her she's able to forget the lure of the razor for more than five minutes at a time. And when she talks to him, she actually feels like she's connecting, not just exchanging words like she does with everyone else.

But Willow isn't sure that she can tell him any of that.

She casts about for some reason she can give him. Something that might convince him to stay, but her mind's a blank. He's moving away from her, a few more seconds and it will be too late.

"Wait a sec!" She grabs on to his leg. "Don't go, okay? Because, because . . ."

"Because what?" He still doesn't sound very friendly, but at least he's not going anywhere.

"Um, because, you know what? You never told me, um, well, which Sherlock Holmes story is your favorite," she stammers.

Willow closes her eyes. She cannot believe how *stupid* she sounds, how *inane*. God forbid that he thinks she's trying to be *cute* or something. Why did she have to drive her only ally away? She squeezes one of the blades that she picked up off the grass.

"Are you serious?" Guy says. Willow opens her eyes and looks up at him. She can see that he's starting to laugh.

"Kind of," she says in a small voice.

"You're just . . ."

Crazy, pathetic, strange.

"You're just so different from anyone else, aren't you?" He's really laughing now, but in a nice way.

"That was your first clue?!"

"Okay." Guy sits down again. "Since you ask, 'The Hound of the Baskervilles.'"

"What?"

"My favorite Sherlock."

"Oh! Oh, right!"

"Willow?"

"Hmm?"

"I meant what I said about . . ."

"About me not keeping my end of things? About this all being way beyond you? Don't worry, I know what a—"

"No," Guy interrupts her. He picks up her hand, the one that's gripping the razor. He doesn't try to take away her blade, he just closes his own hand over hers.

"Then what about?" Willow is confused. "Because I—"

"About being really happy that you hadn't hurt yourself."

"Oh," Willow says after a few seconds. She doesn't let go of the razor, she barely even loosens her grip on it, but she does place her other hand over his.

CHAPTER EIGHT

God that hurts!

Willow grimaces as she tears Guy's bandage off in one smooth motion. It never ceases to amaze her that even after all her sessions with the razor, little things still have the power to cause her pain.

Of course, the sting of the Band-Aid is nothing compared to the bite of the blade. It's only a minor irritation, not enough to give her what she really needs.

Willow examines the wound critically. She's impressed by how innocent this cut looks compared to some of her other lacerations. This one looks like something that anyone might pick up in the course of the day. The other marks that dot her arms aren't nearly so wholesome in appearance.

Obviously Guy knows a thing or two about bandages.

"Willow," Cathy calls from downstairs. "You'd better hurry, or you'll be late for school."

Yeah, yeah.

Willow picks up her backpack and starts down the stairs. She can hear David puttering around the kitchen and the sweet little noises that Isabelle makes as Cathy feeds her. She stops and sits down on the third stair in order to listen more carefully.

Everything sounds normal, everything sounds *good.* This is the way things are supposed to be—they're just a young family getting ready to meet the day.

Willow hates to join them, because she knows that as soon as she steps into the kitchen the illusion will instantly be destroyed. Her presence reminds everyone that there's something desperately wrong, that this isn't just an ordinary family going about its business. This family is different. This is a fractured family.

She sits on the stairs, delaying the moment as long as possible.

"Willow!" Now Cathy sounds irritated.

Willow jumps to her feet. She knows that Cathy has a thousand things to do—feed Isabelle, get ready for work—the last thing Willow wants is to make life more difficult for her.

"Good morning." David looks up as she walks into the kitchen.

"Morning," Willow mumbles. She busies herself with milk and cereal, her eyes on her brother as she does so. As usual he's surrounded by a mountain of books. She wonders what he's reading and briefly considers asking him, but yesterday's experience is still too raw. Clearly talking about books with David is no longer on the menu.

"How's this new thing you're working on going?" Cathy turns to ask him as she wipes Isabelle's face with a napkin.

Obviously Cathy has no such problems talking to David.

"Is it turning out the way you hoped?" she continues between sips of coffee.

"Hmm, hard to tell." David closes the book he's reading with a sigh. "I need to take a look at some other source material before I can go on. Unfortunately, finding some of the books I want is proving just about impossible, given how long they've been out of print."

"What about the library?" Cathy is once more focused on Isabelle. Willow can tell that she's only listening with half an ear, but Willow herself is all attention as she leans against the counter pretending to be totally focused on her cereal.

"They have most of the things I'm looking for, but not the one book that I really need immediately," David says unhappily. "I'm told that an interlibrary loan will take weeks."

"I bet you can find it online." Cathy is reassuring. She unties the little bib that Isabelle is wearing and picks her up.

"You'd think." David shakes his head. "But most of the sites that deal in out of print books don't handle this kind of thing at all."

Willow is sure that *she* can find whatever book he's looking for. Forget online, the easiest thing to do would be to go downtown to their favorite bookstore. The one she talked about with Guy. The one that their father introduced David to years ago, back when he was still in grade school. They have everything under the sun, out of print or not.

Could David possibly have forgotten about that place?

Of course he didn't forget about it!

Willow knows why he isn't going there. It's probably just too painful, it would stir up too many memories. Her actions haven't only deprived them of their parents. So much of the fabric of their daily lives has been changed because of her. Now a simple trip to the bookstore is impossible for David.

"I've got to get ready," Cathy says. "Excuse me, Willow." She puts her coffee cup and Isabelle's dishes in the sink, then starts to walk out of the kitchen with the baby in her arms. "Don't you have a class this morning?" She stops to give David a kiss. "Shouldn't you be getting a move on?"

"You're right." David pushes back his chair. "I'd better hurry."

"What about you, Willow?" Cathy turns toward her. "Are you working this afternoon? Or will you be home early?"

"I'm working," Willow says. She moves out of the way as David brings his own dishes to the sink. She's hoping that he'll leave his pile of books and notes on the table when he goes out of the room to shave or whatever it is that he has to do.

"We'll see you at dinner, then." Cathy smiles at her.

"See you later," David calls over his shoulder. He follows Cathy out of the kitchen.

Willow puts her cereal down and walks stealthily over to the table. If she's lucky, that legal pad that David's scribbled all over will give her some clue as to what he's looking for.

She glances over her shoulder. She definitely doesn't want David coming in and catching her going through his notes, but the coast is clear, and she picks up the pad.

There's a mass of things written down—not only that, but David's handwriting is barely legible. Still, Willow flips through the pages, hoping to be able to make some sense out of it all.

What's this?

It looks like a list of reference works. David's jotted down several different titles, along with notes as to their availability. One in particular is heavily underlined in red. Willow is sure that she's hit upon exactly what she's looking for.

A Study of the Social Origins of Greek Religion? Published in 1927? Sounds right up his alley.

If the bookstore is too painful for David to go to, then Willow will just have to do it for him. Of course, she's sure that it will be difficult for her too, but she doesn't care. She wants to do something for David so badly that she would brave almost anything. And at least this will have meaning for him. Unlike her other attempts to cheer him up, this is something that he truly needs and wants.

If she cuts her last class she'll have time to go down there before her stint at the library. Skipping school isn't the best idea, but school doesn't rank very high on her list of priorities these days.

Willow smiles a little as she rips off a page from the pad and writes the reference down. She's not sure exactly how she'll present the book to him, but she can't believe that he won't at least be somewhat pleased.

Finally, *something* she can do for her brother.

❋

"Oh, Willow?"

What now?

Willow stops dead in her tracks. She'd bolted out of French as soon as the bell had rung—unusual for her—but she simply can't wait to get downtown and scope out that book for David.

"Yes?" Willow turns around slowly. She studies Ms. Benson carefully, trying to figure out what it is that she wants. Does she suspect that Willow is going to cut her next class? Or that Willow cuts *herself*?

"You left the room so fast," Ms. Benson says. Her voice is pleasant, but the expression on her face is rather serious. "I didn't have a chance to give you this." She hands her the quiz she took the week before.

That's all?

Willow is relieved until she glances at it more closely. She can't believe it. She simply *can't* believe it. Just when she'd come up with this idea of how to help David too. . . .

"It's nothing to be too concerned about, it's early in the semester, and you have plenty of time to bring up your grade. However, the school policy is that when any student fails a test it has to be signed off on by a . . ." Ms. Benson doesn't finish, and it's obvious that she's even more uncomfortable than Willow is. "It has to be signed off on," she says after a moment. "I want to reassure you that this doesn't have to affect your final grade. There's plenty of extra credit assignments we can come up with to offset this. If you could bring it back signed tomorrow that would be great. Friday at the latest, okay?"

"Sure thing," Willow says, but she can barely meet her gaze. Her eyes are riveted by the piece of paper in her hand, by the red *F* slashed across the top of it.

It's not that she's failed a quiz—bad enough, since she's never failed anything before—it's more that she's failed her *brother*. The thought of giving this to David, of presenting him with further proof that she's screwing up is too much to bear. She can't add to his worries, she can't give him one more thing that reminds him that he is the parent now. What's the point of even tracking down that book if she's going to hand him *this* at the same time?

She'll have to do a little forgery. Odd that she has qualms about doing something so minor.

After all, a little sleight of hand is nothing compared to murder.

"I'll get it back to you." She nods. "Tomorrow's no problem."

"Terrific," Ms. Benson says, and melts back into the press of students that are crowding the halls.

Willow hurries out of the school and onto the street. Walking is probably the quickest way to get to the bookstore, and she heads downtown as fast as her feet will take her.

She's so intent on getting there that she barely notices the other people on the pavement. Willow zigzags down the street, avoiding people when she can, but bumping into them more often than not. She doesn't care, though, as long as—

"Can you say excuse me?" An irate voice fractures her consciousness. "Oh, hey, Willow, right?" Chloe calms down as she recognizes Willow. "What are you in such a rush for?"

"I'm really sorry," Willow says somewhat breathlessly. "I just . . . I have to get downtown, I wasn't really watching where I was going." She looks back and forth between Chloe and Laurie.

"We're headed that way too," Laurie says between sips of an iced coffee. "Shopping," she confides. "There's some serious shoe stores downtown."

"Shoes?" Willow gives Laurie a look. She never figured her for someone who would skip school to score the latest pair of shoes. "Don't you guys have class or something?"

"We have a study hall at the end of the day three days a week. Technically we're supposed to be in the library, but nobody cares if we just leave," Laurie explains.

"We spent our entire junior year trying to figure out how to schedule that," Chloe adds with a laugh.

"Seniors' privilege." Laurie shrugs. "So, you want to come with us?"

"Yes . . . I mean no." Willow shakes her head. "I mean, I'm headed downtown, but I don't have time to go shopping. Thanks, though."

"Well, walk with us anyway," Laurie urges.

"Okay," Willow says, somewhat reluctantly.

She feels more comfortable around them than she would have a week ago. She's no longer quite so worried about saying the wrong thing. Their time in the park has made her feel like she can be with people without making a complete fool of herself. But she wants to be alone. She needs to think about how she's going to forge her brother's signature. She needs to think about how she's going to find that book. Much as she wishes she could, she *can't* be thinking about shoes.

Won't it be obvious if she forges David's signature? Won't her writing look like a girl's?

Maybe I should just trace it. . . .

"So, Chloe and I want to know, what's going on with you and Guy?"

There's got to be some bill or paper with his signature on it lying around the house. I'll just—

"Excuse me?" It takes a second for Willow to realize that Laurie's asked her a question. It takes her even longer to process just what that question was.

"Sorry." It's clear that Laurie interprets Willow's confusion as embarrassment.

"Oh, don't pay Laurie any attention," Chloe says to Willow. "She has to know everything about everybody. Don't even answer. You'll only encourage her."

"I don't have to know *everything*," Laurie protests. "I was wondering, that's all. It just seems like there's something going on between the two of you." She pauses and looks at Willow.

You have no idea. . . .

"Fine, I'm more interested in shoes anyway," Laurie says. "They'd better still have that red pair that was on sale last week."

"The ones that were half off? With the kitten heels? You'll be lucky."

Chloe and Laurie start debating various heel heights and styles. Willow nods as if she's following the conversation, but she can't stop thinking about the failed quiz.

How can I trace his signature? The paper's so heavy. Will I even be able to see through it?

Without thinking she digs the quiz out of her bag and holds it up, trying to assess just how opaque it is.

"So you agree, Willow? Purple snakeskin stilettos are just too conservative for school?"

"Huh?" Willow doesn't even pretend that she knows what's going on.

"I knew that would get her!" Laurie grins at Chloe. "You're so totally in your own world!" She pries the paper out of Willow's hand. "C'mon, what could possibly be more interesting than shoes? Oh!" She looks at Willow with a stricken expression on her face, and for a moment Willow can't help smiling. Clearly, for Laurie, nothing could be worse than a bad grade.

"I'm sorry," Laurie says after a second. "And I shouldn't have grabbed it either." She hands the paper back to Willow.

"It's okay." Willow shrugs. Having Laurie and Chloe know that she failed hardly matters to her at this point.

"You know what?" Chloe says. "You'll be able to handle this really easily. Benson is totally open to extra credit projects and stuff like that. If you do better on the rest of the quizzes this semester, she'll probably even drop this one."

"Completely true," Laurie is quick to agree. "I did some extra work for her last year, just to lock in a really good grade."

"It's not that so much," Willow says. "It's more that my brother has to sign off on this." She is surprised to hear herself confiding in them.

"Okay." Laurie nods slowly; she's willing to listen, but she looks a little bit confused. And Willow knows that while Laurie is totally sympathetic about the bad grade, she's completely ignorant of the bigger issues at hand.

"I mean, that's something that a parent's supposed to do! Only now he's the one who has to deal with this kind of stuff!" Willow bursts out in frustration.

"Oh." Laurie pauses for a moment. "It's terrible about your parents," she says quietly. "But you know," she continues, "at least your brother's willing to do this kind of thing. I can't imagine mine would. I mean, it's sort of sweet, don't you think?"

Sweet.

Laurie's a nice girl. She's truly *nice*. She's willing to include Willow in whatever she's doing, she's willing to overlook stupid remarks about kittens, she's willing to commiserate about failed quizzes, and she's even, unlike some people, compassionate about Willow's situation.

But it's clear that kind as she is, caring as she is, she's utterly *clueless*!

"Yes," Willow says dully. She stops outside the bookstore. "It's sort of sweet.

"I have to go in here," she says after an uncomfortable pause. "I need a book," she adds unnecessarily.

"Sure," Chloe says agreeably. "If you feel like it, when you're done, you can catch up with us. We'll be across the street, down two blocks." She gestures toward some shops in the distance. "There's a whole row of shoe stores over that way."

"Okay." Willow manages a smile. "And good luck finding the red shoes, Laurie. They'll go with your hair, I mean when you get around to coloring it."

"Thanks." Laurie smiles back. "I'll wear whatever I get to school tomorrow."

Willow watches them walk away, then turns to head into the bookstore.

It's as if there's a plate glass wall standing between her and the entrance.

That's how hard it is for her to bridge the gap that lies between her and the door. Of course she'd known that coming here would be difficult, but she'd thought that she could handle it. As long as she was doing something for David, she figured that she could put up with just about anything.

Except she hadn't counted on the place itself being so overwhelming. Every time she's been here before, *every time*, has been in the company of one of her parents.

Willow stands still and watches as other people go in and out of the store. Suppose she went up to one of them, that cute guy going in right now for instance, and asked him to help her, to take her arm as if she were an old lady and walk her across the street. Would he look at her as if she were crazy? And if he did do as she asked, would it even be enough?

For a second Willow considers abandoning the whole project, running after Chloe and Laurie, seeing if she can help them find the red shoes with the kitten heels. But they're long gone, and besides, she so wants to do this. . . .

She'd better do it soon too, she doesn't have that much time left.

Okay, c'mon, deep breath now. . . .

She's sure that she must actually look like an old lady as she crosses the few feet of sidewalk. She's certainly never walked this slowly, this painfully, before. Someone holds the door open for her, not the way they would in the normal course of things, but more like they can tell that she's terribly sick, and they want to spare her any further pain.

"Thank you," Willow says. She sounds like an old lady too.

Willow looks around. The place hasn't changed since the last time she was here. Well, it probably hasn't changed much in the last fifty years, but still, the stability is unsettling. She can't help thinking that her parents' deaths should have changed everything in their world, not just the immediate world of their family.

She takes a few steps forward and is immediately assaulted by the smells, the crush of people, the sheer energy of the place. But it's okay, she can handle it now. The important thing is to get David's book, and then to head back uptown as fast as possible.

Willow walks over to the anthropology section—she could

find it blindfolded—and pulls out the scrap of paper that she scribbled the title on.

Harrison, J.E.

At least it won't be anywhere near her parents' books.

But after a few minutes of searching the shelves, she's forced to conclude that it doesn't look as if it's anywhere at all.

Fine, so I'll have to deal with the staff.

Willow goes over to the information desk and hands the slip of paper to the clerk. He's probably only about five or six years older than she is. Like the store itself, he's slightly unkempt. He doesn't look like someone who loves books. Willow can see that he's reading an alternative music magazine.

"Whas up?" True to form, he looks irritated at the interruption. Clearly, reading his magazine is much more important than helping a customer. She smiles as she remembers Guy's description of the employees.

"I couldn't find this anywhere," Willow says as sweetly as possible. "Do you think you might have it? Maybe upstairs in the rare book room?"

"Gimme a sec," the guy says between bites of his sandwich. "What is this, anthropology? Archaeology? Religion?" He squints at her handwriting.

"Most likely anthropology," Willow says. "But I guess technically it could fit into—"

"I'll find you, okay?" He interrupts her. "Just hang out in the anthro section and I'll let you know in a few minutes."

Willow wanders slowly back to the anthropology area, stopping at British imports on the way.

She leafs idly through a few books. It's strange, but except for school assignments, she really hasn't read anything in months, not since her parents died. Books used to be as vital to her as food, reading them, talking about them, but now . . .

Although of course, she and Guy did discuss—

"I said to hang out in the anthro section." The clerk startles her out of her reverie. "Anyway, we got it, I mean we *can* get it."

"Great!" Willow is beyond relieved. For a second there she thought that she'd have to leave empty-handed.

"Yeah." He picks his teeth as he looks her over from head to toe. "Special order, a hundred and eighty-six bucks, six weeks max, more like three probably. Oh, you have to pay in full now. You know, it being a special order and all that."

"I . . . Wha . . . It's . . . Huh?"

A hundred and eighty-six dollars? Three to six weeks?

She'd assumed it would be expensive, and figured that she'd pick up some extra shifts at the library, but . . .

A hundred and eighty-six dollars!

Willow is literally speechless.

"So how about it? You want it?"

Willow just stares at him. Her mind is a complete blank.

"You interested?" he persists. "Hey, is something wrong, because you look like you're going to . . ."

"Allergies." Willow swipes a hand across her eyes.

"Yeah? Me too. So you want to order it?"

"I . . . uh . . ."

"You live down here?" he interrupts. It's obvious that he couldn't care less about whether she gets the book or not. "I play in a band a couple doors down. After work. Wednesdays and Fridays. You could come down, listen to us, maybe hang out afterwards."

This isn't happening!

"Thank you, I . . . No. No, I'm sorry, I don't have the money for the book. And I live . . ."

Willow spins away, not sure where she's headed, but she has to be alone. And quickly too.

She pushes past people, desperate for a place that she can be by herself. She looks down each and every aisle, but they're never empty, there's always someone browsing through the dusty old volumes.

Willow is feeling more and more disoriented. She's hot, the dust is making her feel as if she really *does* have allergies. The place is too fraught with memories, and she's horribly, horribly disappointed.

Finally, as she nears the end of the store, she spies an aisle with only one customer who is slowly making his way out.

Willow shoves past him, with barely an excuse me, and collapses against the hard metal frame of the bookshelves. She's breathing heavily and doesn't even notice the way that the books jab into her. She sinks slowly to the floor and buries her head in her hands.

Well, what did you think? What did you think *would happen?*

She should have known better. Nothing else works out for her, so why should this have been the single exception? Why did she think she could succeed where David had failed? Her track record of late has hardly been impressive. Willow ticks off the mistakes that she's made on her fingers. One: She should have known the book would be that expensive. Two: She should have known that something that obscure wouldn't just be waiting for her on the shelf, for her to pick up and waltz off with. Three: She should have known that even if she had found the book, it would have made absolutely no difference.

But I was hoping . . .

Willow raises her head slowly. She hadn't realized just how much she was counting on giving David the stupid book. It had seemed like the perfect thing to do that morning, but really, now that she considers it more carefully, is it any less shallow than her attempts to cheer him up with some fatuous compliments? She's ashamed for thinking that something so simple would make her brother's life better. She's ashamed of herself for being so shallow.

And she's especially ashamed for thinking that buying David a book would be enough to make him love her again.

Willow opens her bag slowly, calmly. There's none of the frantic urgency that she usually associates with her need. Somehow it just seems inevitable now. She is someone who cuts. It's that simple. She's someone who killed her parents. She's someone who has lost her brother. And she is someone who has to cut.

She rolls up her sleeve, then shakes her head. She really will have to wait for some of those cuts to heal before she can work there again. Her legs are a much better bet, but getting to them is not so easy. Still, Willow leans forward and pushes up the leg of her jeans.

"Excuse me."

She jerks her head up as someone steps over her and reaches for a book.

Will nothing work out?

She squeezes the razor in frustration. It slices into her palm as she does so.

Good!

But that is all she can do. And anyway, it's time to go. She has to get to work.

Willow straightens her jeans, puts her things back into her bag, and starts to stand up. As she does so her eye is caught by an old and worn, but nevertheless beautiful, small leather volume jammed in helter-skelter amid all the other books.

She wonders what it's doing in this section and looks toward the end of the aisle, where a small card is posted.

Elizabethan and Restoration Drama.

Willow hadn't realized what part of the store she'd chosen for her little meltdown. She pulls out the book and looks at the blue leather binding, then leafs through the dog-eared copy of *The Tempest*, trying to read the faded purple ink where some earlier reader had annotated the margins.

"Hey, can I get by you already?"

She looks up into the face of an especially cute guy. An actor probably.

"Yes, sorry." Willow scrambles to her feet. She pauses for a moment in the act of putting *The Tempest* back on the shelf. Then she tucks it under her arm and walks toward the cash registers.

Willow isn't really sure why she wants to buy it. She's read the play a million times, she doesn't have time to read anything that isn't related to school right now, and if she did, there are several editions back in the apartment.

Besides . . .

Didn't he say his father was a banker? The last thing he needs is some old moth-eaten edition like this.

He'd probably think it was strange for her to be giving him a used book as a present, all written in and marked up. He'd probably think it was strange for her to be giving him any kind of present at all.

And why is she thinking of getting *Guy* something, anyway?

Unconsciously, Willow touches the cut that he had bandaged.

She doesn't have to give it to him. She doesn't have to do anything with it. She can even toss it out. It doesn't matter, it's just something to have.

Except he really should read *The Tempest*.

Maybe her visit wasn't a total waste, she thinks as she pays for the book and hurries to work.

❋

"Well, look at you." Carlos winks at her as she rushes into the library flushed and slightly breathless, nearly twenty minutes late. "I hope you've been having fun."

"Not exactly." Willow stows her bag underneath the circulation desk. "What kind of mood is she in?" she whispers as she pins her ID to her shirt.

"You're lucky, she isn't here. Emergency root canal."

"Ow." Willow winces in sympathy. She sits down on one of the high stools and tucks her feet underneath the rungs.

"Ask me if anything else interesting happened," Carlos says. He leans back in his chair and gives Willow an arch look.

"Anything else interesting happen?" Willow picks up her

cue, but she's not really listening. She's wondering if she can get some homework done—after all, Miss Hamilton isn't here. . . .

"Someone was asking for you."

"For me?" Willow is surprised. "You mean my brother?"

"Get out of here." Carlos rolls his eyes. "You think I don't know your brother? Younger. Your age. A guy," he adds, anticipating her next question. "I've seen him around before."

"Oh." Willow considers this for a minute. The only other person she can think of is Guy. "What did he want?"

"Wanted to know if you were working today. I told him yes."

"Huh." She shrugs and tries to look indifferent. "Well, maybe he'll come back."

"No maybe about it." Carlos brings his chair back down with a bang and stands up as Guy approaches the desk.

"Hey." Guy smiles at her. "I was working up here and I thought that maybe when you get a break we could—"

"She's got a break now," Carlos interjects.

"I just got here!" Willow protests.

"I'm in charge today," Carlos says. "Besides, things are pretty quiet here. Go on, see you in thirty."

"Well, thanks," Willow says slowly. Of course she's happy to have a break, but she feels a little shy all of a sudden. She takes her ID off and stuffs it into her bag, then pauses for a second.

It's totally safe to leave her bag here. She always does when she takes her break, just takes her wallet and puts it in her pocket.

But Willow can't help thinking about the copy of *The Tempest* that's lying at the bottom of her backpack.

Not that she knows what she's going to do with it or anything, but she might as well take her bag with her for once.

"See you in a bit," she says to Carlos as she slings her backpack over her shoulder.

"That was nice of him," Guy says. They walk down the marble stairs and out of the building.

"Uh-huh." Willow nods. She's sure that she can feel the book weighing down her already heavy bag. It must be her imagination, though. After all, it could hardly be more than a few ounces at most.

"So." Guy gives her a smile. "I was working in the library, and I needed to take a break. I thought maybe I could drag you to that place I told you about."

"That place with the cappuccinos? Sure." Willow pauses. "So what were you working on?"

Willow *is* interested to hear what he's been working on, but there are a million things that she'd rather know first—like *why* he wants to take his break with her in the first place.

Is it because he feels he has to keep tabs on her illicit activities since he hasn't told David?

Is it because he might just kind of want to be with me?

Maybe she should give him the book after all.

"Oh, I'm just doing some reading for the class that I'm taking up here. Hey, watch out." He pulls her back on the curb as a bike messenger whizzes past.

"Thanks." Willow is startled. Not so much by the bike, although it did almost knock her down, but by the feel of his arm on hers. She should be used to his touch, though. After all, he's bandaged her, pulled her up the stairs, held her hand. . . .

Perhaps she's so affected because she's still off balance from her experience in the bookstore. Or perhaps it's because this is the first time that he's touched her for a reason wholly unrelated to cutting.

"This is the place." Guy opens the door.

Willow sits down across from him at one of the green marble tables and picks up a menu, then puts it down and starts biting her nails.

Lovely.

She picks up the menu again, but makes no attempt to open it, then busies herself with the napkin dispenser.

"Are you okay?"

"Oh sure, just a little . . ."

Nervous and uncomfortable.

But that doesn't make any sense. After all, he *knows* about her, she has nothing to fear from him.

Then why is she so edgy?

She thinks back to the other day in the park, when she persuaded him to stay with her. She should have let him go then. She's broken her post-accident resolution. She's starting to feel things. Feel a *lot* of things.

Willow can't allow herself to do that. She should never have let him get to her this way. She has no business talking to him about what he likes to read or where he grew up or anything like that at all.

And what is she doing buying him presents? As soon as she gets back to work, she's throwing it out. First thing. . . .

"Do you know what you want?" Guy asks.

"Huh?" Willow hadn't even noticed that a waiter had shown up. She opens the menu, but it's upside-down.

"Never mind, I'll take care of it." Guy laughs at her, but in a nice way. "Umm, two iced cappuccinos, and two, God, what would you like? Umm, let's see, she'll have . . . a strawberry tart." He looks at her. "That work?"

"Well, sure." Willow nods. "But I really don't have that much time, I have to be back in . . ."

"I know, but something tells me that Carlos will cut you a little slack." Guy looks back at the waiter. "So that's two iced cappuccinos, a strawberry tart, and a—"

"Wait." She manages to turn the menu around. "Umm, he'll have the mocha napoleon."

"Got it in one." Guy hands the menus back to the waiter. "So you know, I was wondering. . . . Wait a sec . . ." He stops talking suddenly and reaches across the table to take hold of Willow's hand. This time his touch is rough, harsh almost, and Willow gives a little gasp.

He opens her hand palm side upward, and stares at the line of dried blood that runs from one end to the other.

"It's not what you think."

"Isn't it?"

"No." Willow squirms a little in her chair. His gaze is too intense, and she looks away. "All right, you want to know the truth? It's not what you think it is, but not for lack of trying, okay?" She pulls her hand away.

"What do you mean?"

"I mean, I wanted to but I couldn't. I wasn't alone. Look, you want to help me?"

"Yes."

"Then talk about something else."

"Okay," Guy says. "What?"

"Well . . ." Willow rests her chin on her hands and thinks for a moment. "I don't know, anything. The weather."

"The weather?"

"Okay. How about the weather in Kuala Lumpur?"

"We already did that." Guy crosses his arms over his chest and gives her a look.

"So tell me about the rest of it. What was it like over there?"

"You're really fixated on that place, aren't you?"

"I like the name." Willow shrugs.

"Whatever." Guy pauses for a second while the waiter sets their order down. "Okay, you want to know what it was like? Everything was really different. I mean *everything*. The people, the buildings, the food, the whole culture. It might as well have been on a whole other planet. But I really couldn't appreciate it, because, well, it was just sort of difficult for me there."

"Difficult? But it sounds like it would be fun," Willow protests. "You were living in this whole other society, you got to read all the time . . ." She trails off as she realizes how shallow she sounds. She might as well be telling him that it sounds *sweet*. "I'm sorry, how was it difficult?"

She can't believe what she's asking. She should get up and walk away instead of getting in deeper and deeper. The last thing she needs is to hear things that make him matter *more* to her.

So much for resolutions. She's like an ex-smoker in a cigarette factory.

"Don't get me wrong." Guy shakes his head. "It wasn't bad exactly. There was a lot about it that was great. We got to do some really incredible stuff, like travel all over the place, go to Thailand . . . Also, it is incredibly interesting getting to see this whole other world up close. But I just never fit in. I mean, I expected Kuala Lumpur to be different. What was weird, though, was that the kids I hung around with and the school I went to were different than anything else I'd ever experienced too. They were all British, all very, very wealthy. They were as strange to me as everything else over there, only the thing is, I was supposed to be just like them. I wasn't. And that was . . ."

"Difficult," Willow says slowly. "That does sound like it would be hard. I'm sorry you didn't have such a great time, but you know what I think?"

"Uh-uh. Tell me."

"Well, being an outsider like that, I think maybe *that's* what made you interested in anthropology. I mean way before you ever read any books or took my brother's class. Observing another culture from the outside, that's sort of what anthropology is about, right?"

"I never thought about it like that." Guy takes a sip of his coffee. "I just complained that I didn't belong, but you're probably right." He stops talking and looks at her for a minute. "You know what? I'm doing a lousy job of distracting you."

"Oh no, listening to someone else's problems . . . believe me, total distraction."

"But it's your problem too. Being an outsider. Well, at least you *think* it is. One of them anyway, and the last thing I want to do is remind you of stuff like that."

"Oh." Willow looks down at her plate. He has a point, of course, but oddly enough, listening to him hasn't made her think of her own situation at all. Still, it would be nice if they could talk about simple things for once.

"All right then," she says. "I don't suppose the weather in Thailand was any better? Wait a sec." Her eye is caught by a flash of red outside the window. "We're in luck, something much more interesting." Willow leans sideways, almost out of her chair, and cranes her neck to look out the glass. "Sorry, false alarm."

"What were you staring at?" Guy looks out the window too.

"I thought I saw Laurie go by, correction, Laurie's new red shoes." Willow relaxes back in her chair. "She went shoe shopping this afternoon, she's going to wear them tomorrow."

"That's more interesting?"

"About a million times. But it wasn't her, so forget it."

"Yeah, I'm totally lost—you went shopping with her?"

"No," Willow sighs. "I should have, but I didn't. She and Chloe were walking downtown to go shopping, and I was going to that bookstore we . . . you like. So we just sort of walked together."

"The one where I told you I bought *Tristes*?" Guy perks up. "Did you get anything?"

"No," Willow says after a moment. "Nothing really."

"I wish I'd known you were going there, I would have gone with you. Were you looking for anything special?"

Willow doesn't answer for a minute. She's too busy thinking about her botched errand. She's too busy thinking about the fact that she has nothing to give David when she sees him later, nothing except a failed quiz, and she *won't* give her brother that.

"Willow?"

"Sorry, I was just . . . Look." Willow grabs her backpack and digs the quiz out. She's careful to keep the bag with *The Tempest* in it hidden from view. "I'm supposed to give David this." She hands Guy the paper. "He has to sign it. I *can't* give it to him, though. I'm going to have to forge his signature or something." She toys with her strawberry tart for a second, then pushes her plate away.

"This must be a new experience for you," Guy says as he takes in the red *F*.

"You're not kidding."

"It will look like a girl's handwriting unless you trace it." Guy holds the paper up to the light. "And the paper's too thick for that." He hands her back the quiz. "I know what you told me in the park, but I think you may be wrong about the whole situation. I mean, are you sure that you just can't give it to him? Okay, it's a really bad grade, but he'll be able to handle it. Signing this isn't that big a deal, is it?"

"It's what signing it *means,* it's what it represents. He could barely handle that parent-teacher conference. How am I going to . . . It's just . . . It's too much. And it's not the grade either, it's more that . . ." Willow shakes her head, at a loss for what to say. Nobody understands, nobody *gets* it. "I bet you think it's sweet, don't you?" Willow says after a moment, a distinct edge to her voice.

"Sweet?" Guy is baffled.

"I mean that he would do stuff like this for me, you know, sign off on a quiz, be the parent."

"Sweet?" he repeats incredulously. "Are you *kidding*? It sounds really, really hard, but I still think that you—"

"I bought you something," Willow blurts out.

"You bought . . . What?"

Willow closes her eyes for a second. She's a little surprised that she's going to give it to him after all, but there's no going back. Now she has to.

"At the bookstore." She reaches into her bag again and pushes the package across the table toward him.

Guy takes the book out of the bag slowly. Willow waits for him to look disappointed, to look confused that she would buy him such a battered, old—

"I love it when used books have notes in the margins, it's the best," Guy says as he flips through the pages. "I always imagine who read it before me." He pauses and looks at one of Prospero's speeches. "I have way too much homework to read this now, but you know what? Screw it, I want to know why it's your favorite Shakespeare. Thank you, that was really nice of you. I mean, you really didn't have to do that."

"But I did anyway," Willow says, so quietly that she's not sure he even hears her.

"Hey." Guy frowns for a second. "*You* didn't write anything in it."

"Oh, I didn't even think . . . I, well, I wouldn't even know what to write," Willow says shyly.

"Well, maybe you'll think of something later," he says.

Willow watches Guy read the opening. There's no mistaking it, his smile is genuine, and she can't help thinking that if she can't make David look like this, at least she can do it for someone.

CHAPTER NINE

"You can only take this out overnight," Willow says as she checks the girl's ID to make sure that she has borrowing privileges.

"That's all I need, because this paper's due tomorrow," the girl responds somewhat breathlessly. She grabs the book. "Thanks."

"Good luck with the paper," Willow says as she watches her dash down the stairs.

She settles back on her stool, careful not to check the clock again. Her shift isn't over for another hour, but she's so bored that she doesn't think that she'll be able to make it.

"So how'd it go?" Carlos comes up behind her.

"Hmm, no big deal," Willow says innocently. "Just a simple checkout, she didn't need an interlibrary loan or anything."

"You idiot!" Carlos swats her arm. "You know exactly what I'm talking about." He sits down and pulls his chair close to Willow's. "Liven up my day, honey. C'mon. Tell me stuff."

"Don't you have anyone else you can bother?" Willow says.

"No."

"All right," she sighs. "Umm . . . it was good. Great strawberry tarts at that place a few blocks from here."

"I want a restaurant review, I'll read the paper."

"Why are you so interested in what happened?" Willow turns to look at him.

"'Cause I've never seen you smile like this before." Carlos tips his chair back and regards her solemnly.

Oh.

"Never mind." He laughs at her. "You're just fun to tease. Why don't you get out of here now?"

"I have almost an hour left!" Willow objects.

"Like I told you before, this place is dead today. Really, I can handle it by myself," Carlos assures her. "Besides, you work too hard."

"A lot you know." Willow thinks of the giant red *F* splashed across her quiz, which is nestled in among all the overdue homework assignments languishing in her bag. "But thanks, Carlos, you're really kind." If he's willing to let her go, then she's not about to argue. Willow slides off of the stool and grabs her things from underneath the circulation desk.

"Don't worry, I intend to collect on this one," Carlos says dryly. "You can cover one of my shifts later on, maybe next week."

"Absolutely," Willow calls over her shoulder as she runs down the stairs two at a time. It must be all the caffeine she had earlier, there's no other reason for her to feel so buoyant.

It can hardly be that she's that thrilled to get off forty minutes early. And it certainly can't be that she has a hundred and fifty pages of the *Bulfinch* to read before tomorrow, as well as finally getting started on that stupid paper.

And it definitely isn't the fact that she has to figure out some way of faking David's signature on that quiz.

Willow slows down, her good mood plummeting as she thinks about the task ahead of her. Tracing seems like the best way to go, in spite of the thickness of the paper. If she rifles through his desk she should be able to find some cancelled checks fairly easily. She'll just have to hold the paper up to a really strong light. . . .

She hates what her life has become.

Willow stops dead in her tracks. There up ahead is David. He sees her too, and gives a brief wave as he heads over toward her. There's nothing strange about bumping into him on campus, after all, it is where he works. . . .

But his sudden appearance affects Willow in uncomfortable ways, and not only because she's planning to forge his signature. It's more that seeing him like this reminds her of all the other times she's met up with him on campus.

She thinks back to the beginning of March, just a few days before the accident. It had been very cold and gray, flurries too, if she remembers correctly. She and Cathy had been shivering because they had expected it to be warmer. Wasn't spring supposed to be around the corner? David had been mad at Cathy for not dressing more warmly. Not really mad, more protective—she was, after all, seven and a half months pregnant.

They'd all gone out to dinner, where David and Cathy had bored her to tears by spending the evening picking out names for the baby. Well, she really hadn't been that bored, she was actually pretty excited about becoming an aunt. At sixteen, none of Willow's friends had any nieces or nephews. Still, acting bored and demanding to talk about other topics had seemed like the thing to do.

Helen. That had been the name they had finally decided upon. Not so surprising; her brother's always been an *Iliad* fan too. David was sure that their parents would approve.

They may have liked the name. Willow never asked them. But they never lived to see their first grandchild.

Isabelle was her mother's middle name. Born six weeks premature, nothing to worry about these days, but nothing that would have happened either, Willow is sure, if Cathy hadn't been under so much stress.

Sometimes she's amazed that Cathy can even look her in the face.

"Hey," David says, walking up to her. "I'm on my way home, but I wasn't expecting to see you. You're out early, aren't you?" He shifts the pile of books under his arm. "Is something wrong? Do you feel sick, or did you get into trouble?"

"Nothing like that," Willow hastens to assure him. "It was just really quiet today, so they let me out early."

"Good." David nods. "We can walk home together. I wanted to—Stephen, what are you doing here?" He greets the tall, slightly disheveled man who's wandered over their way.

"David, how are you?" Stephen shakes his hand. "You know, I had no idea I was going to be here. If I had, I would have e-mailed you ahead of time and let you know."

Willow has no clue who this Stephen is. She's never seen him before, and she waits patiently for David to introduce her.

"So what's going on with you?" David asks.

"I'm interviewing at some local colleges, and I thought I'd stop by here and take a look around the department." Stephen makes a rueful face. "I heard they might be needing someone next fall."

"Yeah, you know, I think there is something opening up." David looks thoughtful. "But it's a little junior for you."

"Get out of here, I'll take anything. Hey! I heard that you were married. Is that possibly true?"

"Married with a *kid*." David nods. "Can you believe it? Remember Cathy? We got married. We have a daughter. Isabelle."

"Good God! It's only been about a year and a half since I last saw you! It's incredible how things can change in such a short time! What else has happened since then?"

Willow looks at her brother anxiously. She knows how uncomfortable this question must make him, how much pain it will give him to answer.

"Yes, it's amazing what can change in such a short time," David says after an appreciable pause.

"Like what else could possibly happen besides getting married and becoming a father?" Stephen laughs. "Please don't tell me that you've got tenure already—even you're not that much of a prodigy."

"God no, I wish." David laughs along with him.

Willow is the one who is amazed. It's true that she was not looking forward to David reciting the litany of woe that has been heaped upon him since he last saw this guy, that she was worried about how it would affect him . . . but for him to say *nothing*?

"And who's this?" Stephen looks at her. "A student?"

"Oh sorry, I'm not thinking clearly today. Stephen, this is my sister, Willow."

"Your sister!" Stephen extends his hand. "Do you go to school here?"

"No, I—"

"Willow's living with me and Cathy now," David interrupts. But that's all he says. He offers no explanation as to why this is so.

"That must be fun for you." Stephen smiles at her. "God, when I was a teenager I would have given anything to get out from under my parents. Speaking of which, I didn't even think to ask, how are your parents? You know it's been ages since I spoke with them, but I'll never forget that recommendation your father wrote for me. It was years ago, but I still think about it, and him too."

Willow closes her eyes for a second. Stephen's careless good cheer is just awful under the circumstances. She steps closer to her brother. She wants to take his hand, reassure him by some gesture if possible, do *something* to support him through this ordeal. Unlike a few moments ago, there is no way he can avoid answering this with anything less than the full and brutal truth. The silence stretches out, Stephen looks at David expectantly.

"He . . . He thought very highly of you," David says finally. That is *all* that he says.

Willow is stunned. She can't believe it. She honestly can't believe it! Why didn't David tell him what happened? Why didn't he let Stephen know that the man he admired so much is gone? Gone! His wife with him. That Willow was there at the end. That she was driving. That the reason she lives with

David and Cathy is *not to get out from under their parents,* but because their parents are *dead*?

What is wrong with him? Why is he in such God-awful denial?

For once, Willow is angry with her brother. Furious, in fact. What is he hiding from? Why is he always, always acting as if *nothing ever happened*?

Something inside her snaps. Gone is the girl who's desperate to make his life better. She is not the same person who left the house that morning. She no longer has the desire to flatter him on the off chance of seeing him smile, she couldn't care less about finding him a book in the vain hopes of making him feel better. She has no wish to comfort him—or worse, collude with him in his rejection of the facts. At that moment she almost hates him. Almost as much as he must hate her.

She's desperate to set the record straight. To say . . . No, to *yell* the truth in her loudest voice. She'll do it too.

Sorry, Stephen, David's not letting you in on all the details! Our parents are dead. I killed them. That's why I'm living with him and his wife, because I killed our parents! Okay? That's what's happened in the past year!

Unfortunately it's not so simple to break the training of seventeen years. Willow can't, she simply can't just stand in the middle of campus and start shouting at the top of her lungs.

If only there was someone she knew walking around. Laurie, say. Or Andy, even better. Someone she could grab and introduce to David. Someone to whom she could tell her version of events while David and his friend stood there and listened.

Willow looks around wildly, but of course, nobody she

knows is around. She's simmering with rage, completely powerless to do what she wants. She just stands there and listens to David's stupid friend carry on about his stupid job search.

"So, I'm hoping that I can get something around here, I mean I'm from this area originally and . . ."

Suddenly Willow has an idea. She knows just what to do to shock David out of his complacency, to force him to tell Stephen the truth about their situation. Forget about not wanting to remind him that he is the parent now, forget about trying to spare him! She rummages frantically in her bag. "Here," she says loudly, as loudly as she dares, interrupting Stephen mid-sentence. "Here!" she repeats, thrusting the quiz under David's nose. "You need to sign this!"

Both men look startled.

Good!!

"Go on, David," Willow insists, shoving a pen into David's hand. "You have to sign this for me. I need a *parent or legal guardian* to sign it." She looks triumphantly back and forth between her brother and his friend, expecting Stephen to ask what she means by legal guardian, expecting David to look stricken with horror.

But the moment has fallen flat. Stephen does not seem to have picked up on the key words, and David is too busy studying the quiz to pay her much attention. It's true that as the meaning of the paper sinks in, he looks concerned, but it's also clear that unlike Willow, he has no intention of making a scene in front of his friend. She realizes that the only thing she has accomplished is looking crazy, or at the very least, extremely rude.

"I should get going," Stephen says after an uncomfortable pause.

"Best of luck with the job search," David says as he scribbles his signature on the quiz and hands it back to Willow.

Willow watches Stephen walk off with a twisted little smile on her face. Maybe her actions didn't have quite the effect that she wanted, but still, she's sure that there will have to be some reckoning now. She has to believe that David will finally give her hell. Not just for failing a quiz, but also for being so incredibly ill-mannered. And once he does, she'll have her opportunity. At last they'll be able to get things out in the open.

"Let's go home," David says after a moment. It's abundantly clear from the expression on his face and the tone of his voice that he's livid. But it's also clear that he has no intention of calling Willow on either her behavior, or her grades. He doesn't even look her way as he heads out of the campus gates and toward the park.

And Willow really has no other choice but to follow silently after him.

❋

"Well, you two are home early," Cathy calls out from the kitchen as they walk into the apartment. "Good, I'm starving—in fact, I already ordered."

"Hi, Cath," David says, coming into the kitchen. He puts his books down on the table, then goes to Isabelle's high chair to gives her a kiss before turning to his wife and wrapping his arms around her.

"I hope you're up for Japanese." Cathy smiles over David's

shoulder at Willow, who has followed him into the kitchen. "It should be here any minute."

"Great," Willow says as unenthusiastically as possible. She wishes she could get away from them, go up to her room and be alone for a while. But clearly that's not on. There simply isn't time before they all sit down to eat. She'll just have to try to act like everything's fine, just like she always does, except she doesn't think that she'll be able to tonight, not after what just happened.

"Oh, you know what else?" Cathy continues, handing Willow place mats and cutlery. "Markie called again. I got the feeling that she'd really like to hear from you."

"Huh." Willow could hardly give less of a response. She starts laying the place mats and silverware around the table, dumping David's books unceremoniously on the floor as she does so.

"There's the food," Cathy says as the doorbell rings. She hurries to answer it.

"It would probably be good for you to see Markie," David remarks as he gets some plates from the cupboard and joins Willow in setting the table. "Why haven't you been returning her calls?" He almost trips over the pile of books, but manages to grab the table just in time. David picks them up with a frown and puts them on one of the empty chairs, then sits down and puts his napkin on his lap.

Is that all he's going to say to her? He's *still* not going to mention what just happened? She finds it incredible that he's not even bringing up the quiz. After all, her schoolwork is the one thing he has been able to talk to her about. Maybe the scene rattled him more than she thought.

Good.

"Because she doesn't get what it's like to be an orphan," Willow replies after a moment. She bites each word off succinctly. She sits down on the opposite side of the table from David, crosses her arms over her chest, and looks at him evenly.

Now, this isn't the whole reason that Willow has lost touch with her old friends, but she wants to state their situation as baldly as possible. She wants to rub David's face in it, get a reaction out of him. Somehow, some way, she's going to force him to respond.

David doesn't reply to this, but she does have the satisfaction of seeing him flinch.

He leans back in his chair and regards Willow thoughtfully. He looks confused, and maybe even slightly angry. One thing is for sure, though—her antics are finally starting to get to him.

"I got California rolls for us," Cathy says, coming back into the kitchen. "And tempura for you, Willow. Is that okay?" Neither David nor Willow answers her.

"I'll take that as a yes," she mutters, opening the food and placing it on the table.

Except for the sounds that Isabelle makes as she fusses in her high chair, there is total silence.

"So how was work today?" Cathy asks David. Clearly, she senses the tension around the table, and is hoping to dispel it with small talk.

"It was fine," David replies after a moment. He looks away from Willow. "Nothing really special."

Willow wonders if she should mention the incident with Stephen. Would Cathy be surprised that David didn't say anything to him about their parents dying? Would that finally bring things to a crisis?

"Wasn't seeing your old friend—"

"I thought that we could—"

Willow and Cathy speak at the same time.

"Sorry," Willow says after a second. "You go first."

"I was just going to say that *I* had a really hard day at work, and I'd really love to do something tonight." Cathy sounds a little on edge.

Willow gives Cathy a sideways glance. She does look like she's had a hard day, there are circles under her eyes, and her hair is somewhat disheveled. Not so surprising, she has a job working in a law firm and a six-month-old. She looks like she needs a break, maybe a movie or something. Willow knows that she should offer to babysit.

Odd that they've never asked her to before.

In fact, it's *extremely* odd that a young couple with a six-month-old wouldn't ask the *seventeen-year-old* to babysit at least once in a while. Wouldn't having a live-in babysitter make more of a material difference to their lives than the few measly dollars she gives them each week?

Although, now that she thinks about it, hasn't *Cathy* suggested that she take care of Isabelle a few times? But somehow, they've always coordinated their outings with other couples who have infants, either bringing Isabelle along with them, or leaving her with the other couple's babysitter.

But that's okay, Willow doesn't care that she's never taken care of her niece before—in fact, she's glad, because now she has the ammunition she needs.

"You do look kind of stressed, Cathy," Willow says. "You

should take a break, why don't you guys go out to the movies or something?" She looks over her deep-fried shrimp at David, all big eyes and innocence.

"I'd *love* to go to a movie." Cathy brightens up. "Wouldn't that be great?" She smiles at David.

"Well, I guess so. . . ." He trails off uncertainly.

"What time would work for you?" Cathy asks as she reaches behind her for the paper. "I think there's a show in about half an hour."

"Tonight?" David puts down his fork and looks at Cathy as if she were crazy. "We can't go to a movie *tonight.*" He makes the idea sound ludicrous, as if Cathy had suggested going skydiving or something equally outrageous.

"Why not tonight," Cathy answers distractedly as she leafs through the paper. "Too much work?"

"Why not tonight?" Willow echoes her.

Willow knows goddamn well why David won't go out of the house, but she wants to hear him say it. She'll *make* him say it if it's the last thing she does.

"No, not too much work." He shrugs. "I just don't feel like it."

"Why not?" Willow asks again.

"I'm really not in the mood for the movies," David says, but he's never been a good liar and his voice sounds hollow.

"Why not?" Cathy sounds annoyed. "It would be so great to do something spur of the moment."

"Why not?" Willow spits out the words. Her chair makes a hideous scraping sound as she pushes it back and stands up.

"What's gotten into you?" David looks at her in confusion. "Why do you want us out of the house so badly?"

"Willow," Cathy says, "maybe you should—"

"Why don't you tell Cathy why you're so desperate to *stay in,*" Willow cuts Cathy off with a savage gesture.

"I'm not so desperate to stay in. . . ."

"Fine." Willow's hands are shaking. She places them on the back of the chair to steady them. "I'll tell her." She turns to look at her sister-in-law. "You see, Cathy, David is afraid to let me be alone with Isabelle. He's too scared. I guess he thinks that I want to finish off the rest of the family. Mom and Dad weren't enough."

For a second there is total silence. Even Isabelle stops fussing in her high chair. Willow can't believe that she had the guts to say it, but judging from David's ashen face, she's *finally* hit a nerve.

"Willow!" Cathy exclaims in horror. "How could you possibly think something like that?!" She looks back and forth between the two of them. It's clear that she expects David to make some kind of denial, but he isn't saying anything.

"I'm right, aren't I?" Willow says. She stares at David, but he's focused on his plate and refuses to meet her eyes.

"Well?" she persists. "Why don't you just say it? Why don't you just tell Cathy that you—"

"It was a hideous accident," David interrupts her, his face even whiter than a few moments ago. It's clear that he's having a hard time controlling his voice.

"Really? Then why are you afraid to leave me alone with—"

"It was a hideous accident," he repeats. "But staying with a six-month-old . . . Well, you have to be on top of things, it's—"

"Oh, c'mon David," Willow interrupts him. "You've got to do better than that! It's not like I haven't babysat for years.

Admit it. You're scared to leave her alone with me. You're *scared* because you think I'm a—"

"I think that you're still raw," David cuts her off. "You have a lot going on right now, it's unfair to expect you to . . ."

"Stop it!" Willow is breathing heavily. "Just stop it!" She can't bear to hear him lie like this. "Tell the truth! Just say it already! Admit that you blame me for killing them! Admit that you hate me now!"

Willow claps a hand over her mouth. She's close, *dangerously* close to completely falling apart. If anything could make her feel the absolute horror, the pain of her situation, it's this—knowing for sure that she's lost her brother's love. If she weren't grasping the chair so tightly, she'd collapse on the ground in a flood of tears, and that is something that she simply cannot allow to happen. She's not equipped to process that kind of grief.

She shuts her eyes tightly, desperate for some kind of control. She pushes herself away from the chair, which falls to the floor with a loud crash, and heads for the stairs.

Willow knows that David and Cathy are calling after her, but she doesn't listen. She's too intent on reaching her sanctuary. She gets to her room and shuts the door behind her, grateful for the lock that a previous owner had put there.

She can still hear them shouting her name as she sinks down to the floor, covering her ears with her hands. Anything to shut out the noise. Because the noise is threatening to overwhelm her. Not just Cathy's and David's voices, but the squeal of the brakes. The crack of her mother's head hitting the dashboard. The silvery sound of the windshield breaking into a thousand pieces.

Willow can't take it anymore. She has to make it stop, she has to block the tidal wave of feelings that are starting to engulf her. Unfortunately she's left her bag downstairs, but thankfully her room has everything she needs. She crawls across the floor toward the bed and fumbles under the mattress for her equipment, knocking the phone off the bedside table as she does so.

Some part of her registers the sound of the dial tone piercing the air. But it's not enough, nowhere near enough to drown out the sounds that are filling her head. She grabs the razor convulsively, ready to do what she has to.

Willow pauses for the briefest instant. She doesn't know what she's thinking, she doesn't know what she's doing, but suddenly she's dialing the phone, punching in the numbers that she's already committed to memory.

"Hello?" His voice sounds like it's coming from incredibly far away.

"Hello?" Guy repeats.

Willow can't speak. She leans against the bed and unbuttons her shirt with trembling fingers. She looks down at her stomach, searching to find a likely place, and makes the first cut, waiting for the moment when the pain of the razor erases everything else. It's not happening as fast as it usually does, and her breath comes in little gasps as the razor sinks deeper and deeper into her flesh.

"Willow?" Guy asks. His voice is louder.

Willow closes her eyes, trying to let the sound reach her. It's a struggle. She can't stop hearing the windshield splintering, and it's getting worse. Now the pictures are starting. She sees her father's face crushed beyond recognition, a bloody pulp.

She sees her mother, intact, but with her eyes glazed over. She sinks the blade deeper, as if her blood could wash away theirs.

"Willow?" Guy repeats.

Willow doesn't talk, she's breathing shallowly. She watches as the blood springs from the cut she's making, but it doesn't change anything. Not this time. She swipes again, deeper. Now she feels pain, but will it be enough?

"Willow," Guy says a third time. Only this time it's not a question. This time it's clear that he's just making his presence known.

Willow tries to focus on his voice, on the lifeline he's throwing her. The pictures aren't fading, but as she listens to Guy's breathing, the sounds of the accident grow dim.

She stops cutting. The razor dangles uselessly from her hand; it has finally done its work. Willow watches the blood trickle over her skin through half-closed eyes.

Her breath deepens, becomes more regular, in concert with Guy's. The sound of their breathing in tandem is shockingly intimate, and soon, the only noise that filters through Willow's pain is the gentle swoosh of their shared inhalations as she drifts off to sleep grasping the phone as if it were a living being, as if it were her lover.

CHAPTER TEN

The first thing that Willow thinks when she wakes up is that the light fixture isn't where it's supposed to be. It takes her a second before she realizes that it is she herself who is in the wrong place. Instead of being in bed, she's lying on the floor, still dressed in all her clothes, grasping a dead phone. She hasn't felt this dazed, this bewildered since she woke up in the hospital after the accident.

But that momentary disorientation over the light is the only confusion that she feels. Everything else is crystal clear. She knows why she's on the floor, she knows why she's still in her clothes, she knows why those clothes are sticking to her, and she knows why there's the faint metallic smell of blood in the air.

Willow remembers everything from the night before. The look on her brother's face, the look on Cathy's face . . .

And Guy's voice on the other end of the phone, the sound of his breathing as she cut.

She rolls over onto her stomach, dropping the receiver

and wincing as the hard floor makes contact with her fresh cuts. She rests her chin on her hands and thinks about the fact that she called him. It never occurred to her, when she took his number, that she would actually phone him, but then again she never expected to sit in the park with him, or buy him a book, or do any of the things that they've done together.

But none of that means that Willow feels good about actually having called him. Shame washes over her as she remembers the inarticulate noises that she makes when she hacks at herself. Why *did* she decide to make him privy to that? Why did she give him a day pass into her world of pain? He deserves much better.

Willow knows that Guy was the one who told her to call in the first place, but she has to believe that he couldn't have known what he was letting himself in for. Maybe Guy knew that she was a cutter, but knowing and witnessing—even through the filter of a phone line—are two vastly different things.

She wonders how he'll act when she runs into him at school. Will he bring up the phone call? More to the point, how will *she* act? Of course, it's possible that she won't even see him at school.

In any case, she has more pressing things to think about. Forget *Guy's* reaction. How is she going to face David and Cathy?

Willow glances at the clock. She's overslept, so there's a chance that they've already left. On any other day either Cathy or David would have made sure to wake her up, but surely they must be as anxious to avoid her as she is them.

She hauls herself to her feet, not an easy task given how worn and tired she feels, hangs up the phone, then tiptoes to the door. She unlocks it as quietly as possible and sticks her head out.

Silence greets her.

They must have left already. Good. She has a little breathing space. Maybe, with enough time, she'll be able to figure out what to say when she sees them. Should she apologize for the night before? Maybe David will be the one to apologize. Maybe she should just act like it never happened.

Yeah! That'll be easy!

Willow shuts the door quietly, even though she knows there's no one to hear, and heads toward the bathroom. It's time to get on with the day. She stops for a second to pull some clean clothes out of her dresser.

The first thing that comes to hand is a short-sleeved T-shirt—not at all the kind of thing she can wear these days, given how much it reveals of her arms. Willow pauses in the act of stuffing it back into the drawer.

Of course, if she doesn't go to school, she can wear anything she wants. . . .

Maybe she should stay home, actually open her French book, or see if she can finally get some work done on the *Bulfinch,* like finish the reading or get started on the paper. Wouldn't that make more sense than going to school, where she'll only sleepwalk through her classes, still dazed from the events of the night before? Not only that, but if she does skip school, that would solve the problem, at least for today, of how to act when she sees Guy.

Fine, one problem solved. Too bad she just can't skip the

rest of her life. She slings the clothes over her shoulder, walks into the bathroom, and turns on the shower.

She leans against the wet tiles as the water cascades over her and watches in sick fascination as the dried, scabbed blood swirls down the drain. Unlike the act of cutting, which never fails to soothe her, this sight offers no comfort. In fact, it makes her more than slightly ill. Willow knows that there's a terrible disconnect between what she does and what she feels when she sees the fruits of her labor, but it is not so easy to be rational when the urge to cut is upon her.

Willow turns off the shower with a sigh, gets dressed, and walks down the stairs into the kitchen.

There's not much to eat, beyond a half-empty bag of pretzels and a few jars of baby food. Cathy never has time to shop, that's part of why they order in so much. Maybe she should go shopping later, that could be like a peace offering, of sorts.

Right. As if that'll make everything better!

Willow takes a handful of stale pretzels and wanders over to the table. There, propped up against the sugar bowl, is a note with her name on it in Cathy's handwriting.

She stares at it for a moment, too frightened to open it up. But really, there's nothing Cathy could say that could possibly make things any worse. Willow wonders if the letter is a reprimand, or an attempt to smooth things over.

Only one way to find out.

She grabs the paper before she can change her mind.

Dear Willow,

I decided to let you sleep in today. . . .

You must know how much David and I both love you. Don't ever think that he blames you for what happened or that he doesn't trust you! Nothing could be further from the truth.

David said that he thought you were so overwrought because you've had some trouble in school. You mustn't worry about that! You have plenty of time to bring up your grades. In any case, we both think you're doing incredibly well in the given circumstances. Take the day off if you want. Maybe you should go to the park and do some watercolors.

Try and feel better.

Love, Cathy

Willow folds the note carefully and puts it into her pocket. She knows that she should be relieved, and she's touched by Cathy's concern, but still, in many ways the letter only depresses her. Cathy's assurances prove that she just doesn't get what's going on. In a way, her protestations of love are no different from David's unwillingness to discuss what's happened. In both cases, there is simply a huge failure to connect.

She's turning away from the window, about to go back upstairs and get to work, when something outside catches her attention. There's always a lot to look at—young mothers with strollers, harried-looking businessmen rushing to work, joggers in colorful outfits, but this morning there's something more. Because this morning, Guy is part of the commotion taking place on the other side of the street.

At first Willow is sure that she's imagining things. But no, he's really there, standing just outside the park, watching her building. The obvious, the *only* explanation she can think of is that he's waiting for her.

So much for skipping school....

Willow isn't sure what her move should be. She could always stay in the apartment and avoid him that way, but who's to say he won't cross the street and ring the bell?

And besides, she's not really sure that she wants to avoid him.

Yes I do.... I mean... Well, don't I?

Willow is ashamed that she called him, no doubt about that, and ashamed that he's heard her in the throes of an... episode. Still, along with the shame is another feeling. She's connected to him—maybe by a thread of blood, maybe by the bond of the razor, or maybe by something else again—but whatever has caused it, it's something that she cannot deny.

And it would be kind of rude to ignore him....

Willow doesn't stop to analyze the situation further, but grabs her keys and heads out the door.

She pauses in front of the building and stares at him, a thousand questions forming in her mind. She wants to know why he's there, she wants to know what he thought about her calling him, but somehow, the only thing that she manages to say as she stands there shivering in her shirtsleeves is:

"How did you know where I lived?"

"There's this thing called the phone book," Guy says as he crosses the street. "And your brother put his address on the website for his class."

"Oh. Right." Willow nods as she rubs her arms.

"What are you doing barefoot?" Guy says as he looks her over.

Willow glances down at her feet on the pavement. She hadn't even realized that she wasn't wearing shoes.

"I . . . I just ran out of the house when I saw you. I didn't stop . . ." Willow trails off. She wonders why they're discussing such trivial things. Is it because he's also reluctant to bring up the phone call?

"Well, don't you think you should put some shoes on?"

"Yeah, well, I guess so." Willow shifts back and forth uncomfortably. "Come on, let's go inside," she says after a second, and leads him back into the building.

Guy is staring at her intently as she unlocks the door to the apartment. His scrutiny makes her very nervous. He must be thinking about the phone call, about what the phone call meant, but he's not saying anything, he appears to be—

"Your arms," Guy interrupts her thoughts.

"Yes?" Willow stops at the entrance to the living room and turns to face him. "What about them?" She looks down at her arms and tries to see them as he might. There are plenty of marks, but so what? Guy's seen her cuts before, surely he's the one person in the world that she can wear a T-shirt in front of.

"There's nothing new," he says after a moment. He gestures at the thin red lines that score her flesh. "Those aren't recent."

Willow knows exactly what he's getting at, but she has no intention of answering his unspoken question. "In here," she says as she walks over to the couch and collapses against it. After a moment, Guy sits down too.

"Well, where did you do it then?" Clearly now that he's brought the subject up, he has no intention of letting it drop.

"On my stomach," she says, having decided that in the long run, it would just be easier to tell him.

"But that's . . . I thought . . . I mean, you said that you only did it on your arms!" Guy objects.

Willow stares at him, confused by his protests. Is he saying that it would be *better* if she had cut her arms? Is it that he doesn't *believe* that she cut her stomach? Does he—God forbid—think she made the whole thing up? That she was pretending when she called him in order to get his attention or something? Willow is horrified at the thought.

"I said that I *mostly* do it on my arms." Her voice is rough. "Here, you don't believe me, you want to see?"

She pulls her T-shirt up over her bra, unzips her jeans, and pulls them down to just above her underwear. "Here!" she says angrily, practically shouting. "Take a look if you don't believe me!"

Willow is surprised by her own actions. She can't help thinking how different the scene would be if she were taking off her clothes for the normal reasons. If that were the case, her concerns would be about whether her underwear looked good enough, whether she looked good enough, not whether her scars looked recent enough for him to believe her.

Guy, however, is determinedly not looking at her stomach. His face averted, he stares at the faded Persian carpet, the bookshelves, anywhere but at her naked skin.

"Go on!" she admonishes him once again.

Guy turns his head slowly, careful to keep his eyes on her face. "I never said that I didn't believe you, I just was wondering . . ." He trails off miserably.

Willow looks steadily back at him. She doesn't think that

she's ever seen anyone look as unhappy, as uncomfortable, as he does at that moment.

Finally, his eyes drop down and he looks at her stomach, *really* looks at it, takes in each and every cut.

Willow leans back and watches him through half-closed eyes. He appears transfixed. She knows that there is something perverse about this scene. The reason that he's staring at her, completely speechless, is not because he's captivated by her beauty, but because of the horror of what he sees.

Guy slowly reaches out a hand and places it on her abdomen. His hand is large and it covers every slash that she's made. Placed like that, with her scars concealed, it's easy to pretend that there is nothing out of the ordinary about the skin that he's touching. It's easy to pretend that his hand isn't there to hide her cuts but for another reason entirely.

But Willow *can't* pretend. It's true that Guy's hand, as it rests on her stomach, is affecting her in ways that are completely new. But those wondrous sensations are mixed with the pain that he is causing as he irritates the freshly broken skin.

And as for Guy, he does not look as if he is enjoying or even grasping the romantic possibilities of their circumstances. If anything he looks more than slightly sick. His face is white as a sheet.

He whips his hand away suddenly and claps it over his mouth.

"Do you want me to hold your head?" Willow asks, a distinct edge to her voice. She remembers the time in the stacks when Guy offered to hold her hair back, how struck she had been by his incredible kindness, how struck she is by it now. She wishes that she could be as considerate in return, but she is too traumatized by recent events to behave with such grace.

"No, no." Guy shakes his head. "I . . . No."

"Good." Willow yanks down her shirt and zips up her pants.

Guy doesn't speak for a moment. He's sitting the same way that she is, slumped against the couch, his expression dazed.

"What . . . Could you tell me *what* made you do it?" he says haltingly.

"I had an argument with my brother," Willow responds. She doesn't quite know how else to describe what happened.

"What . . . About what? The fight. I mean . . . what was it about?" Guy asks. His normal facility with speech seems to have deserted him. Willow realizes that she's never heard him sound so inarticulate before.

"About whose turn it was to do the dishes," Willow says. She's much too tired to go into it all.

"Fine," Guy says. "That's just fine." He struggles to an upright position. "Don't worry about being honest with me, I couldn't care less. I mean, I just came over here this morning for fun, right? This stuff doesn't matter to me. It's no big deal. Don't knock yourself out trying to give me a straight answer or anything."

Willow nods. His anger doesn't faze her; she certainly didn't expect him to buy what she was saying.

"Look, I'm sorry," he says after a second. "I shouldn't have gotten so angry—"

"No," Willow interrupts him. "You *should* be angry. I'm not being very nice to you, and you're being . . ."

Kinder than I ever had a right to expect from anyone ever.

She's more moved than she can say by the fact that he showed up at her door. Ambivalence has turned into gratitude. She wants to ask him why he's there, but is a little afraid to hear the answer. Would he tell her that it's because she frightened him? Willow knows that she has forfeited the right to be called normal, but still, she hates to think that he might consider her . . . *crazy* or something.

Is he there because he promised he wouldn't tell her brother, and that makes him feel responsible?

Is he there because he *cares* about her?

Willow sighs deeply. She feels unable to talk to him about any of this. She feels unable to tell him what his actions mean to her, and she realizes, given all that, that the least she can do is tell him the truth about the night before.

"The fight was about the fact that David hates me now." Willow says this simply, without drama. "He hates me because I killed our parents."

Willow waits to hear the inevitable. To hear Guy say, like everyone else does, that it was just an accident, that she didn't set out to kill their parents. That her brother loves her more than ever now that she's an orphan. She's heard the empty words countless times before.

But Guy is silent. He just looks at her.

"I can't imagine how hard it must be for you," he says finally. He looks stricken. "For both of you, actually," he adds after a moment.

"You're right, you can't," Willow says in a small voice. She should have known that he wouldn't fob her off with some pabulum answer, that he wouldn't try to talk her out of her feelings, or tell her that she was imagining things. "But . . .

thank you for, well, at least for not telling me that it's all in my head."

"Well, you're welcome, I guess." Guy pauses for a second. "Look, maybe I shouldn't say this after what you just said. I know I can't really get what you're going through, and I believe that *you* believe that your brother hates you. I mean, I totally don't think that it's all in your head. I'm sure that things are really . . . well, hard between the two of you." He shifts around on the couch and turns to look her in the face. "But are you sure that maybe you're not, well, maybe, I don't know, misinterpreting things somehow? I'm just thinking about the David Randall that I took a class with last year. There's no way he would hate his sister. I mean, who would, right? But him especially, I just don't see it."

"I think I know him better than you do," Willow says stiffly.

"I'm not trying to tell you what you feel or don't feel. I guess I just wished that I could make you feel *better,* and maybe looking at things in a different way . . ." He doesn't finish the sentence.

"It's not that simple," Willow says. Now she is the one having a hard time looking at him. It's painful for her to see just how miserable he looks, because she knows that she's responsible. "Look, don't go thinking that talking to you doesn't make me feel . . ." She fumbles for the words. "Well, you don't talk to me like anyone else does," she finishes lamely, but that isn't what she really wanted to say, not by a long shot.

"Yeah well, you don't talk to me the way that anyone else does either," Guy says.

"I don't?" Willow is surprised.

"Oh sure, discussions about *Tristes Tropiques,* sandwiched in between talking about where on your body you cut yourself, because you think that you're a murderer. Totally standard, every other girl I know is *just* the same. What is it with you people? I mean really, if I have to sit through one more conversation like that, pretending not to be bored . . ." He shakes his head.

Willow cannot believe, she really cannot believe that she's laughing, Guy is too, and for a moment they are both literally convulsed with laughter. "That isn't why I cut myself," she says after she calms down.

"Then why don't you just—" Guy begins, but Willow interrupts him.

"Look, what I was trying to say a minute ago is that, well, you're the only person who listens to me, who doesn't have to pretend that everything is okay." She stops, not sure if she should go on, but really, it's the least that she can do for him, considering how much he's done for her.

"You know, I realized something after my parents died." Willow's voice is a little shaky. "I realized that what people say, the way they react, tells you more about *them* than it does anything else. People may think that they're offering you condolences or whatever you want to call it, but really, they're letting you see what *they're* all about."

"I'm not getting you, exactly." Guy frowns.

"Well, okay, here's what I mean." Willow takes a deep breath. "After the funeral, this one old lady came up to me to tell me how sorry she was. I barely knew her, but my parents did a little bit. Anyway, she said that she was sorry, and then she said *at least they didn't die alone.*" Willow closes her eyes as the sights and sounds of that day come rushing back to her. It's not easy, but she collects herself after a moment and goes on.

"Now, that's a bizarre thing to say when you think about it. I mean, *my parents were dead,* they'd died in a car crash, that's a horrible way to go, and she was saying that at least they didn't die alone, she was saying that it was good that they died together." Willow stops talking for a second and looks at Guy. She can see how intently he's listening.

"When I say she was old," Willow continues, "I mean she was *old,* mid-eighties, I'm guessing, and I knew, everyone knew, that her husband had died thirty years before, and that her only son had died in Vietnam right before that. And I realized that all she had in front of her was the knowledge that she was going to die alone. She wasn't being insensitive—for her, my parents really did have it easy.

"And here's another example, the other day I told Laurie about my brother, how he has to do all these parent things, and you know what she said? That he was being *sweet.* She wasn't being insensitive either. It's just that she doesn't get it." Willow pauses and shifts her gaze away from Guy. "But with you, well, the things you say . . . You *do* get it, and that does make me feel . . . better." Willow can feel herself starting to blush.

"You blush a lot," Guy says after a moment.

"I can't help it."

"Well, don't help it. I mean, blushing. I think *that's* sweet."

"Oh."

"And I'm really happy if anything I do makes you feel any better."

"Oh." Now Willow is really red, but she doesn't turn her

head away from him, she just lets him look at her, flushed face and all.

"We're going to be so late for school," Guy says. "We definitely missed first period."

"I'm not going to school today," Willow tells him. "I just can't, not after last night, and anyway, I'm so behind in my work that I should really just stay home and try to catch up."

"Maybe I won't go either." Guy stretches out his legs and crosses his hands behind his head. "It might be nice to take the day off."

"You don't have to do that because of me," Willow says hastily. "I mean, you don't have to worry that I'm going to do something. . . ."

"Maybe I'm doing it because I feel like it," he says. "But now that I am, is there anything you want to do? I mean before you get started on all this homework?"

Willow thinks of all the things that she would like to do: go to sleep for about three days straight, get her work done—finally. Maybe even do something for Cathy and David, like clean up the house or go shopping, but all those things pale in comparison to the one overriding need she has right now.

"You know what I'd really love to do, more than anything?" Willow leans forward. "I'd *love* to have breakfast. I'm completely starving."

"That sounds really good," Guy says. "I'm starving too. Let's get out of here." He stands up and pulls her to her feet.

"What are you in the mood for?" Willow asks, grabbing a sweater from the hall closet. "Do you even know anyplace near here that we can get breakfast?" She locks the door and walks down the stairs in front of him.

"I know the *best* place," he assures her. "And it's only a couple of minutes away."

"There's no place a couple of minutes from here," Willow objects as they walk along the pavement.

"Shows what you know," Guy says as they turn the corner and stop in front of an old-fashioned diner. He pushes the door open with his shoulder. "Two bacon, egg, and cheese sandwiches to go," he gives their order to the guy behind the counter. "We'll take them to the park, okay? Sit on a bench or something."

"This is pretty good," Willow says as she bites into her sandwich a few minutes later.

"You've never had a bacon, egg, and cheese before?" Guy is incredulous. "They're like a classic hangover remedy."

"Yeah well, I've never been hungover before."

"What was all that stuff about Jell-O shots with your best friend?" Guy looks at her suspiciously as they enter the park. "No benches, c'mon, I know a nicer spot anyway."

"If you remember, I told you that I threw up when we did Jell-O shots, no hangover," Willow says as she follows him through the park. "And if you really want to know, that was pretty much the only time I did anything like that."

"This is perfect," Guy says. They sit down at the top of a small hill, underneath a Japanese maple with their backs against the tree. It's a particularly pretty place, shady, surrounded by flowers and with a view of a small man-made pond. "So, do you still see any of your old friends, anyway? I mean, what happened to this Jell-O shots girl?"

He shifts around, trying to get comfortable. Willow is sensitive to every move that he makes. He stretches his legs out, jostling hers, and for an instant they are joined at the hip.

Willow's first reaction is to move away, give him more room. But after a second, she edges back and lets her leg fall into place against his. He doesn't appear to notice. Why should he? It's very tame, especially after what happened on the couch, but Willow is acutely aware of the way her body feels against his.

"No, I don't really talk to my old friends anymore," she says after a while. "Markie, that's who I did the Jell-O shots with, I haven't spoken to her in months." Willow finishes her sandwich and wads up the wrapper.

"Don't you kind of miss them?"

"Well, yes, but . . ." Willow thinks about the phone calls she and Markie used to have. She wonders what Markie would think of Guy, and imagines the kind of conversations the two of them would have about him. Too bad she won't be talking to her any time soon. "You know why I don't talk to my old friends anymore?" Willow turns to look at Guy. "I can't because it just hurts too much. At first I thought it was because they just didn't get my situation, but then I realized it's because they remind me too much of the life I used to have. Seeing them with their parents, doing the kinds of things we used to do, whatever, it's all too hard. Things seem the same, and then at the end of the day, they go back to their same old lives, their same old world that they've always known, and I'm stuck on my own, in this new world that I've woken up in. I'm just a tourist in theirs." She starts shredding the wadded-up sandwich wrapper nervously.

Guy takes the paper from her gently and throws it along with his own in a nearby garbage can.

"You say that I'm wrong about my brother," Willow goes on. "But that's part of how I know that I'm right. I'm a constant reminder to him of what his life used to be like. He can never get away from it, not even for five minutes at a time. I've invaded his world. Every time he sees me, he knows that something has changed forever." She pauses. "I'm sorry. You ask me a simple question and I . . . Look, even I don't want to talk about this stuff anymore. Do me a favor, okay?"

"The weather in Kuala Lumpur?" Guy raises his eyebrows.

"Well, something, anyway."

"Okay . . . You know what I was doing when you called?"

"Uh . . ." Willow thinks for a minute. "Watching the game?"

"What game?" Guy looks confused.

"I don't know, isn't there some game?"

"You mean the World Series?"

"That'll work."

"You're about ten days ahead of schedule."

"Okay, so what were you doing?"

"Reading *The Tempest*."

"Oh." Willow thinks about this. "And . . ." she prompts.

"You may have a point," Guy concedes. "It is better than *Macbeth*."

"I told you!"

"I said you *may* have a point. You can't really compare because they're so different. I mean, *The Tempest* really is this magical, romantic—Hey look at that," he interrupts himself. "Look, over by the pond."

"What?" Willow follows his gaze but can't see what he's interested in, unless it's the man getting out of the rowboat.

"He's just leaving it there," Guy says. He sounds excited. "You're supposed to return them, I know because I've rented here a couple of times. It's really expensive, but that guy's just leaving it! C'mon." He grabs her hand, jerks her to her feet, and starts running down the hill.

"Do you know what you're doing?" Willow says as she watches him get into the boat.

"Excuse me." Guy looks at her. "I row on the *river* three mornings a week, you think I can't handle a pond?"

"Whatever." Willow shrugs, then climbs gingerly into the boat and sits down as he grabs the oars and steers them toward the center of the pond. "So did you and Andy ever, I don't remember, shave three minutes off your time or something?"

"Try ten seconds." Guy pulls on the oars. "We do the 2500 in eight minutes and twelve seconds right now. If we took three minutes off of that, we'd be beating the world record by a pretty wide margin. Anyway, I'm not expecting to beat eight twelve. Andy doesn't work hard enough, and I don't care enough. I really just row because I love being out on the river early in the morning."

Willow watches the deft action of his arms as he rows. There's something incredibly soothing, almost hypnotic, about his movements. She can't take her eyes away from the smooth motion that his strong, lightly tanned forearms make as they manipulate the oars.

She reaches her hand down into the water and lets it trail behind her in the little wake that they're making. Maybe it's the fact that she's worn out from the night before, or maybe it's the gentle sound that the oars make as they dip into the water, Willow doesn't know and she doesn't care. The only thing she's certain of is how peaceful she feels, better than she's felt in days, weeks even. She watches Guy through half-closed lids, and the last thing she sees before she drifts off to sleep is his smile.

CHAPTER ELEVEN

"Now, that one looks like a rabbit."

"Are you out of your mind?" Willow turns her head to look at Guy as they lay side by side on the grass staring up at the clouds. "If anything it's a swan."

"You're the crazy one, look." He points toward the sky. "See the ears?"

"No, that's the *neck*."

"Ears."

"Listen." Willow rolls over onto her stomach and props her head on her hands. "I don't know how to break this to you, but you might be in serious trouble."

"Oh yeah? How's that?"

"You know those inkblot tests? You must have read about them somewhere, the ones where a shrink makes you look at all these pictures of, well, of *inkblots*?"

"Yeah, sure." Guy turns on his side to face her.

"Okay, so the way they work is that most people will look

at some splotch of ink and think that it looks like a house or something, but then you get someone else who thinks that it looks like a . . . I don't know, a spider . . ."

"Or a rabbit."

"Exactly! And *those* people are certifiable."

"Your point?"

"Well, thinking that cloud looks like a rabbit . . . that's a bad sign."

"Maybe thinking it's a swan is more worrisome," he says with a yawn and flops down on his back again. "So what's this homework you're supposed to be doing now?"

"Please, don't remind me," Willow groans. When she decided to skip school that morning, she really *had* intended to spend the day looking over her French quiz, or getting to work on her paper. She never expected that she would spend it hanging out in the park with Guy. But in the three hours since they had breakfast, they've done nothing more demanding than rowing, taking a long walk, and then finally, just sitting around and talking.

Willow knows that she shouldn't be doing this, and yet, it would be impossible to tear herself away. Because in spite of the fact that she still hasn't really processed what happened the night before, in spite of the fact that she's so far behind in her work, she doesn't feel the need to do anything beyond sitting and talking to him. The girl who killed her parents, the girl who cuts, that girl's a million miles away. Right here, right now, Willow is simply and only a girl spending a day in the park with a guy.

"Well." Guy gives her a nudge. "C'mon, tell me."

"I'm way behind in that class all of you like so much, Myths and Idiots, or whatever it's called," Willow says as she pulls a couple of blades of grass from the lawn. "I have tons of reading, and I've got to get started on this paper already." She tries to use the grass as a whistle. "How come this isn't working? I thought you could use grass as a kind of whistle or something."

"Myths and Idiots?" he laughs. "That's good. Andy would appreciate that one. And yeah, you can whistle with a blade of grass, but I haven't done it since I was about five, so don't ask me to show you how."

"Some help you are." Willow lets the grass scatter in the wind. "You know what this paper is supposed to be about? About Demeter and Persephone, loss and redemption, how after Persephone is abducted to the underworld they're dead to each other. I mean, this should be pretty easy for me. I'm probably the only one in the class with personal experience, right?" Willow pauses for a second. "Except you know what? It's not about loss, it's about rebirth, how they get to be reunited . . ."

"Did you pick the topic?" Guy seems surprised.

"No, what's his name . . . Adams? He gave it to me."

"Yeah, well, that was really sensitive of him."

"Oh you know, he probably wasn't even thinking about what he was doing."

"Obviously not." Guy turns his head and looks at her carefully. "Well, listen, if you're really having a hard time, maybe I can help. I'm sure that I still have my old papers hanging around somewhere, maybe looking at them would make it easier for you to get started." He turns back and stares at the clouds again.

"Thanks," Willow says. "What . . . What are you doing?" She looks at him suspiciously. He's flat on his back staring up at the clouds, but his arms are outstretched and he's moving them as if he's . . .

"What does it look like?"

"Uh, if I had to guess, I'd say you were trying to direct traffic or conduct a symphony."

"Sort of. Actually, I'm trying to move the clouds closer together," he says. He looks serious too. "See? That one that looks like a rabbit, *okay*, swan, and that one that looks like a layer cake. I'm pushing them closer together."

"All right." Willow sits up abruptly. "I told you seeing a rabbit was a bad sign, you've obviously completely lost it, this is just the . . ."

"Did you see that?" Guy interrupts her. "It moved, you can't deny it! And relax, I'm not crazy, this is a very old and respected technique that I'm using."

"Huh?"

"It's from the *Boys' Book of Magic,* out of print since 1878, I bought it downtown. Trick number nineteen. How to control the weather and astonish friends at outdoor tea parties."

"Tea parties?"

"I told you, it went out of print in 1878. Besides, it was English. It was full of references to things like garden parties and playing cricket, and how to behave when doing tricks for your betters."

"Uh-huh, and you umm, bought this recently?"

"I bought it when I was twelve," Guy says. "And, okay, this is really embarrassing, but I actually believed that stuff like spells for controlling the weather would work. There! Did you see that! I'm telling you, I'm moving these clouds!" He looks at her with a triumphant expression on his face.

"Please." Willow doesn't even bother to glance up at the sky. "It's the wind. It's been getting windier and colder for about the past hour." She lies back down on the grass. "*Boys' Book of Magic*? It sounds like something that tutor of yours would have liked."

"I'm sure a long-lost relative of his wrote it," Guy answers her, but he's totally focused on the sky. "Actually, I think it was the last book I bought before we moved to Kuala Lumpur."

"I would have thought that it would have helped you fit in with all those British kids," Willow says as she watches him. He's infinitely more interesting than the clouds. She wonders what he must have been like when he was twelve.

"Maybe if we'd all been living a hundred years ago, and maybe if I ever learned any good tricks. But the only magic I ever figured out how to do was really stupid card tricks that would irritate your friends and make you look like an idiot at outdoor tea parties." Guy makes a face. "I haven't actually even thought about the book since then. I got bored with it pretty fast, but reading *The Tempest* reminded me of it. Remember the way that Prospero conjures up that storm? See! You're not watching." He gives her braid a little pull. "C'mon, give me some credit here. Obviously the book had something going on, and I was just too young to really grasp how hard it is to control the weather. I'm telling you, those clouds are moving, we are definitely on the way to having a storm here." He stops and turns to face her. "You see? Just like Prospero."

"You're not at all like Prospero!" Willow objects. "If anything, you're . . ."

Well, he's exactly like Ferdinand.

Willow is struck by just how true that is. Of course he's like Ferdinand: He's a *perfect* romantic hero. She's reminded too of Miranda's words when she first sets eyes on Ferdinand:

Oh brave new world that has such people in it . . .

Unlike Miranda, Willow *is* in a new world, and though she would never have chosen to be there, it is amazing to her that it has such an incredible person in it.

"Look," Guy says, interrupting her thoughts. "It *really* is going to rain. We should get out of the park. Unless you want to stay. It is pretty fun to be outside during a storm. You should see the way the lightning looks over the river."

"No," Willow says shortly. "I hate the rain."

"No! Don't say that!" Guy looks genuinely distressed. "I mean, that's a really serious category, people who get how great the rain is and people who just get mad because it screws up traffic. Please don't say that you hate the rain."

"I used to love it." She thinks back to all the times at home, when she would spend hour after hour curled up on the window seat with a book, while the rain beat against the glass.

"Then why don't you—"

"It was raining that night," Willow says suddenly. "It wasn't supposed to rain, but it did. And it wasn't *beautiful* rain, the kind you're talking about. It was torrential. I've always wondered what would have happened if the weather had been just a little bit better." She doesn't elaborate further. She's sure that he'll understand which night she is referring to.

"Why were you driving anyway?" Guy clearly picks up on

the reference. He moves closer and takes her hand. "I don't get it. You told me that you didn't even have your license yet, and the weather was so awful. What was going on?"

"Nothing. There was nothing going on. What do you mean? We were out. My parents felt like drinking." Willow shrugs. "It's just so awful, what I did. There's just no way to ever . . . Last night, I had this . . . scene with my brother. This argument. You know what started it? We ran into some friend of his and he asked David about our parents, and David didn't tell him. He *couldn't* tell him. He can't face what I did. He can't face what I am."

"Maybe he just didn't want to get into all of it. Maybe he was trying to protect *you*. Spare you from this guy asking any more questions," Guy says.

Willow stares at him without speaking, considering this for a moment before rejecting it as implausible.

"We should probably leave the park," Guy says as the rain starts falling. He stands up, pulling her with him. "Do you want to go back to your house, or maybe get some lunch? I'd say go to my house, except my mom will be there, and she'll wonder what I'm doing home in the middle of the day. She's a painter," he adds. "So she works from home."

"I'm not ready for lunch," Willow says. "And my house is too far away." They start walking faster to avoid the rain, but it's a losing battle.

"You know where we could go?" Guy says suddenly. "We could . . ." But he doesn't finish the sentence, and he has a hard time meeting her eyes as they exit the park and cross the street.

Willow is sure that she knows what he's thinking. It's the obvious place, barely a block away, free if you're a student, fascinating, and, unfortunately for her, full of memories.

They could go to the museum. The one where Guy heard her parents lecture, the one where she herself has been countless times.

"You were going to say the museum, weren't you? C'mon, that's a good idea. Let's go." She tugs on his sleeve.

"Are you sure?" He looks worried.

"No, but let's go there anyway," Willow says over a peal of thunder. The rain is coming down in driving sheets, it's madness to stay on the streets, and it's by far the most sensible option.

"Okay."

They run as fast as they can down the block and up the stairs into the museum.

"I'm soaked!" She shakes her head and droplets of water fly all over. Guy is also dripping water over the polished marble floor.

"I have that sweatshirt that I lent you the other day in my backpack," he says. "We could use that as a towel."

"Please." No sooner is the word out of her mouth than she finds herself swathed in his sweatshirt and being given a vigorous rubbing. "Ow! Stop!" Willow laughs. "Not so rough!"

"Don't you want to get dry?"

"Yeah, but I'm not a puppy!"

"I wouldn't be so—"

"Ssh!" A security guard admonishes them.

Willow stops laughing—not so much because of the guard's reproof, but more because she's suddenly become aware of her surroundings. She looks around slowly, testing out how she feels. Will this be like the bookstore?

But as she gazes around the great marble entrance hall, she experiences none of the feelings that she did in the store. Maybe it's because, unlike the bookstore, the museum seems completely different than she remembers. Willow has never visited on a weekday afternoon before. It's practically empty. She's never seen it be anything but crowded, but now it seems as if they have the whole place to themselves. Maybe it's because she has memories of this place that are separate from her parents, having been many times without them.

Or maybe it's just because she isn't alone.

"So what do you want to do?" Guy says as he finishes drying himself off. "What do you feel like seeing?"

"Forget what I want to see," Willow responds as they head toward the stairs. "I know exactly what *you* want to see. The dinosaurs, right?"

"Got it in one."

They walk through the vast corridors, past rooms filled with jade ornaments and tribal masks, past the lecture hall where her parents spoke, until finally they reach the dinosaur exhibit.

"These are my favorite," Guy says as he leads her over to a pair of ornithomimids. He leans over the velvet rope, and for a second Willow thinks that he's going to pet one.

"No touching," a bored guard cautions.

"As if I would," Guy mutters under his breath. "I guess I can understand it from his perspective, though." He stands up straight and turns to Willow. "I've been here on the weekends and the place is packed with little kids. You should see them, they practically climb all over these things. Especially the T. rex. They go crazy for that one." He walks across the room to examine another skeleton.

Willow can't help smiling a little. As far as she can tell, he's no different from the five-year-olds, at least when it comes to dinosaurs, anyway.

"So." Guy tears his eyes away from a model of a reconstructed jawbone and looks at Willow. "Where to now? What's your favorite exhibit? Wait, don't tell me. I know I'm going to get it, just gimme a sec. Okay, you probably like the gems and minerals, right? I'm not talking about that room with all the really fancy stuff, the crown jewels or whatever, those are too formal for you, I mean the semiprecious stuff, those great hunks of amethyst and topaz."

"You're right," Willow says. In fact, the massive purple and golden crystals with their peculiar luster are among the things that she likes best in the museum. She's not surprised that he's guessed that, not after everything that they've shared. But still, the fact that he can so easily pinpoint her wants and desires makes her slightly uncomfortable. The ambivalence she felt earlier that morning comes rushing back.

She steps away from him a little, twists her hands together, and thinks. It's not like she feels ashamed the way she did before. His knowledge of her isn't necessarily bad, far from it. The bond that they've forged is the only positive thing in her life. It's more that he knows *everything*. He knows the most awful thing about her, and, as she stands there in front of him, it is impossible for her not to feel horribly vulnerable.

"So, how about it, do you want to go downstairs?"

"You know everything about me," Willow bursts out. Guy looks startled and she realizes that she's not making any sense, that as far as he's concerned what she's just said came out of nowhere. "I mean, it's not just that you knew that I'd want to see the amethyst . . ." She trails off, unsure of how to go on.

"Well, you knew that I'd want to see the dinosaurs, I don't get—"

"That's different," Willow interrupts. "You're a guy, you're hardwired to like dinosaurs."

"You know, if I said that because you're a girl you're hard-wired to like jewels, you'd be telling me that was some sexist—"

"You're not getting it," Willow says somewhat wildly. "I mean that you know the worst thing about me, and I . . . don't know the same about you. I know all the good things, but I don't know what you're ashamed of, I don't know something about you that you'd want to hide from everyone else."

"Oh." Guy still looks a little surprised at the turn the conversation has taken.

"Never mind," she mutters after a second. "Look, let's just go look at the gems, okay? C'mon." She tugs his hand. "Forget I said anything."

But Willow is having a hard time forgetting. Unfortunately, holding his hand isn't making things any easier. With anyone else, holding hands would be so innocent, but that isn't the case with Guy. His hands, his big and beautiful hands that have bandaged her arm and felt her scars, only remind her that he knows her deepest secret.

"This is it," she says as they enter the hall of gems and minerals. As with the dinosaur exhibit, they're alone, without even a security guard, most probably because everything here is behind shatterproof glass.

The room is underground, without windows. But the whole place is illuminated both by artificial lighting and the luminosity that the jewels give off. The strange ghostly radiance and the uneven crystal formations have always made Willow feel as if she were walking on the surface of the moon.

"You know, there's a huge oyster here somewhere. You might not like it, but I think it's fascinating. It had the biggest natural pearl ever. I forget how much it weighed, but . . . Wait a sec, it's right over here, if I remember . . ." Willow feels like she's babbling, but she doesn't know what else to do. The things that she said upstairs are still hanging in the air, and she's desperate to get back to the carefree banter that they shared in the park.

"What do you think?" she asks with artificial brightness as they stop in front of the oyster.

"I don't think that I'm, well . . . I don't think that I'm *ashamed* of anything," Guy says, completely ignoring the oyster and turning to look at her. "There's nothing I've *done* that I have to hide from other people. Or nothing that's not completely trivial anyway. I'm sure I cheated on some algebra test back in eighth grade or something else like that."

"Oh," Willow says faintly.

"What I mean is, it's not like there's some particular act that I'm afraid people will find out about," Guy continues. "That isn't the way things are for me. I'd say that it's more like I'd hate for people, my friends, Adrian even, to know what's going on inside me most of the time." He pauses and looks into Willow's eyes, and she can see that even with all his strength, he's just as vulnerable as she is.

"You see, I'm . . . well, I guess the best way to describe the way I feel is that I'm scared, *completely* scared. And I know that deep down a lot of people are, but still . . . I mean, I know Laurie would tell you that *she's* scared. She's afraid that she won't get into the right school, or that she and Adrian will have to go to different schools. And I'm not saying that those fears aren't real for her, but with me it's something different. I'm more afraid that maybe I'll get into the right school, and maybe after that I'll get the right job, and that from the outside everything will look great, but I'll never really do anything or think anything special. And even if it all looks good on the surface, *I'll* know I've failed, and not at something unimportant like school, but at *life.*" He stops talking for a second.

"Keep going," Willow says. She squeezes his hand.

"Okay, remember when we were in the stacks that day and you were telling me about what fieldwork is like?"

"Yes." Willow nods.

"Well, we were joking, and I know that this sounds like a meaningless example, but I said maybe I wouldn't like fieldwork either, because I like my showers. Well, sometimes I worry that my whole life will be based around what's comfortable and easy. I'll care too much about what makes me feel good to ever really reach for anything. And then I worry that even if I do, I won't succeed."

Willow doesn't say anything. She's too busy mulling over everything that he's told her and she can't figure out why, when he's exposed himself so completely, made himself so vulnerable, he only seems stronger.

"But these days, I haven't been worrying about those things so much," Guy says. "I guess what scares me the most now is the thought that I won't be able to protect you."

Willow stares at him. She doesn't know how to respond to this extraordinary thing that he's told her. She squeezes his hand more tightly and she's aware that he's slowly moving closer to her, very slowly. She feels as if they're both underwater, and she knows that he's going to kiss her.

"Ahem." They jump apart as a security guard comes into the room and clears his throat.

Guy gives her a lopsided grin. Willow can tell that to him, the interruption is unwelcome but amusing.

But Willow feels differently. As much as she would love to have kissed him, she is also somewhat relieved that the guard prevented it from happening. Her heart is beating wildly, both from anticipation of how that kiss would have felt, and from fear.

Because now she's the one who's scared, *very* scared. Not of him, but of herself, or rather, of her feelings for him.

Didn't you know? Well, didn't you know that this is the way things would go?

She should have known better. Couldn't she tell from the first time she talked with him in the library—talked to him the way she's almost never talked to anyone else—couldn't she tell *then* that this would happen? And she tried to prevent it too. That first day when he wanted to walk home with her, she tried to send him away then.

What happened to her resolve? She should never have called him last night. She can't believe that she's spent so much time talking to him and finding out about him, that she practically begged him to show her the deepest recesses of his soul.

And most of all, she can't believe that she let him get under her skin and mean so goddamn much to her.

Willow knows that a year ago, if she found herself in such

a situation, with such a guy, she would be happy beyond belief, but her life is not as it was a year ago.

It is nothing less than astonishing that her new world—so far from brave—has such a person in it. But most unfortunately for Willow, she cannot let herself feel for him the way she would have if she were still living in her old world.

The silence between them is starting to become awkward. Willow knows Guy is expecting her to say something first. That he's waiting to hear her response to the things that he told her, and maybe even more, her response to his attempt to kiss her. She should say *something* to him, she should respond to this gift that he's offering her. But she can't. She can't tell him that she's moved, because she won't let herself be moved. She can't tell him that she cares, because she's trying very hard not to care.

Willow doesn't know what to do. She needs to get away from him, get away before things get any more complicated, but she doesn't know how to make a graceful exit. She doesn't know how she can ignore the appeal that's written so clearly on his face.

"I bet it's stopped raining by now. I should head on home and see if I can get anything done on that paper," is what Willow finally does choose to say. She can tell from the change in his expression—he looks like he's been slapped—that it's possibly the worst thing she could have come out with.

"Your paper?" he says incredulously. "Are you kidding me? *That's* your response? Fine." He backs away from her, *pushes* her away. Unlike before, his movements are quick; clearly he can't wait to get away from her either. "Fine, you do that. I guess I'll head up to the library, see if I can get some work done too." His voice is cold, and Willow can tell that he's hurt and confused.

"I'll walk you there," she says in a rush. Now he looks more confused than ever. And why not? She knows how crazy she must sound given the rejection that she's just handed him. But Willow's not quite capable of walking away from him yet.

And she can't bear to leave him with that look on his face.

"If you like," he says diffidently. "C'mon, let's get out of here."

It has indeed stopped raining. Once again the sun is shining and there is a light breeze, but they are both oblivious to the beauty of the day. Neither one of them speaks a word during the entire walk to the library.

"Well, I'm headed for the stacks as usual, you want to come?" Guy doesn't look at her as he says this, and Willow wonders why he's even bothering to ask. If their situations were reversed, she doesn't know if she would bother to talk to him. Maybe, like her, he feels that there's something unfinished in the air.

"All right." She nods.

They walk silently through the campus and into the library. After flashing their ID cards for Carlos, they take the elevator and get off on the eleventh floor. As usual they're alone. Guy presses the button for the lights and Willow blinks in the sudden glare.

"It's not that I wasn't moved by what you said," she says suddenly, grabbing his wrist and pulling him close. "It's not that I didn't want you to kiss me. It's that I can't let myself be kissed. You don't understand, I can't *let* myself."

Guy gently disentangles his arm and places both hands on her shoulders. "You're right," he says. "I don't understand." But the coldness is gone from his voice.

"I want to tell you something. I'm *going* to tell you something," she amends. Willow has made a decision. He's done so much for her, given her so much, that she simply has to give him something in return. She reaches up and covers his hands with hers. "C'mon, let's be comfortable at least." She walks him over to the place where they sat and talked about her parents' lecture.

"I'm going to tell you something," Willow repeats. She sits down cross-legged on the floor, and pulls him down alongside her, close, so close that it is as if they are joined from shoulder to hip.

"I'm listening." Guy seems reserved, but attentive.

"All right." Willow takes a deep breath. "After the accident, I was in the hospital for a week. There wasn't anything wrong with me, but, you know they keep you in there for *observation* or something. Anyway, the one good thing about it was that I was so drugged that I didn't really get what had happened. Oh, I knew, all right, but I didn't *get* it. I was conscious maybe two, three hours a day, I just slept all the time." She pauses for a moment to gather her thoughts.

"Then David and Cathy came to pick me up. Of course they'd visited me all the time, I mean that they came to take me home, well, to *their* house. Obviously I had to move in with them, I couldn't go back home and live by myself, and David didn't want to leave the city. He worked out how I could finish the school year by sending in some extra papers and things. I was always ahead in my classes, and anyway, my old school got out mid-May, so there were only about eight weeks left." Willow stops talking. She knows what she's going to say, it's just hard to come out with things that she has never before spoken of to anyone.

"It was terrible after the hospital. The hospital was, I don't know, oblivion. But being with David and Cathy, not having sleeping pills or pain pills, was just awful. I was dazed all the time, not from drugs anymore, but because now I really knew what I'd done. I mean, I got it in my head, I understood what had happened, but I didn't feel any pain, not then anyway. I guess I was still in shock.

"Well, after about another week of just hanging around in my bathrobe and sleeping all day, David decided that he wanted to go home and pack up our parents' books to take to his apartment. You can imagine that our house has a lot of books—I'm talking thousands upon thousands. Anyway, when we got home, David gave me a screwdriver. He wanted me to take apart this old bookcase down in the basement, while he got to work on some of the ones upstairs. Now that I think about it, what he did doesn't make any sense. I mean, there's no place in his apartment for all of those books, and why would I have to dismantle this crappy old bookcase anyway? Why not just pack up all the books? You know what I think was going on? I think for David, destroying the bookcases that way was like when the ancient Greeks would rend their clothes and tear their hair as a way of mourning. I think that's what it was all about, even though, in the end, we didn't get very far with it.

"So I was downstairs in the basement, with this screwdriver. Now, me and a screwdriver is not a good mix, it's like high heels on Everest, something you never want to see together, and I'm trying to take this stupid bookcase apart and it's just not happening. And all of a sudden, maybe it's being back home, I don't know, maybe it's what books meant to my parents, and the fact that I'm trying to dismantle their collection, but all of a sudden, I start to *get* it. I don't mean *think* it, I mean *get* it. It was like there was this extraordinary pain just knocking at the door of my consciousness—this overwhelming, extreme sensation, and I knew that if I let it in, I would go under.

"And then, just when I thought that I had no control over what was about to happen, I realized two things. The first is that the emotional pain was going away, it was leaving, it *wasn't* going to consume me, and the second was that I was stabbing myself, really *attacking* myself with the screwdriver, and that the physical pain that I was causing was better than the best drug the hospital had. It was just forcing everything else out. This pain, this *physical* pain, was flowing through my veins like heroin, and I was numb, immune to the rest of it, I couldn't feel anything but the pain, and I knew that I had found a way to save myself.

"When you found me out, you thought that I wanted to kill myself, that all this slashing was like target practice until I got up enough courage for the real thing. You don't understand at all. You just don't get it. I'm *saving* myself.

"I've taught myself, I've trained myself, not to feel anything *except* physical pain. I'm completely in control of that. Do you understand? Do you get what that means?"

Guy doesn't say anything. He is ashen-faced. Willow is also silent, spent from having revealed so much, but something else is happening too. As she sits there next to him she is acutely aware of the way his body feels, of the way his arms look with his sleeves rolled up, of the texture of his bare skin as it brushes against hers, and of the sensations all of those things evoke deep inside of her. And she realizes that try as she might to prevent it, try as she might to only feel pain, now there is something else she feels as well, and there is nothing she would rather do than kiss him.

She's shocked that her mood has swung so wildly. How did anguish suddenly morph into desire?

Maybe it's because she has never revealed so much of herself to another person. Maybe it's because she wants to test if her hypothesis is true. Is it really so dangerous for her to feel anything? Will kissing him, feeling for him, *falling in love with him,* really be so disastrous?

This time she is the one who leans forward. She is on her knees in front of him, grasping his shirt collar, pulling him close to her. He is clearly as startled by this as she herself is, but he allows himself to be drawn in. Their mouths meet, she moves even closer still until she is sitting on his lap, takes his hands from her waist and puts them on her breasts, does everything but devour him, desperate to see if she can have something beyond her bondage with the razor.

Willow doesn't know the exact moment that the extraordinary pleasure she's feeling turns into the pain of her worst fears. Pictures of the accident start writhing beneath her closed lids, competing for attention with the image she holds of his face. A tidal wave of emotion threatens to engulf her. She is suddenly back in the basement with the bookcases.

"I can't." Willow pushes him away. "I can't!"

She's breathing heavily. She barely even registers that Guy is on his knees in front of her. The bloody dashboard, her mother's crushed limbs, these are the things that she sees.

Willow claps her hands over her ears in a vain attempt to drown out the dreadful sounds of the accident.

She jumps up, wheels away from him, fumbles in her pocket for the razor that she always keeps there.

But just as she's preparing to slice, to save herself, to end the nightmare visions, Guy's hand clamps down on hers. He pulls her down on the floor again roughly.

"No." He's shaking his head. "Not here. Not now. Not with me around."

"I have to." Willow is gasping. "Just let me be. Let me do it!"

Guy sits back on his heels and regards her solemnly. "All right then," he says finally. "You can cut yourself, but not like this, not like some cornered animal. You have to do it in front of me."

"You . . . You want . . ." She stares at him openmouthed. She can't imagine cutting herself in front of him. It is something so intimate that it makes their kiss seem like nothing more than shaking hands. She can't do it. She just can't. She just sits on the floor in front of him, the razor dangling uselessly from her hand.

But the pictures in her head won't stop, and there is only one way she knows of ending them.

Willow doesn't flinch as she presses the blade into her flesh. She stares at Guy, aware that although she is fully clothed, she is completely bare before him. It hurts. It hurts badly, and within seconds the pain is swirling through her like an opiate, completely crowding out everything else.

"Oh my God. Oh my God!" Now Guy is the one who is clapping a hand over his mouth. "Stop it! I can't watch!" He grabs the razor and flings it across the room, grabs her arm and stares at the blood, grabs *her* and crushes her close.

Willow is so close that once again she's sitting in his lap. She's so close that they might as well be sharing the same breath.

"You won't let yourself feel anything but pain?" He holds her more tightly than she would have thought possible.

Willow leans back against his chest. Now that the razor has done its work, it's not so overwhelming to be there with him. She watches through half-closed lids as he wipes the blood on her arm with his shirttail. Now that she's numbed herself, she'd like nothing more than to stay there with him, like this, forever.

Instead she does the next best thing. She stays there, like that, long after the lights flicker out and leave them in the darkness. She stays there long past the time that she should go home. She just stays there, like that, for as long as she possibly can.

CHAPTER TWELVE

Willow was sure that she had perfected the technique of pretending to pay attention in class when her thoughts were completely elsewhere. She knew how to make it look like she was industriously taking notes when she was doing nothing more than scribbling, she knew how to make it look like she was following along in the text even when her book was open to the wrong page, and she knew how to nod along at key moments to make it look like she was listening.

But somehow those dubious skills seem to have deserted her. Because today, Willow knows that it's all too obvious to anyone who cares to look, that although she may physically be in French class, her mind is far from present.

She can't stop thinking about what happened in the stacks. She can't stop thinking about what happened with David the night before that, and she can't stop wondering how she will behave, how she *should* behave the next time that she sees either Guy or her brother.

At least she'd been given a small reprieve with David. When she'd finally gone home the night before, dreading the confrontation that she was sure would take place, Cathy had reminded her that David had gone to yet another conference, and wasn't due back until much later today. As for Cathy, she hadn't said much of anything to her about the whole mess. She'd already expressed her feelings in her note, and Willow was grateful that she clearly didn't see the need to discuss it any further.

Willow is sure that when she sees David again, things will be very uncomfortable, but she's nowhere near as sure of what seeing Guy will be like. There's no reason that things shouldn't be fine, better than fine, actually . . . except for the fact that she herself is far from fine.

Willow closes her eyes as unbidden images of their afternoon wash over her. It is impossible to think of their day together with unmixed emotions: It was wonderful to talk to him. She should *never* have talked to him about how she became a cutter. It was wonderful to kiss him. It was *terrifying* to kiss him. It was incredibly moving to hear about his hopes and fears. She's not strong enough to take on someone else's pain.

Things were simple before she met him. There was the accident, and there was the razor. Life revolved around both of them. Now things are far from simple.

She sighs deeply, miserably aware that the girl next to her is looking at her strangely.

Maybe she just needs a little time to sort things out. Who's to say that she's going to see him today anyway? This is her last period, he may or may not be outside afterward, he's never called her or anything, she's the one . . .

Willow starts to laugh. Not really loudly, but enough for the same girl to give her another look.

This time it doesn't bother her, though. It is absurd to her that after everything that's happened, all she can think about is *Will he call or should I call him first?* It's the sort of thing that she and Markie used to spend hours obsessing over. For a second she feels just like a regular girl again.

Class ends and she leaves the room with everyone else. She looks over her shoulder as she walks down the hall, both relieved and disappointed that he doesn't seem to be around.

Well, you wanted some time alone to think about things, didn't you?

There are plenty of students milling around on the pavement outside school, but again, no Guy. Willow does see Laurie and Chloe, however, and she walks over to them.

"So, whaddya think?" Laurie smiles at Willow as she pivots on one heel. Willow is confused for a moment until she realizes that Laurie is asking about her new shoes.

"Oh, they're absolutely fabulous!" Willow says in admiration. "And I really love the color."

"Aren't they amazing? I couldn't believe that they had a pair left in my size. They're comfortable too."

"You should have come with us," Chloe joins in. "They had a lot of great things on sale. I got two pairs, but I'm not wearing either of them today," she adds as Willow glances over at her feet.

"What did you get?"

"The same ones as Laurie, only I promised not to wear mine until next year when we're at different schools." Chloe makes a rueful face. "And then a pair that are way too fancy to wear to school, but they're really great. Black. *Super* high. *Super* strappy."

"We're headed to the park right now," Laurie says. "No money left to do anything else. You want to hang out with us today?"

"Sure," Willow responds after a few seconds. This is probably exactly what she needs. No scenes with her brother, no rehearsing those scenes beforehand, no wondering about Guy and how things are going to proceed with him, just hanging out in the park and talking about nothing more emotionally demanding than shoes. Perfect.

"So, did you ever get that internship you were interviewing for?" Willow asks Laurie as they cross the street and start walking toward the park.

"Haven't you figured out by now that it's dangerous to ask her questions about stuff like that?" Chloe says, kicking a stone out of her path.

Willow looks at Chloe with a question in her eyes, which quickly turns to a shared grin as Laurie launches into a diatribe regarding the pros and cons of working for a recommendation versus working for cash.

"I mean, it would look so good if I had that kind of experience." Laurie chews on her lower lip fretfully. "But I'd love to have some money right now. Especially now, since I spent practically everything I had the other day. The thing is, though, I don't even know if I've gotten the internship. I'm supposed to hear this week—"

"What do you think of Andy?" Chloe interrupts suddenly.

"Who, me?" Willow asks.

"Yeah, well, I already know what Laurie thinks."

"How is Willow is supposed to know?" Laurie protests. "She's barely exchanged two words with him!"

"True," Chloe concedes. "Great arms, though, huh? Rowing is the best for arms, it really develops them."

"It sure does." Willow doesn't remember *Andy's* arms at all, but she has to agree with Chloe. Rowing really does give people amazing arms. She turns her head away, aware that not everyone finds blushing sweet. "Are you . . . interested in him?" Willow asks after a moment.

"Let's put it this way." Chloe sighs. "He's the only one who's interested in me right now."

"Maybe you should give him more of a chance," Laurie interjects. "After all, we hardly know him any better than Willow does."

"He's not new, is he?" Willow frowns. "I mean, how come you guys don't know him that well?"

"No, he's not new or anything like that," Chloe says as they enter the park. "We just never really spent any time with him before."

"He used to go out with the most horrible girl," Laurie adds as they all sit down on the grass. "Elizabeth something or other. She left last year, though." She takes off her new shoes and starts rubbing her feet. "I shouldn't have worn these two days in a row."

"Yeah, it's sort of like a worrisome sign that he's interested in me after her." Chloe represses a shudder. "I mean, am I like *Elizabeth* in any way?" She looks at Laurie.

"Yeah, just like her, that's why we've been best friends for three years now. God, these blisters are killing me."

"Weren't you just saying how comfortable they were?" Chloe raises an eyebrow.

"Comfortable for *heels*."

"I have some Band-Aids," Willow offers. She starts rooting around in her bag for the box that Guy bought her.

"You're so well prepared," Chloe observes.

"What do you mean?" Willow asks warily. She tosses the Band-Aids over to Laurie.

"I don't know." Chloe shrugs. "You just seem to have stuff that people need, like when we were here with Andy and you had those handy wipey things."

"Oh." Willow nods. She wonders if Chloe notices that it's a rather odd assortment of things that she carries around with her, far more unusual than the nail polish and other paraphernalia that Chloe obviously packs. She feels exposed, guilty even, like a heroin addict who's been caught with her works.

"Anyway, getting back to Andy—Ouch!" Laurie exclaims as she pops a particularly nasty-looking blister. "Don't make up your mind about him yet, who knows, he may turn out to be okay. I'm sure that when Adrian shows up, he'll be tagging along and—"

"Adrian is showing up?" Willow blurts out. She doesn't know why that surprises her. It makes total sense, obviously he and Laurie are together but . . .

"Yeah, he had to do some stuff after school, so he said he'd meet us here." Laurie tosses the Band-Aids back to Willow.

"Oh." Willow wonders if Guy will be along for the ride too.

"I'm pretty sure that Guy will be coming with them," Laurie says, as if she can read Willow's mind. "Because I know that he was going with Adrian on whatever errand it was he had to do."

"Whoever shows up, I hope that they brings some Diet Cokes." Chloe yawns.

"That should be good though, right?" Laurie looks at Willow. "I mean, and don't give me a hard time, Chloe," she says as the other girl starts to speak. "You do like him, right? I didn't mean to bother you the other day, but, c'mon, tell us."

"Yes," Willow says. "I like him." Privately she thinks how bland and pallid the word *like* is as a way to describe her feelings. But as much as she might feel for him, she hopes that he won't show up. She was expecting some time alone to sort things out, she wasn't counting on their first meeting after the stacks being in mixed company.

"Now *he's* someone to have interested in you." Chloe leans forward, her eyes sparkling. "Oh, don't worry." She touches Willow's arm. "I've known him for three years and nothing . . ." She shrugs eloquently.

"Well, it's not really like what you're thinking," Willow says. "I mean, it's just—"

"Speak of the devil," Laurie interrupts, looking over Willow's shoulder.

"And no Diet Cokes." Chloe groans. "Maybe I can get Andy to go find one of those hot dog carts. There's usually a couple in the park, somewhere. It shouldn't take him too long."

Willow turns to watch the three of them approach.

Her hands tremble a little and she drops the box of Band-Aids in the grass. She curses under her breath, annoyed at herself for being so flustered. Well, at least now she doesn't have to wonder how she'll feel when she sees Guy.

"Ah, that brief blissful time when you can get them to do your bidding." Laurie laughs.

"Right, like finding me a Diet Coke compares to the stuff that Adrian does for you."

"Sssh!" Laurie elbows Chloe in the ribs. "He thinks everyone is that way. *Please,* it took me *months* to train him, don't go giving him any ideas." She stops talking as they come within hearing distance.

"Do something for me," Chloe says as Andy drops his backpack down next to her.

"Sure," he says easily.

Willow watches Adrian give Laurie a kiss. She feels rather than sees Guy sit down across from her. She shoves the Band-Aids back into her bag. There should be nothing awkward about this. He's someone she really likes, and unless she's completely mistaken, he likes her too, so what's the big deal? There's nothing so unusual about that.

Except everything about their time together has been unusual.

"Get me a Diet Coke," Chloe begs. "No, *two* Diet Cokes, please?"

"Hi," Guy says to Willow. He smiles at her. Not the same way that he's smiled at her when they've been alone. There's nothing particularly intimate about it, but it is genuine.

Willow looks at him. Okay, so *he* doesn't feel uncomfortable. *She* won't feel uncomfortable either.

"Hey, get me a Sprite while you're at it." Laurie fishes in her pocket for some change.

"Hell—" Willow starts to say.

"Anyone else want anything?" Andy interrupts as he moves

between her and Guy. He not only cuts her off verbally, but physically as well. "What about you, Willow?"

"Huh? Oh, nothing for me." Willow knows that he's just trying to be nice, but still, she finds him irritating. Did he have to get in the way like that?

"Okay, be back in a second."

Now Willow has her chance to smile at Guy, but he's too busy looking in his backpack for something to even notice. As he shifts things around, Willow can see the blue leather corner of *The Tempest* stuck in there among his other books. The sight of it makes her feel better. He wouldn't really be carrying it around unless it meant something to him, would he? Unless *she* meant something to him?

He looks up suddenly, their eyes meet, and she can't help it, she starts to blush. Willow glances away for a second, embarrassed, but then turns to him, determined to get over her awkwardness and to finally say hello. Only, as she looks at him, it is impossible not to think about everything that happened. The memory of what it was like to kiss him washes over her, blotting out the here and now. His features become fragmented, images of their time in the stacks are suddenly superimposed over his face.

Willow's blush deepens as she remembers grabbing his hands, forcefully *grabbing* them and placing them on her breasts. And then, as if that weren't bad enough, she remembers starting to cut in front of him. She can't think about these things right now—it would be one thing if they were alone together, but surrounded by everyone else? Willow drops her head in her hands for a second, as if by covering her eyes, she can blot out the pictures.

"Willow!" Laurie sounds alarmed. "Are you okay?"

"Oh." She jerks her head up.

This just isn't working.

"I have a headache, I get the most terrible migraines," she stammers. She avoids looking at Guy, avoids looking at any of them.

"And you don't have any aspirin in that bag of yours?" Chloe asks.

"No, well, the thing is, it's more that I just have so much work . . . I should get going." Willow shakes her head regretfully. "I'll see you all later, okay?" She gets her things together and stands up. Slowly, calmly, as if she really does wish that she could stay there with them.

Willow turns and walks out of the park, resisting the urge to run.

Well, that went well, huh?

If she was embarrassed and uncomfortable before, there simply aren't words to describe how she feels now. She briefly considers ramming her head into the stone wall that borders the park. It would make a novel change from cutting anyway.

The thing to do now is go home, forget the last twenty minutes, erase it. Get home and . . .

She wonders if Guy will follow her, or if he's had more than enough already.

Well, it's not like he hasn't already picked up on the fact that I'm a little different. . . .

If he does follow her, what will *she* do? Maybe her first instincts were right, maybe she has room for only one relationship.

Too bad that relationship just happens to be with a sharp piece of metal.

Don't think about it! Figure it out later! Get home! Open your French book! Get to work on your paper!

Willow can't stop herself from reliving the incident throughout the entire walk home. She goes back and forth between convincing herself that nothing so very dreadful happened and being sure that she's completely ruined everything.

Ruined what anyway?

Do I even have anything to ruin?

She's looking forward to sitting at her desk. Maybe getting to work will prove to be the distraction that she needs. But unfortunately, as she unlocks the door she's confronted by the sounds of Isabelle, screaming as if her lungs are fit to burst. Cathy is holding her while she paces back and forth on the phone. She looks completely overwhelmed. Willow drops her keys on the hall table and goes into the kitchen.

"Cathy?"

"I'm glad you're here," Cathy says above the screaming. "What?" she speaks into the phone. "Okay, thank you, yes, call it in to the pharmacy." She hangs up and looks at Willow.

"What's going on? What are you doing home? Is Isabelle sick or something?"

"She's burning up, poor little thing." Cathy presses a kiss against Isabelle's forehead. "They called me at work to come and pick her up. It's just an ear infection, the doctor said that there's nothing to worry about, that super high fevers are really common . . ." Clearly she's trying to reassure herself as much as Willow. "I have to go to the pharmacy and pick up her prescription. Will you be okay with her until I get back?"

"Of course," Willow says, taking Isabelle from Cathy. Now

is not the time to remind Cathy that David wouldn't approve of her staying with the baby. "I'll be fine," she says calmly. "Go to the pharmacy."

"Thank you," Cathy says, pulling on her sweater and grabbing her purse. "I don't know how long this will take, sometimes they make you wait while they make up the prescription. I'll be back as soon as I can." She dashes out the door.

Willow walks over to the window, Isabelle in her arms, and watches as Cathy runs down the street. "I'm sorry you feel so sick," she says, bouncing the baby up and down on her hip. But Isabelle seems a little calmer than she did a few minutes ago, she's no longer crying quite so forcefully. Her tears are subsiding, punctuated by little snuffles. Willow thinks how wonderful it would be, and not just for poor Isabelle's sake either, if when Cathy came home, everything was under perfect control, Isabelle calm, sleeping even, the kitchen clean. . . .

"Wouldn't that be nice, sweetie? Wouldn't you feel better?"

Willow wants rather desperately to repay Cathy's faith in her. Not only that, but she's sure that taking care of Isabelle, taking care of her *perfectly* that is, might go a little way toward smoothing things over with David when he finally comes home.

And if she's totally focused on Isabelle, then she won't even have time to think about what just happened in the park.

Of course, she's not exactly sure what taking care of Isabelle perfectly might entail. There's only so much she can do with a sick baby, after all, but maybe feeding her, and changing her, would be a good start. She does feel wet.

"So, let's get you changed, and then make you something to eat. You'll like that, won't you?"

Willow walks into Isabelle's bedroom and lays her down on the changing table. Now, she may have changed many diapers in her time—she's been babysitting since she was thirteen—but she's never changed Isabelle. Although it's not the most challenging activity, it is a little more difficult than she would have thought, since Isabelle, alone among all the babies that Willow has ever met, wears cloth diapers.

David gives Cathy a hard time about this, since they're incalculably more expensive than disposable diapers, difficult to even find, and more inconvenient in every way possible, but Cathy, who studied environmental law, always insists.

"Okay, so this shouldn't be so difficult. . . ." Willow grabs a cloth diaper and two diaper pins.

But Isabelle is not as cooperative as she might be. Clearly the poor little girl doesn't feel well. Instead of lying still she fusses and kicks, and Willow, unused to diaper pins, manages to stab her. Rather sharply too, if the baby's screams are anything to go by.

"Oh, no!" Willow is horrified. How could she do such a thing? She stares transfixed at the minute pinprick blossoming red that mars her niece's perfect, tender flesh. There's something absolutely obscene about damaging something so flawless.

Willow slowly reaches out her hand and touches the spot where she pricked Isabelle. Just as when Guy touched her, Willow's hand completely obliterates the mark that she made. Well, that's not very surprising. What she has inflicted on Isabelle greatly differs from the gashes that score her own stomach. But what if that tiny little mark were to grow? For a second she imagines Isabelle's skin scored all over, savaged by a razor, the way that her own is. How would she feel if, say, ten or fifteen years from now she found out that *Isabelle* was a cutter?

Willow jerks her hand back.

And what if she killed David and Cathy, then what? Would you still think her being a cutter was so bad?

She finishes diapering Isabelle without incident, although her hands are trembling, and carries her into the kitchen.

"Well, we're off to a great start here, don't you think?" she says in a shaky voice. So much for taking care of her niece perfectly. At least Isabelle has stopped crying. Willow can't help feeling that the baby has recovered from the episode far better than she herself has.

"How about something to eat?" She opens the cupboards and rummages around. Today even the pretzels and baby food are gone. "Yeah, so much for that." Willow slams the doors shut and moves to the refrigerator.

At least the refrigerator is more promising. There are half a dozen eggs, and some butter among other things. Willow puts Isabelle in her high chair and grabs a couple of the eggs and a bowl. She sets a pan on the stove and throws some butter in. As she beats the eggs she thinks about what just happened. She absentmindedly pours the eggs in the pan, then dumps the bowl in the sink.

Willow stares out the widow, but she barely even registers the park outside. The only thing she sees is Isabelle's perfect skin. She's so lost in thought that she forgets about the eggs for a second.

Willow turns back from the window and gasps in horror. The eggs are on fire. The pan is on fire. The kitchen is on fire.

Not again!

This is her first thought. *She has done it again*. David was right, she really will finish the rest of the family off. As her eyes start to tear from the acrid smoke, she has another thought as well. What if this time around she managed to save Isabelle? What if this time things are *different*?

The vision of herself as a heroine is delicious.

But the smoke starts to dissipate, and Willow can see that really, of course there is no fire. How likely would it be that some burned scrambled eggs could turn into a three-alarm fire anyway?

There is no fire, she will neither kill nor save Isabelle in some dramatic gesture. She is simply a girl who has made a filthy mess, a girl who is incapable of taking care of her niece, as incapable of that as she is of everything else these days.

Willow takes the smoking pan and tosses it into the sink, where it hisses and splutters angrily. As she stares at the smoke that drifts toward the ceiling, it occurs to her that maybe for once, David was being completely honest when he said that his reservations about leaving her alone were simply because she is too overwrought to take care of a six-month-old. Based on the evidence she'd have to agree with him.

The doorbell rings. Willow can only hope that it isn't Cathy, so weighed down by packages that she can't manage her keys, or even worse, David, home from his conference.

At least give me time to clean up, for God's sake.

But when she opens the door, it is Guy who is standing there.

This time Willow doesn't blush, and she doesn't feel flustered either. She's much too relieved that it's him as opposed to David or Cathy.

"Migraines?" He leans against the door jamb.

"Yeah, well, I thought the plague might sound suspicious. C'mon in." She steps back and opens the door wider.

"Something smells like it's burning."

"Tell me about it," Willow says. She walks in front of him toward the kitchen.

"What are you doing?"

"Umm . . ." Willow surveys the smoky kitchen. Her plan, to take care of Isabelle perfectly, could not have backfired more spectacularly. "I guess I'm continuing to screw up my life and anyone else's who comes into contact with me." She goes over to the sink and picks up a sponge, intending to scrub the burned pan. "That sounds about right, what do you think?"

"Just 'cause you burned some . . ." He joins her at the sink and glances into the pan. "Hmm, I'm guessing these were eggs at one point?"

"No, that's not the only reason." Willow attacks the pan with the sponge. It's tough going. She should have soaked it first.

The whole process of washing the pot seems futile suddenly. She wonders what would happen if she just threw it out the window. Instead she settles for the trash can under the sink. Maybe if she covers it with enough garbage David and Cathy won't even notice.

"You're just throwing it out?" Guy seems to find this funny.

Willow shrugs. "Oh, by the way, this is Isabelle."

"About those migraines in the park—" Guy starts to say, but they are interrupted by the sound of a key in the lock, and David's voice calling out.

"Hey, I'm back. Who's here?"

Willow is glad that the smoke has cleared somewhat, and that she has managed to get rid of the pan, but she'd prefer it if he didn't enter the kitchen just yet. She picks up Isabelle and walks into the foyer.

"Hi," she says warily. This is, after all, the first time that she has seen David since her fit a couple of nights ago. She has no idea how to act toward him. Given how close-mouthed David's been lately, she can hardly expect him to start something in front of Guy. Still, she imagines that he will make reference to the other night *somehow,* if only because her being left alone with Isabelle would have to reactivate the argument.

"Hello." David nods to Guy, but it's clear that he's preoccupied. "What's going on?" He looks confused. "Where's Cathy?" David reaches out to take the baby from Willow.

"She went to the pharmacy," Willow says. "Isabelle's sick, an ear infection, I think she said."

"You didn't try and put her down for a nap?" he asks mildly.

Willow can't believe how stupid she's been. Of course it would have made much more sense to do that than anything else. She braces herself for David's condemnation.

But David doesn't seem as if he cares very much about reprimanding her. He's far more interested in Isabelle's welfare. Willow knows that this is only natural and correct. Furthermore, she has no interest in having any kind of replay of the other night. Yet as she watches David kiss his daughter, she is struck by a pain so sharp, so brutal, that she nearly doubles over.

She clutches her stomach. For a second she is sure that she is going to faint. The ache is so intense that she is surprised, when she looks down at herself, to see that there is no blood springing through her clothes, that this pain is not self-inflicted. This is the pain that she has been fighting for so long.

Of course David's first concern would be for his daughter. Willow is not hurt by the fact that she is not first with *him*. It is that she will *never* be first with anyone again. She will never be anyone's child again. This happens to everyone, it will happen to Isabelle too, but surely not as soon as it has happened to her.

"Willow?" David grabs her arm, no easy feat since he is still holding Isabelle. "What's wrong?"

"I'm okay, just . . ." Willow straightens up. The pain is gone. She has no idea how, she can only be thankful that it is so. "I'm just a little . . ." She searches for the right thing to say. Migraines won't fly with David. "I'm really tired, that's all. We're . . . I'm going to go upstairs and lie down." She winces at her choice of words, and wonders if David or Guy has picked up on them, but David has already turned back to Isabelle.

"C'mon," she says to Guy. "Let's go."

Willow walks up the stairs to her room. The episode has left her feeling completely drained. She feels like she could sleep for a thousand years. She opens the door and eyes her bed longingly. She wonders what Guy would do if she just got under the covers and closed her eyes.

Instead of doing that she sits at her desk and Guy is the one who gets the bed. He doesn't get under the covers, but he does sit down and lean against the pillows. The sight of him on her bed is anything but comfortable and she has to look away for a few moments to compose herself.

But even though she is uncomfortable, even though she is

still reeling from what happened downstairs, seeing him like this, without the complications of other people, she knows, suddenly, what her feelings are. She can't rationally say that being with him is too complicated, that her fidelity is only to the razor. She is powerless to make such a decision. She cannot do otherwise but be with him.

"So about the park," Guy says. "I was wondering if your getting these migraines was a way of—"

"Oh," Willow interrupts him. "I . . . was . . ." She wishes she could tell him that she ran out of the park because she was so overcome by the memory of the way that they kissed, but saying those words is nearly as overwhelming as the act itself. "It was just that I was . . . Well, I wasn't going to *do* anything." She hopes that he will get her oblique reference. Surely this must be why he is asking, because he's worried that she had a date with her blades?

"Yeah, that isn't what I was thinking. I was just wondering if you really get migraines or if you were just trying to avoid me. Either way, you were kind of rude." There is a definite edge to his normally calm voice, and Willow is sure that she can hear something else beneath the words.

"I was . . . Huh?" She blinks as the meaning of what he's said sinks in. But she has to admit that while she wouldn't necessarily brand her behavior as rude, she knew, even as she was doing it, that it was at least very odd.

"I asked if you were trying to avoid me."

Now Willow *knows* that he has something going on. She wants to reassure him, she wants to tell him that she can't stop thinking about the day that they spent together, that right now, she wants nothing more than to crawl underneath the covers with him. But the words die in her throat, so instead she says:

"It's just sort of complicated . . . I mean *you're* complicated and . . . difficult . . ."

"*I'm* complicated? *I'm* difficult?" he asks incredulously. "Are you out of your mind?"

"Apparently," Willow says unhappily.

"You think you're not *complicated* and *difficult*?" Guy goes on as if he hadn't heard her. "You think you're easy to deal with? You think what happened after we kissed is the way things normally go?"

"No, I never thought that." Willow shakes her head vehemently. She knows that he's right, she'd be the first to say so, but she can't help feeling hurt. Was the only thing that he took away from the other day the *strangeness* of it all? Didn't he feel any of the things that she felt? "But I did think that maybe . . . maybe you had some fun. . . ."

Fun? Fun! Okay, guess it's back to asking about kittens!

Willow cannot believe that she has said something so profoundly stupid, and judging from the look on Guy's face, he can't either.

"Fun? Fun! Oh yeah! It's been really *FUN*! You think that this isn't playing hell with my *mind*? Fuck that!" Guy practically spits the words out. Willow blinks. She's not used to hearing him talk that way. "You think that this isn't playing hell with my *life*? I've barely slept since the first time I saw your arm, let alone gotten any work done. You think I like this? That this is all fun? Fuck all of it, and *fuck you too*!"

Willow feels as if he's slapped her. She didn't realize that calm, easygoing Guy could get so angry. She didn't realize that their day together didn't hold any magic for him. She didn't realize that he had the power to wound her quite so deeply.

"I don't think that this is all fun," she says after a few moments. Her voice is cold and hard. She is no longer interested in reassuring him. "But guess what, Guy, I never asked you to hang around either. Nobody invited you here today. You can just walk away. You can just leave."

"Right, I can leave," Guy says sarcastically. "You think I could just walk away after what happened in the library?"

Willow is dying to ask him which part of their time in the library he's referring to. Does he feel that he can't walk away because of their kiss, or because of her cutting? But she doesn't say anything.

"Yeah, okay," Guy continues. "Maybe I would like to be around somebody who doesn't need talking down all the time, but then what? I don't need you on my conscience."

Willow has her answer. She doesn't like being his community service for the semester, and, if that's all that's keeping him, then she wants no part of it.

"Don't make me your project, Guy. That's what this is about? You don't want to feel guilty? You don't want me on your conscience? You look a little too old to be a Boy Scout." Willow tries to make her voice as harsh as possible, but she is no more successful at this than she was at taking care of Isabelle. In fact, she sounds nothing so much as scared and vulnerable. "Go back to the other things you said you had going on this semester. The things you said I was going to complicate. All those classes you take up at the university, your rowing. Go ahead. Go somewhere else. Knock ten seconds off your time, but don't worry about me anymore."

"Don't worry about you?" Guy shakes his head. "So you'll be okay, no slicing and dicing? You're all together now?"

Willow has no answer to this. Instead she thinks about all the things that she's told him, all the things that he's told her, and all the things that they've done together. How did it all get to be such a mess right now? She wishes that she could press the rewind button and simply erase the last ten minutes, but unfortunately that's not possible, and she realizes that, difficult as it may be, it is up to her to salvage the situation.

"I'll be all right," she says after a moment. "If you're staying here because you think you're going to stop me from cutting, then leave. If you're afraid that if you do leave I'll *always* be a cutter, then that's another reason for you to get out of here as quickly as possible. I don't want you to stick around because of that. I don't even know how that part of the story ends, but I do know if you go . . ." She trails off, puts her elbows on the desk, and rests her head in her hands. It is far easier to cut herself, to *mutilate* herself than to tell him how she feels.

"Then what? If I go, then what?" Guy's voice is angry, angry enough so that Willow almost backs down from what she is going to say.

"Go on. Tell me, if I go, *then what*?" Guy says once again.

There are many answers that Willow can give to this question. She can tell him that if he goes she might be better off. She won't be afraid of experiencing the things that so overwhelmed her in the stacks, that are starting to overwhelm her even as she sits there with him now. She won't worry that there is someone who is intent on weaning her off of her extracurricular activities. She won't have to worry about protecting someone else's feelings. But she will have no one to talk to, no one who knows her, no one who understands. Willow looks at him, and the only answer that she can give, the truest answer is simply:

"If you go, then I'll miss you . . . *terribly.*"

"Oh," Guy says. He gets up from the bed, crosses over to where she is, and lowers himself until he is sitting on his heels in front of her. Willow wonders if he is aware of how closely he is mimicking her posture from yesterday. "You're not my project," he says finally. "You're not my project," he says again more forcefully. "And I don't want to go anywhere else."

Willow is speechless. She had no idea, she really had no idea that anybody would ever look at her in that way.

She leans forward, until her forehead is brushing his. The most natural thing right now would be for them to kiss each other once again, but Willow knows that she can't do that, she simply can't risk it. She wonders why he wants to stay. He can get so much more somewhere, *anywhere* else, without all of her added complications.

"I . . . I don't want you to go anywhere else either," she says finally.

"Then what do you want?" Guy asks.

Willow isn't sure if she has the energy to answer this. She's bone weary. Exhausted. Trying to take care of Isabelle wore her out. The scene they just had wore her out. Just telling him the truth wore her out. Her *life* is wearing her out. But all of that fades away as she looks at Guy. She thinks that he's beautiful. And as she remembers the way that he looked on the bed, so calm, so strong, so *right,* there is only one thing she wants to do. It may not be the answer that he was looking for, but it is the only one that she can give him.

"I want to go to sleep," she says finally. "Just to sleep, for a long time, and not wake up until I'm ready."

Guy doesn't say anything. He just nods as if this is not only the most natural response she could give, but the only one.

"Okay." He gets to his feet, pulls her up off the chair, and walks her to the bed. Guy lies back down in his former position, but Willow just sits on the edge and looks at him. She wonders if he can possibly feel her secret stash hidden under the mattress. She offers him a shy smile, because as much as she wants this, it is still difficult for her. *He* doesn't appear to be having any difficulties, however. He just smiles back at her and holds out a hand.

Willow kicks off her shoes and, grasping his hand, crawls across the bed toward him. She has moved far beyond exhaustion and his chest is the best pillow she could ever imagine. But for all that, she's trembling. What she has told him has left her naked; she feels as if she has ripped off a layer of her skin. Willow feels things, good things, to be sure, even wonderful things, but she is used to being deadened, anesthetized, and she knows of only one way to process this.

Guy is asleep within moments. But it is not so easy for Willow. She stares up at the ceiling. She tries to mimic his calm easy breathing. But she can't quite do it, her breath remains a little panicky. She tries to focus instead on how wonderful his arms feel. She even laughs a little as she remembers Chloe's comments about rowers. But still, she can't stop trembling. Her hand strays to the edge of the mattress, goes underneath, feels for her supplies.

You can handle this, can't you? It's not so difficult.

It occurs to Willow that she has handled far worse. Whatever it was that happened downstairs with David just now, however savage, was *survivable*. The realization makes her bolt upright. How is that she managed to endure that pain without any recourse to her trusty equipment?

Willow knows that she should find this comforting, but in fact it scares her more than almost anything. She breaks into a cold sweat. The idea, however fleeting, that she could possibly survive without her constant companion of the past seven months is simply too unsettling. She searches under the mattress more frantically. When her hand finally closes around the razor she squeezes it tightly. She has no need of more right now, but she does need to know that more is possible.

Guy shifts in his sleep, moving both of them, and somehow manages to dislodge her grip. The razor falls to the floor with a faint metallic ping.

Willow gets out of bed to retrieve it, and as she does so her gaze falls upon Guy's backpack. An idea occurs to her. She checks to make certain that he really is asleep and when she is sure that he is, walks over to her desk and gets a pen. She pauses for a moment, looking at the box of still unused watercolors. It would be wonderful to do some kind of illustration, something that would go along with what she's about to write, but it would take too long to dry, and besides, she's in too much of a hurry to get back in bed with him. She goes over to his bag, unzips it as quietly as possible, and takes out the copy of *The Tempest*.

She doesn't even have to think twice:

For Guy,

Oh brave new world that has such a person in it . . .

She smiles a little as she imagines his reaction when he finds it, and she wonders when that will be—tonight, tomorrow?

Willow gets back into bed, still clutching her razor, but it doesn't matter, because she finds that this time her breathing does match Guy's, and she too sleeps.

CHAPTER THIRTEEN

At first Willow thinks that it is a nightmare that has woken her up so suddenly. Then she is sure it must be the sounds of the late-night traffic that filter through the window. But as she looks out onto the moonlit street, she sees that there are no cars, that the road is completely empty.

Willow is used to waking up in the middle of the night with a start, but this time seems different. There is no reason that she should be sitting bolt upright in bed at three in the morning. There are no hideous images that permeate her dreams, no sounds that recall the accident.

Is it just that she is overwrought by the events of the past few days? The stacks, her nap with Guy, the pain she felt as she watched David with Isabelle. *Especially* the pain she felt watching the two of them. These are disturbing things, but are they enough to startle her awake in the middle of the night?

Willow hugs her legs to her chest, rests her chin on her knees and thinks. Should she—

What's that?

She raises her head at a noise, faint but unmistakable.

Oh.

Now Willow knows exactly what it is that has woken her up so abruptly. It is nothing that would rouse anyone else, being barely audible, but the sound goes straight to her heart. Once again her brother is weeping.

She swings her legs over the edge of the bed and reaches for her bathrobe. She has no conscious plan, no thought that she is going to help her brother, and indeed, not only would she not know how to do such a thing, but she knows that her appearance would be a profound invasion. Still, though, she cannot stay in bed when her brother is crying, and when she herself has caused his tears.

She creeps down the stairs, pausing on every step, determined not to make any noise that will alert him to her presence.

The sound of his crying is even more painful than the sounds she remembers from the accident.

Willow sinks down on the steps, careful to position herself so that David cannot see her if he were to look up. Although it seems unlikely that he would do such a thing. His head is buried on his arms, which are folded on the table, and his glasses lie off to one side.

Willow doesn't think that she has ever seen anyone weep with such total abandon. It is a punishment to watch, and she knows that she cannot witness his grief, she cannot see such naked emotion, without succumbing to her crutch, her remedy, her razor.

She reaches in her bathrobe pocket for the blade she keeps

there, but stops just before she sinks the razor into her flesh.

It occurs to her that finally, there is something that she can do for her brother. She cannot bring their parents back, her attempts to help him in even the most superficial ways have failed completely, but here, *now,* there is something that she can do.

She can sit and watch him, bear witness to his pain. She can *force* herself to sit through this, live through every sob with him, without resorting to the one thing that has protected her from feeling such pain herself.

He will never know what this will cost her, the entire act will go unacknowledged, but Willow will feel as if she has finally done something for David.

Willow remembers the last time that she saw him cry, how shocked she had been, frightened almost, to see him reduced to such a state. She is not so much scared now as awed. Impressed, as she had not been that other time, by how strong he must be in order to withstand such misery. She knows better than anyone what kind of inner fortitude it must take to let oneself be so overcome.

It is something that she will never be able to do. Even to watch it without allowing herself the luxury of cutting is almost more that she can bear.

His sobs wound her far more than anything she can inflict on herself, but it is not only pain that she feels as she watches him. She takes a bittersweet comfort in the fact that her brother is capable of feeling such grief. That he will never have to resort to the kind of remedy that she does, that he has an endless reservoir of strength that allows him to weep in such a fashion.

No, she herself is far from being that strong. But she will sit there and watch him, watch every tear, until he is spent.

It takes a long time, a very long time, but finally, David stops crying. He sits at the table resting his chin in his hands and stares at the wall for a few moments before he gets up and walks out of the room.

Willow gets up too. She walks back up the stairs as silently as she came down them, crawls into her bed, and stares at the ceiling. She is still awake when the sky starts to lighten outside her window. She is still awake when the sun comes up. She never falls back asleep. She just lies in bed and stares at the ceiling, until the rest of the household wakens and Cathy calls her for breakfast.

*

The image of David crying stays with Willow throughout the day. She is so tired that she can barely keep her eyes open, but every time that sleep threatens to overtake her, she manages to jerk herself awake by remembering the way he looked seated at the kitchen table. Willow is able to make it through her classes by doing this, but she is absolutely exhausted by the time she gets to the library.

"Hey, Carlos." Willow can barely get the words out, she's yawning so hard. "I'm sorry!" She covers her mouth. "I barely got any sleep last night."

"Well, this is your lucky day then," Carlos says as he takes in the dark circles under her eyes. "Because I'm in charge this afternoon. Maybe you should just stick with shelving today, okay? It's probably easiest."

"Whatever you think," Willow says, stowing her bag underneath the circulation desk. She knows that Carlos is trying to be kind, and shelving *is* often easier than dealing with people and their questions, but she would rather not be up alone in the stacks right now with nothing but her thoughts to keep her company.

"You've got more than enough to last your whole shift." Carlos waves his hand at the pile of battered metal carts overflowing with books that are blocking the entrance to the elevator.

"What did you do, save them all for me?" Willow grumbles as she grabs the first cart and wheels it into the elevator.

But to Willow's relief, shelving so many books proves to be more than distraction enough to blot out all thoughts of the previous night. Certainly it is more pleasant than torturing herself with memories of her brother's misery. The time passes quickly and uneventfully, and Willow is grateful that Carlos gave her the job, until she sees the last batch of books, destined for the eleventh floor.

As she gets off the elevator she can't help but think of all the things that have happened there between her and Guy. From the first conversation that she had with him to their kiss the other day, she feels as if these walls have witnessed the most important events in her life since her parents died.

Willow leaves the cart and walks over to the area near the windows. She kneels down and touches the floor where they sat. She knows she's being fanciful, but it seems strange to her that the concrete is so cold and raw, when the heat they generated was so intense.

She closes her eyes and allows the memory of their embrace to wash over her, but jumps up with a start as she hears the whirr of the elevator. Having other people up in the stacks while she's working makes her uncomfortable enough, but she would die of shame if anyone were to walk in on her communing with the floor.

She races back to the cart, grabs it, and is in position in front of one of the bookcases with a volume in her hand, when the elevator doors open. Willow glances over her shoulder, mildly curious to see who it is.

"Oh!" She is startled to see that it is *Guy* who is getting off the elevator, and for a brief moment she thinks that he is just a vision conjured up by her intense longing.

"Hello," she says after a second. "I didn't know that you'd be up here today."

"Hi." He walks over to her. "That guy downstairs at the circulation desk said you'd be on eleven."

"Carlos?"

"Yeah, sorry, I forgot his name. Anyway, I brought you something."

"Really?" Willow puts the book she's holding back on the cart and looks at Guy. "That was nice of you. What?"

"Contraband." Guy takes his hands out from behind his back. He's holding a brown paper bag, from which he removes a container of iced coffee.

"Oh my God!" Willow laughs. "That is the sweetest thing! It's just what I needed too! How did you know? And how did you manage to sneak it up here?" She pushes the cart out of the way and moves closer to him.

"Umm, Carlos said you were really tired, and I got the feeling that he wouldn't care if I brought you this."

"Oh, it's perfect." Willow takes the coffee from him and sits down with her back against the wall. She closes her eyes and takes a sip. "You even put the right amount of sweetener in."

"I'm observant." Guy sits down next to her.

"You're not kidding." Willow shifts so that their legs are touching. "Want some?"

"No thanks." Guy shakes his head. "Too sweet for me. So how come you're so tired? I thought maybe we could do something together after work, but if you're not up for it . . ." He trails off.

"Oh no, I'm not too tired. I mean, I am." Willow yawns between sips. "But I'd really like to do something, and besides"—she gestures with the coffee—"this is helping."

"Were you up all night working on your paper or something?"

"Not exactly." Willow sighs. "I haven't even started on that. I just . . ." She pauses for a moment. "Well, I couldn't sleep, that's all." She wonders why, when she's told him so many important things, she is hesitant about letting him know the real reason she stayed up all night. "That was amazing," Willow says as she drinks the last of the coffee. "Thank you so much." She smiles at Guy for a second, then stands up reluctantly.

"Hey, you know what?" Guy gets up too. "I finally finished reading *The Tempest*."

"Really?" This perks Willow up even more than the coffee. "What did you think? Did you love it? Admit it, it's his best play, isn't it?" She takes a handful of books and starts sorting through them.

"Yeah, I really did like it. *Okay,*" he amends quickly as he sees her smile fade. "I loved it, no seriously, I did. Is it his best play? I don't know 'cause I haven't read them all, but I'll tell you what, I like imaginary places too. And I'll tell you something else."

"What?"

"I'll tell you what my favorite part of the whole thing was."

"Don't tell me, let me guess." Willow stops shelving and leans against the stacks as she considers this. "Umm, one of Prospero's really great speeches because—"

"Nope." Guy shakes his head. "Not even close."

"No?" Willow is surprised. "Okay, you're not going to tell me you liked Caliban better? You like categories so much, *that* would be a really weird one. I mean, people who think he's a better character than Prospero?!"

"Forget Caliban," Guy says. "You're still about a million miles away." He folds his arms, rests them on the edge of the metal cart, leans forward, and smiles. "Want to try third time lucky, or should I just tell you?"

"Just tell me."

"Okay. My favorite part was the dedication."

"The *dedication*?" Willow frowns. "Shakespeare didn't write a dedication for *The Tempest*. I don't think he did for any play, did he?"

"I'm not talking about any dedication that *Shakespeare* wrote."

"Oh." Willow bites her lower lip as the meaning of his words sinks in. "Okay." She smiles and starts shelving again.

"You know what?" Guy says slowly. "You're—"

"I am not!" she protests.

"How do you know what I was going to say?"

"You're going to say that I'm blushing, and I'm *not*."

"Yeah, you are." Guy leans even closer.

Willow is dismally aware of how perfectly romantic the

moment is, and of where the moment should lead. She wishes more than anything that she could lean in toward him, let things develop the way they ought to, but she can't, she knows what the consequences would be.

"Well, anyway, I'm glad you liked what I wrote," Willow says awkwardly. She moves a few feet away and stares at the bookcases as if they hold the secret of life. Her hands tremble as she shoves the volumes in any which way, and she manages to drop several on the floor.

"Did you ever look at any of these titles?" Guy says as he picks up the fallen books and hands them to her. "*The Research Activities of the South Manchurian Railway 1907–1945*. Someone actually *wrote* this? Someone actually *took this out*? And I thought I liked weird stuff!"

"That's nothing." Willow manages to laugh. "If you were here an hour ago you could have helped me with *The Proceedings of the Fourth International Congress of Lithuanian Entomologists*."

"Okay, you had to have made *that* one up."

"I didn't, I swear! Fifth floor if you don't believe me!"

"I believe you." Guy smiles. "So when do you get out of here, anyway?"

"Oh." Willow looks at her watch. "In about . . . Well, *now* actually."

"You want to go to the park? It's really gorgeous out. Or I don't know, maybe you want to go back to that place and have another coffee?"

"I'd much rather go to the park. Who'd want to be inside if it's so beautiful outside?" Willow says as they walk to the elevator. "But if you'd like to get something, then I'm happy to go there." The doors open and they get on.

"No, don't worry, I'm good," Guy reassures her as they exit the elevator on the main floor.

"Hey Carlos." Willow gets her things from under the circulation desk. "I guess I'll see you in a couple days."

"Have fun," he says, giving her a wink, which Willow pointedly ignores.

"Have you ever been out on the river?" Guy asks as they leave the building and start walking across campus. Willow is relieved that he doesn't seem to have noticed Carlos's gesture, or that if he did, he's not about to mention it.

"You mean like in a boat?" She's a little confused.

"Umm, okay, so tell me, how else would you go out on the river?"

"Don't ask me." Willow shrugs.

"You should try it," Guy says as they enter the park. "I'll take you sometime. Anyway, let's at least walk by the water now, okay? This way." He leads her down a narrow path, underneath an arcade of chestnut trees, to the river.

"It's beautiful here," Willow says. "I've never even walked this way before." She leans her elbows on the stone wall that separates them from the water and stares out at the sailboats.

"You should see it when we go out rowing in the morning. It's perfect. It's like there's no one else in the world." Guy jumps up on the wall.

"You're going to fall in!" Willow exclaims in alarm.

"Right, this thing's got to be like two feet wide at least."

"Try half of that, *maybe*," Willow looks dubiously at the narrow expanse of stone. "Really, unless you're going to tell me that along with that *Boys' Book of Magic* you bought the *Boys' Book of High Wire* or something, you should get off."

"You think I haven't fallen in the water a million times since I stared rowing? C'mere." He extends his hand. "No." Willow shakes her head. "Have you really? Fallen in, I mean? I thought it was so polluted?"

"Of course I've fallen in, and it is polluted. I told you, that's why I had that peroxide and stuff with me, everybody carries it, so you can disinfect any . . ." He stops talking for a moment. "Anyway, you wouldn't believe how cold the water gets by the end of October."

"Yeah, I would believe it! That's why I'm staying where I am!"

"Get up here," Guy says. He ignores her protests, grabs her hands and hauls Willow onto the stone parapet. "It's not so bad, is it?" he says above her outraged shrieks as he pulls her close to him. "You're not going to fall, and even if you did, I'd catch you."

"I know," Willow says slowly. "You would." They stand face-to-face. Willow is sure that they must look like a postcard, silhouetted against the dying rays of the sun, but she knows too that there is something wrong with this picture, and that something happens to be her.

"Hey, Guy! Over here!"

Willow turns to see Andy waving at them. Chloe, Laurie, and Adrian are walking a few feet behind him.

"Do you see that boat?" He hurries over to them and scrambles up on the wall, nearly knocking Willow over as he does so.

"Watch it, will you?" Guy says, tightening his grip on Willow.

"Yeah, sorry." He barely glances her way. "Come on, look at that!" He points at a racing sloop in the distance. "Could you imagine what it would be like to sail something that big?

That's got to be about seventy, eighty feet. You'd need a crew of, like, twenty."

"I thought you were interested in *rowing*," Willow says.

"Yeah, you know, I do it for school." Andy shrugs. "But I love to sail. That's how I spent the summer."

"It's all he ever talks about too," Chloe says, coming over to join them. She shields her eyes from the sun and looks up at Willow on the parapet.

"I'd kill to crew on a boat like that." Andy shakes his head. "It would be so amazing."

"Well, first you'd have to—" Guy begins.

"Hey, you guys want to come with us and get something to eat?" Andy changes the subject abruptly. "I'm tired of hanging in the park, I'd much rather be inside somewhere."

Of course you would, Willow thinks as she disengages herself from Guy and jumps down from the wall.

"Willow." Chloe tugs on her sleeve. "Come with us." She says under her breath, "C'mon. I need a second opinion."

"About what?" Willow is confused.

"Him." Chloe nods toward Andy, who's still standing on the wall with his back to them. "Laurie's no good. She's too desperate for things to work out between us. She won't rest until everyone is a couple like her and Adrian." She looks over to where the two of them are kissing. Willow's eyes follow hers and she feels a pang as she watches Laurie break away and smile. Obviously she's thrilled by her boyfriend's attention.

"You want to go?" Guy jumps down beside her.

"I . . . well . . . Sure," Willow says. She wishes that they hadn't run into everybody else, but she *is* flattered that Chloe wants her along.

"We can go to that place right next to the boat basin," Andy announces as he gets down from the wall and stands near Chloe.

"It's so expensive," Laurie says as she walks over.

"Who cares?" Andy responds with a shrug. "It's near here, and it's good."

"He has a point," Adrian says. "We might as well just go there." He takes Laurie's hand and starts walking in the direction of the boat basin. Andy and Guy fall into step behind them.

"So are you that interested in sailing?" Willow asks Chloe. They hang back a few feet behind the others.

"Depends. Do you mean would I like it if he took me out on a boat like that? Sure. Do you mean would I like it if he talked about something else occasionally? Sure."

"Got it."

"*We* should talk about something else." Chloe sighs. "I have so much homework, I shouldn't even be here now. It's just, I don't know, I'm like the opposite of Laurie. Now that I'm a senior I'm less and less focused."

"I know the feeling." Willow chews on her nails fretfully, then shoves her hands into her pockets.

"You could really use a manicure," Chloe says as they approach the cafe. "Don't take that the wrong way or anything! It's just that I usually do Laurie's nails for her, and if you wanted I could do yours sometime. . . ."

"Oh . . . thanks. I'm not offended at all. I know they look terrible, but to be honest they always have. My best friend from home used to give me a hard time about them too," Willow admits with a rueful smile.

"It's way too crowded, we're never going to get a table,"

Laurie calls over from where she and Adrian are standing at the entrance to the restaurant.

"So we'll wait a couple minutes," Andy says, clearly unconcerned.

Guy walks back to Willow. "We don't have to stay if you don't want to."

"Oh, that's okay. Thank you, though," she says, too softly for anyone else to hear.

"Hey, they have a table if we're willing to sit out back," Adrian says after conferring with the waitress.

"Then we won't be able to see the water," Andy complains.

"You're the one who's insisting on eating here," Chloe points out.

"Fine, forget the water." Andy follows Adrian and Laurie as they walk into the cafe.

"This is actually really nice back here," Laurie says as they crowd around a small table set underneath a striped umbrella.

"Who wants what?" Andy looks around for a menu.

"I just want dessert," Chloe says.

"Me too," Laurie agrees. "No, sorry. A salad."

"Then I'll have to get one too! C'mon, stick with dessert. What are you having, Willow?"

"Umm. Maybe a . . ."

Willow sees her before any of the others. A walking skeleton, the victim of some terrible wasting disease, like something out of the history books, a death camp survivor. It takes Willow a moment to realize that the girl is none of those things. She's just a girl, a girl like Willow, who's chosen to inflict terrible pain on herself. Only this girl's weapon isn't a razor, it's starvation.

Willow can hardly bear to look at her, but she's transfixed, spellbound. Every lineament of the girl's wasted body is a testament to her inner turmoil. Willow can only imagine what kind of pain she must be in to destroy herself that way. She knows there's something ironic in her compassion for the other girl, but she can't help feeling that this utter mortification of the flesh is far worse than anything that she herself has done.

"Oh my God, that poor girl," Laurie whispers. Clearly she has noticed the apparition as well.

"Who?" Adrian asks, his voice unnaturally loud in contrast with Laurie's.

"Ssh!" Laurie elbows him.

Guy twists his head to see what they're talking about, and Willow can see that he too is affected by her appearance, as anyone would be, really.

Willow turns away from the spectacle and her gaze falls on Andy. He is also riveted by the girl, but his reaction is very different from Willow's and the others'. It's clear that he looks at this walking skeleton and sees only that she is breastless, sexless, *ugly*.

"Yeah, I wouldn't go feeling too sorry for her," he says to Laurie with a smirk.

"Excuse me?" Chloe gives him a look.

"C'mon, she's in someplace like this, she obviously has the money to eat. It's not like she's some poor starving kid from Africa, you know?"

"No." Chloe shakes her head. "I *don't* know. What are you talking about?"

"I mean it's something she's doing to herself . . ."

"Yeah, it's called an *eating disorder*," Laurie says angrily.

"Right, I know, okay? Don't talk to me like I'm an idiot."

"Why not? You're acting like one," Chloe snaps.

"Oh, sorry if I don't *genuflect* because some girl who can't handle whatever problems life is throwing at her hides behind the disease of the week."

"What the hell could you possibly know about what *life is throwing at her*? What the hell could *you* possibly know about why she's doing that to herself?" Chloe demands.

The rest of the table is silent. Willow is sure that she's not the only one who wishes she was someplace else. She doesn't look at Adrian or Laurie, she can barely bring herself to look at Guy.

"Look, I know the type," Andy continues, not even bothering to lower his voice. "Society, the media, everybody else is responsible for her problems. It's like it's become this hip thing to starve yourself and complain that the rest of the world is driving you to do it. Trust me, it's just that she can't deal with things, so she manufactures this problem—"

"Stop it!" Willow bursts out. She can't help herself. She can't listen to another word. Willow rests her forehead on her palm. Maybe she really is getting a migraine. She feels Guy's hand on her shoulder and raises her head to look at Andy.

"Thank you, Willow," Chloe says.

Willow knows that Chloe is upset because of how insensitive Andy is being. But she herself is bothered for more selfish reasons. It's as if Andy is addressing every word straight to her. What would he say if she were to lift up her shirt and show him her cuts the way she did for Guy? Would he say that she has manufactured her problem?

Would he be right?

"Yeah, okay. Look, I'm outta here," Andy says after a few moments.

"Me too, but guess what, I'm headed in the *opposite* direction." Chloe throws her napkin on the table. "See you guys tomorrow."

"Can we leave too?" Willow says to Guy. "I'm sorry." She looks over at Laurie and Adrian.

"*You* don't have anything to be sorry about." Laurie gives Andy a dirty look. "I thought you were leaving?" she says pointedly.

"Yeah, let's get out of here." Guy stands up. "Hey Andy, just so you know? I totally agree with Chloe on this one."

"So I guess Chloe won't be needing a second opinion," Willow says as they walk out of the cafe. The sun has set completely now, and it's a beautiful, mild night.

"Huh?" Guy looks confused. "What are you talking about?"

"Chloe wanted to know what I thought of Andy," Willow explains. "You know, if she should go out with him or something."

"You guys talk about stuff like that?" Guy looks at her incredulously. "I mean, she can't just make up her own mind?"

"I don't know." Willow shrugs. "I guess not." She doesn't really have the energy to make small talk. She's too upset, the scene in the cafe is too fresh. She's angry, and not just about what Andy said regarding that poor girl, but because of what his words imply about *her.*

"I don't feel like walking right now," Guy says. "Do you mind?" He sits down on the grass and pulls her down next to him. "Is this okay? We can see the water from here."

"I don't just make my own problems," Willow says suddenly. "I don't just do what I do because it's hip, because it's the *fashion.*" She pauses for a moment. "I do it because I have to," she says finally. "There's no other way."

"No." Guy shakes his head. "You won't let yourself have any other way. There's a difference."

"I *can't* let myself have any other way! You know that! You *saw* that!" Willow insists. Guy doesn't say anything and the two of them sit in silence for a few minutes and stare at the water shimmering in the moonlight.

"Maybe Andy was right," Willow continues. "Me and that girl, we just can't face what life is throwing us, so we hide behind our sickness. Maybe everything he said about *her* is true about *me*."

"Why would you even listen to anything that he has to—"

"My brother cries at night." Willow interrupts suddenly. "Don't laugh," she says hurriedly. "I know that you're not like Andy, you would never say anything insensitive or stupid, but well, some people think a guy crying is . . . I don't know."

"I'm not laughing."

"That's why I didn't sleep last night. He cries. And I watch him."

"Why are you telling me this now?" Guy asks.

"I have no idea." Willow is surprised herself. "I have no idea," she repeats. "I just . . . He's so strong, if you think his crying like that is anything else, you're wrong. I don't even know how he manages to do it, to get through it, I mean." Willow pauses. "Do you think I'm like that girl?" She searches his face, barely visible in the faint light from the stars.

"I don't know," he says slowly. "But I do know this. The way her body affected you, that's the way your scars affect me."

"Oh." Willow doesn't know how to respond to this. How

wonderful that she should affect him so strongly, how awful that it should be in that way. She can't help thinking that almost any other reaction would be preferable, and that it is her own fault that when he looks at her he doesn't just see a girl, he sees a *cutter*.

She rolls up her left sleeve and examines her cuts, really looks at them the way she might if she were alone, tries to see them the way that she imagines he does.

There's no denying that they're hideous. It's very clear why he told her they were ugly that day in the stacks.

That shouldn't matter. Her cuts serve a purpose and that purpose is independent of such trivial considerations. She knows this as deeply as she has ever known anything. But still, for a moment she wishes that they looked different, that they *did* look like the kind of scratches a cat might make.

She starts to roll down her sleeve, but Guy stops her. He holds her arm, looks at her cuts, traces the pattern of her razor marks with his hand.

"Don't, it's . . ."

Willow stops speaking as he bends his head and kisses the scars.

She knows she should tell him to stop, but she can't because she wants him to go on forever. She knows too that she will probably pay for this feeling with other less pleasurable ones, but still she can't bring herself to pull her arm away.

And then Willow does something that surprises herself more than anything she has ever done. She moves her other arm, and, very tentatively, holding the side of his face with her hand, raises his mouth to hers and kisses him. She can't believe that she is willing to risk this, not after what happened in the stacks. Given that, this act is even more shocking to her than when all those months ago, she found herself stabbing her arm with the screwdriver and knew that she had found her calling.

She waits for the cataclysm to happen, to be overwhelmed the way she was in the library, but, at least for that moment, feels only how wonderful it is to kiss someone, to kiss *him,* underneath the stars, and how odd it is, how *refreshing,* that after all she has been through she can at last respond to something the way anyone else would.

"Will you do something for me?" she whispers against his mouth. She is trembling slightly, both from excitement and fear, and she cannot yet bring herself to believe that her act will not have consequences.

"Yes," he whispers back. "Just tell me what."

"Take me home."

Willow has no idea why she has requested this, where this desire has come from, if it has been building for a long time or if it is a sudden need. But she is sure that it is genuine, she is sure that it is what she wants.

"Now?" Guy pulls away from her. "You mean you want me to walk you back to your brother's apartment?"

"No." Willow shakes her head. "I want to go home. Back to my parents' house, where I grew up. *Home.*"

"Oh." Guy nods. He looks confused, but thoughtful. "It's not far, is it? I mean, you could borrow your brother's car and drive out there, couldn't you?" He stops for a second. "Sorry. Have you driven since . . . I wasn't thinking."

"No, I haven't. I can't go there by myself and I can't borrow my brother's car. He'll want to know what for and I can't tell him. I need *you* to take me, Guy. Please."

"Why do you want to go home? Is it, is it because maybe you're afraid that now your home has become a place you can only visit in your imagination?"

"No, I don't think that's it . . ." She trails off.

Willow wishes that she could answer him. That she herself knew the answer. She thinks about the two times she's been home since the accident, the time with David and the bookcases, and the time that she gathered her clothes. There is no reason to think that going home now will be any different. Willow has no idea what she is looking for, what she hopes to get out of such an excursion. And why does she think that if her brother, her *unbelievably* strong brother, has been unable to withstand the emotional impact of being in their parents' house, that *she* will be able to?

Maybe she just needs to drive along the road where it all happened again. Maybe she needs to bury her head in her mother's closet and see if she can still smell her. Maybe she needs to look at those bookcases again.

"I want a book," Willow blurts out finally. She supposes that this answer makes as much sense as any other. "*Bulfinch's Mythology*. I want my father's copy."

Guy nods slowly, as if this makes perfect sense. He doesn't say, as someone else might, that she can walk into almost any bookstore and buy a copy, he doesn't say that he knows that she already owns a copy, that he's seen her with it any number of times, or that he can lend her his own. Instead he just turns to her and says: "Okay then, looks like I'm the one who's going to have to find a car to borrow."

CHAPTER FOURTEEN

Of course it would be raining.

Willow stares listlessly out of the window, but there's really nothing to see. Nothing, that is, except the driving sheets of rain, the futile back and forth of the windshield wipers, and the occasional flash of lightning.

Even though the weather report had promised nothing but blue skies, even though the past few days have been perfect fall weather, Willow had known that the second she got in the car with Guy it would start to pour.

She wonders if Guy's nervous, if he's worried about driving in such nasty weather—the only time the rain had let up was when it had started to hail. Or maybe he's worried that *she's* worried, worried that she'll be in an accident. *Another* accident.

Willow isn't concerned about anything like *that,* but she feels distinctly uncomfortable. There's just something unsettling about so much rain.

"We turn here, right?"

Willow doesn't respond. She's staring out the window, straining to see beyond the rain-streaked glass. It's useless, of course—she can barely make out the road—but it's also unnecessary. She doesn't need to see. She would know where she was even if she were blindfolded.

"Hey, aren't I supposed to make a turn here?"

"Stop."

"What?"

"Stop the car."

Guy pulls the car over to the side of the road, next to a wide-open field. "Are you okay? Are you going to be—"

Willow doesn't wait for him to finish, she opens the door and hesitates for only an instant before plunging into the driving rain.

She isn't dressed for this kind of weather—within seconds she's soaked through to the bone, but she hardly notices as she stumbles across the field. There, maybe five or six yards from the road, is an enormous old oak.

"What are you doing?" Guy calls after her. He gets out of the car and walks through the rain to where Willow is standing in front of the tree.

"Willow," he has to shout to be heard over the thunder. "Come on, get back in the car." He takes her arm.

Willow looks at him without seeing. She reaches out her hand and touches the side of the tree, touches a huge section that has its bark sheared clean off, leaving in its stead a smear of midnight blue paint.

Odd that after all these months, after all this rain, the paint would still be there.

She sinks on her knees before the tree. The crackle of cellophane makes her look down and it takes her a second to realize that she is kneeling on the remnants of dozens of floral offerings, now turned into compost, unrecognizable except for their soiled ribbons and plastic wrappings.

The scene should be affecting, disturbing, *shattering* even, and yet Willow feels nothing so much as uncomfortable as the rain sinks through her clothes and drenches her skin. She is unmoved, the drama of the weather, the import of the place, they have no power over her. She doesn't know what she was expecting, what she was looking for, but it certainly wasn't this, this emptiness, this meaninglessness.

Guy appears to be much more affected than she is. His face is white as the meaning of the sheared bark, the traces of paint, and the rotten floral tributes sinks in.

"Let's go." She stands up. "C'mon." Willow takes his arm. His clothes are soaked too. "Let's get out of here." She pulls him back to the car.

Guy gets in and slams the door, gives her a searching look, but doesn't say anything beyond: "About a mile and a half, right?"

"That's right. Take the next left and then it's just straight on from there."

Neither of them says anything else for the rest of the trip. Willow hopes that Guy doesn't feel as cold and uncomfortable as she does.

"Is this it?"

"Um-hum. That's right. It's that mailbox up ahead."

Guy turns into the driveway and turns off the engine. She's home. After all these months, she's home.

Willow gets out of the car, slowly, gingerly, as if she's suddenly become old and infirm. She's transfixed, staring at the house, no longer noticing the rain as it drips unchecked down her face and plasters her already sodden clothes against her skin.

"Maybe we should go inside?" Guy suggests tentatively.

"Oh, yes." Willow stares at him without really seeing him. "We should go inside."

She starts forward, but trips on the gravel. "You sure this is okay?" Guy catches her arm. "You sure you want to do this?"

"Maybe . . . Maybe . . . I don't know." Willow shakes her head—she's *not* sure all of a sudden. "Maybe we could go somewhere and . . . um, I don't know . . . have lunch first?" she says finally. Willow knows the suggestion is idiotic. It's just past ten in the morning, they're both soaking wet, the house, while daunting, at least offers the *possibility* of comfort. They would certainly be able to dry off and change inside. Almost all of her clothes are still there, and she's sure that she could find something for Guy as well.

"Whatever you say. It's completely up to you."

"You're so . . . You're too . . ." Willow trails off.

Perfect, wonderful, heavenly. . . .

"I'm too what?"

"Nice," Willow says finally. The word is completely inadequate. "You're too nice."

"Well, I'm not exactly going to drag you in there. Look, whatever you want to do, it's your call. Totally. But maybe you could decide soon. This rain is really starting to get to me."

"Let's get back in the car." She walks to the passenger side.

"Now what?" Guy turns to look at her as he gets in and turns the key in the ignition. "You really want to go and get *lunch*?"

"At least it's dry in here." Willow doesn't answer him directly. "Whose car is this anyway?"

"Adrian's brother's."

"Did you tell him what it was for?'

"Nope. And he didn't ask."

"Oh." Willow nods. "Listen, what I said out there . . ." She drums her fingers on the dashboard. "It's true. . . ."

"What?"

"That you're too . . . You're so . . ." To Willow's astonishment her voice breaks. She is shocked that Guy's kindness has the power to move her so much. How strange that he can affect her like this when the scene of the accident left her cold.

"Willow?"

"Yes?" Her voice is steadier and she is once again in control.

"You are too."

"Oh." She puts her elbows on the dashboard and rests her forehead against her palms. "If you say so."

"Are you crying?" Guy touches her shoulder.

"No." Willow lifts her head up. "You should know by now, I don't cry. Look, let's go and get lunch, okay? I know it's really early, but let's just go. There's this place everyone at my school used to hang out at. It's only about two miles from here." She glances at the clock. "It will be completely empty now."

"Okay." Guy backs the car out of the driveway. "I guess I could use something hot. Do they have good coffee?"

"Hot chocolate."

"Huh?"

"Hot chocolate. It's this little place run by this couple from France, and that's what they do best. Or at least it's what everyone from school used to order. But you can get the half espresso, half chocolate. You'll like it, I promise."

"Keep going straight?"

"No, make a right, and then another right. You'll see it after that."

"Is this it?" Guy pulls up outside the cafe. It's nestled among a row of shops that form one side of a semicircle set around a statue of a Revolutionary War hero. "My clothes are sticking to me," he says as he gets out of the car.

"I'm sorry." Willow can't help feeling guilty. "Mine are too. Maybe we'll dry off a little inside."

The cafe is as empty as she had hoped. They have the whole place to themselves, and Willow picks her old favorite spot, a booth near the window.

"Is it too early to get dessert?" Guy asks, looking at the menu.

"Go ahead." Willow shifts uncomfortably against the banquette. Her wet jeans are making her miserable. "I know what you want, that mocha cream thing, I can't even pronounce it. You should definitely get it."

"Is there a waitress around here?"

"You have to go to the counter to order."

"And you just want hot chocolate?"

"Umm, yeah, because—"

"Willow?!"

"Markie?!" Willow is so stunned that she can hardly speak. She half stands up as she stares at what must surely be a ghost, because she can't quite believe that what she's seeing is real. After all these months, after all the phone calls she's avoided, she's finally face-to-face with her best friend.

"What are you doing here?" she asks as Markie walks over to the table. "I mean, why aren't you in class?"

"What am *I* doing here? *I* live here. How about what are *you* doing here?" She looks at Willow in disbelief as if she too can't believe that what she's seeing is real.

"You cut your hair," Willow says stupidly.

"Yeah, about a foot. . . ." Markie pauses; she looks back and forth between Willow and Guy.

"Oh, uh, sorry, this is Guy, and I guess that you've figured out by now that this is Markie."

"I've heard about you," Guy says, clearly more comfortable with the situation than they are.

Willow is surprised by the remark. It's such a cocktail party kind of comment, but she is grateful to Guy for saying it. She can see now, as she looks at Markie, that she has hurt her old friend. Willow hopes that Guy's words will at least show Markie that she has not forgotten her, that she has thought about her and talked about her over the past eight months, that all the things that they have done together over the years still matter to her.

"Hi." Markie nods at him. "So what *are* you doing here?" She shifts her attention back to Willow.

"I . . . had to pick up something at the house," Willow answers after a second. It's the only thing she can think to say, and in fact, picking up the *Bulfinch* is really the only concrete reason she has for being back home. "So what are you doing here in the middle of the day?" She turns the question back to Markie.

"Oh, I'm getting some stuff for my mom." Markie shrugs. "She's having a dinner party. There was a water main break in school. The whole place flooded. We have the next two days off while they clean up." She speaks in short staccato bursts.

"That makes sense, I guess. . . ." Willow tries to smile, but it comes out all wrong.

"I'll go give them our order." Guy stands up and looks at Willow. Clearly he is waiting to see if she will ask Markie to join them.

"I have to hurry back," Markie says. The words come out in a rush—it's obvious that she doesn't want to give Willow the chance to reject her yet again. But as soon as Guy leaves, she slides into the banquette. She stares at Willow, but neither of them speaks, and the silence between them is not the comfortable silence of two friends.

"I like your hair that way," Willow finally says.

"Thanks." Markie doesn't seem particularly flattered. She looks at Willow closely. "I haven't seen you with your hair in a braid since you were about six years old. I remember your mom used to do it for you."

Is that true?

Willow had completely forgotten about that, but now an image comes back to her. She remembers squirming on a footstool, desperate to go out and play with Markie, while her mother sat behind her with a brush.

She blinks to clear away the vision, bringing her focus back to the present. "So is your hair easier to deal with now it's so much shorter? I mean, it used to take you forever to blow it dry. . . ." Willow can't believe that this is all she can say to her friend after so many months, that their relationship has been reduced to this kind of small talk, and she knows that it's all her fault.

But Markie's having none of it. Now that the two of them

are alone, she gets right to the point. "My mom said that the reason you never called back or e-mailed me or anything, is just that things are so hard for you right now. . . ."

"She's right," Willow begins eagerly, glad to have the chance to explain. She leans across the table. "You see—"

"But I said that was impossible," Markie cuts her off. "Because I told her if that were the case, then you would just say something to me, like 'Hey Markie, I can't deal with you right now, the second I'm ready, you're first . . .' I told her that you wouldn't just *ignore* me, that you weren't like that. You wouldn't be so . . . dishonest. *Emotionally* dishonest, I mean."

Willow pulls back in shock. "I'm . . . I'm *really* sorry," she stammers. She feels as if she's been slapped, but she can't be mad at Markie, because she knows that her friend is right. "I should never have . . ."

"I hate saying stuff like this to you!" Markie bursts out. "I don't want to be talking to you like this! I feel like you're my ex or something and I'm begging you to call me! And I feel so selfish too! I should be asking you how you've been holding up, not getting mad at you." She pauses. "So, how have you been holding up?" she says after a moment.

"Not always so great."

Talk about an understatement!

Willow wonders what would happen if she showed Markie her arms. Would she forgive her for not calling? Would she understand what her life has become?

Would she tell her mother? *Of course* she would. She wouldn't even think twice. She wouldn't be like Guy. Markie has known her whole family since they were both five. She wouldn't listen to Willow's protests. She would tell her mother. Her mother would tell David. Her razors would be taken away. *Something* would be done. That part of her life would be over.

Willow is not yet ready for that to happen, but for the briefest instant she is overcome by an urge so powerful that she literally has to restrain herself from flinging her arms out at Markie. All she would have to do is roll up her sleeves and the thing would be set in motion. . . .

Instead she jerks her hands off the table. Puts them in her lap. Starts twisting her napkin, does anything to keep them occupied.

"I . . . I miss you," she finally says, her eyes firmly fixed on her napkin. "I miss you and I miss the way things used to be between us. And even though your mother was right . . . you were too." Willow looks up at Markie. "I should have just let you know that I couldn't talk to you." Once again, to her amazement, she feels her voice start to break. But as before, the moment passes quickly.

"What about now?" Markie asks.

"I'll . . . I *will* call you," Willow says. "I'd like to see you."

"Really?" Markie looks skeptical.

"Really," Willow assures her. "But listen . . ." She blushes as she thinks of Markie's earlier reprimand. This time she's determined to be straight with her. "I don't think that it's going to be anytime soon."

"Oh," Markie says slowly. "Well, I guess I'll just have to wait then. I . . . Well, I really hope that it's not going to be another seven months or anything. And Willow . . ." She gives her a funny little half smile. "I did kind of buy what my mom was saying. If I hadn't, I wouldn't have kept calling you all these months."

They look at each other across the table without saying anything, but this time the silence isn't nearly as uncomfortable.

"So." Markie leans forward and looks at Willow with a little of her old sparkle. "Is he part of the reason you haven't called?" She gestures at Guy, who is standing near the counter, with his back to them. "Because I might forgive you for *that*."

"No, but I *have* wondered what you would think of him," Willow confides as she too leans across the table. Their elbows touch and for a moment it is as if they have never been apart.

"He's incredibly cute." Markie glances over at him again. "Is he your . . . boyfriend or something, or just a friend? I mean, who is he?"

"Well . . ." Willow follows Markie's eyes. How can she possibly explain what Guy means to her? He's something far more than a friend. Something other than a boyfriend, a lover maybe, in everything but the technical sense. . . .

And then she looks back at Markie and says the truest, most honest words that she has ever said to anyone: "He's someone that *knows* me, and someone that I *know*."

"Oh." Markie nods thoughtfully as she takes this in. "Umm, maybe we should talk about something else," she murmurs. "'Cause he's headed back this way. You know what?" she continues in her normal voice as Guy approaches the table. "I have to get going, I mean I really don't want to. I wish I could stay, but my mom's expecting me, and I'm guessing that you would rather not have her know that I saw you . . ."

"Definitely, don't mention it. Please."

"Okay, so, I mean, I can't use running into you as an excuse for why I'm late." Markie stands up. "Well, I guess that I'll just have to save everything I wanted to talk about until I hear from you . . ." She says this awkwardly, but her earlier hostility is gone.

Willow stands up too. "I hope that . . ." she begins, but words fail her. She reaches out to her friend, tentatively, afraid of embracing her when she is so wet. But Markie is not hesitant at all. She grabs Willow in a fierce hug.

"See you." Markie lets go after a moment. She looks at Guy, smiles a little, and walks off.

"Good-bye." Guy smiles back at her. He sits down in the spot she has just vacated. "Our stuff will be ready in a couple minutes," he says to Willow.

"Oh . . . good." Willow stares at him vacantly. She's too focused on what happened with Markie to really take in what he's saying.

"Everything okay?" he asks. "I mean, was it good to see her?"

"Well, I'm glad I did, anyway. . . . Listen, do you mind getting the stuff to go?"

Guy just looks at her.

"I know, I'm complicated and difficult, but look, you said it was all up to me. I just feel like getting home now. Sorry."

"No, no, I mean it's not that hard to get our stuff to go, and I don't exactly need to sit in some girly place, but are you sure that this time, you're ready?"

"You think this is a *girl's* place? All the guys in my school used to love it!"

"Uh-huh. What kind of guys went to your school? Anyway, are you sure this time?"

"I'm sure."

"Hey, could you wrap that stuff up?" Guy calls over to the woman behind the counter.

"Well, wait a sec." Willow tugs on his sleeve. "What's so girlish about it here?"

"Describe your napkin."

"Pink linen with violets embroidered on it." Willow shrugs.

"Right. Okay, let's go." Guy gets up and pays at the counter.

The drive back to the house is uneventful, except for the fact that the rain is coming down as heavily as ever, and that their clothes got even more drenched as they ran to and from the car.

"Can you hurry up and open the door?" Guy says, his teeth chattering.

"Sorry." Willow fumbles in her pocket for the key. "Got it."

She opens the door and they both step inside. The house smells musty, it seems obvious somehow that it's unlived in, empty. "Well," Willow says as they stand in the entryway shivering in their wet clothes. "We're here." She puts down her bag and the cup of hot chocolate, still untouched, on the floor.

"Okay," Guy says slowly. He steps closer to her. "What do you want to do now?"

Willow has no idea what she wants to do. She still hasn't figured out why she needed to come home in the first place. She'd expected that the moment she entered the house she'd know, that she'd open the door and everything would become clear.

But nothing is clear. There is no great epiphany. The moment seems as flat and meaningless as before when she stood by the side of the road staring at the place where her parents' lives ended.

Willow's at a loss. Guy seems anxious on her behalf, curious as to what her next move will be.

"Do you want to see my room?" she asks suddenly.

Guy looks surprised. It's clear that this isn't what he was expecting.

"Sorry." Willow shakes her head at how stupid that must have sounded. She isn't in first grade and she doesn't want to show him her doll collection. "That didn't come out right. I meant I have some stuff up there, and we can change into something dry."

"Oh great." Guy nods. "Only, I'm not sure that we're the same size."

"Stop it." She laughs. "My brother has some things here too. C'mon." She takes his hand and leads him upstairs.

"You do have a lot of books," he says as they enter her room. "I've got to say, though, I never pictured you as having black walls." He wanders over to the bookcases, still holding her hand, and looks at the different titles.

"Oh, this used to be David's room, he painted it black," Willow explains. "When he went to college I inherited it. Now he uses my old room when he visits." She pauses, aware that she has just used the present tense.

"Let's go to my *old* room," she says, pulling him down the hall. "My brother keeps his things there. In here." She opens a door on the right. "Some of this should fit." Willow frowns as she rummages through the chest of drawers in the corner. "I mean, you are the same *height*. . . . Here." She tosses him a sweatshirt and a faded pair of jeans. "I'll see you in a few minutes. . . . Umm, I'm going to uh, change in my room." Willow closes the door hurriedly as Guy starts unbuttoning his shirt.

Willow undoes her braid and runs her fingers through her hair. Markie's comment had made her feel self-conscious somehow. In any case, it should dry much faster now that it's loose. She goes through her closet searching for something to wear. She is amazed at all the things she owns, clothes that she has forgotten about, and she wonders if David or Cathy would notice and question her if she brought some of them back with her.

Maybe I should put a dress on.

She runs her hands through the folds of the many skirts hanging in her closet. Guy has never seen her in anything like that. . . .

Willow shakes her head at how frivolous she's being. The purpose of this visit is not to stage a fashion show. . . .

Except she really doesn't know *what* the purpose is. . . .

"Hey, are you ready in there?" Guy knocks on the door.

"Uh . . . Just a sec." Willow steps into a dry pair of jeans and buttons up a shirt. "Come on in," she calls out.

"What should I do with these things?" he asks, walking into the room with his wet clothes in his arms. "Hey, your hair is different."

"Easier to dry this way." Willow shrugs.

"I've never seen it like that. It looks beautiful."

"Thank you." Willow blushes, then she looks at him and starts to laugh. "I guess you and David are the same height, but that's about it."

"What's wrong with what I'm wearing?"

"Nothing, absolutely nothing, it's just, well, that sweatshirt is a little small."

"Hey, you're the one who gave me this stuff. . . ."

"No, no, it's great." Willow can't stop laughing. "Listen, promise me that you'll never stop rowing, I mean really. Even if you end up doing fieldwork, pack a pair of oars or something."

"Whatever." Guy shrugs, but Willow can tell that he's flattered.

"Umm, you know what?" She looks at the bundle of wet clothes in his arms. "I guess we should do a load of laundry." She gathers up her own assortment of dripping things. "C'mon, it's in the basement."

As they walk through the empty rooms, Willow can't help thinking how strange, how lifeless the house is. No one coming in for the first time would mistake it for the home of a family that has gone on vacation. There is a quality in the air that absolutely forbids such a notion. It is as if the house senses that its occupants are gone, dead, scattered, and has reacted in sympathy.

Willow stops dead in her tracks halfway down the stairs to the basement. How could she have forgotten what was here? She sinks down onto the steps and stares at the half-dismantled bookcases. The screwdriver, her first accomplice, lies off to one side.

"What is it?" Guy sits next to her.

Willow shakes her head. Once again, she feels that she should be overcome, that the sight of this, like the site of the accident, should be her undoing. She wonders why she isn't in desperate need of her razor, why everything is leaving her cold. She turns to look at Guy and is shocked to see how strongly the sight is affecting him. He is pale, ghostly almost, as he stares at the screwdriver. He is the one who needs to be talked through this.

"Are you okay?" she asks, concerned. "Guy, are you all right?"

"I don't know." He turns away from the screwdriver and looks at her. "I just know that that has to be the ugliest thing I've ever seen in my life."

"I'm sorry. I don't know why I dragged you here." Willow brushes the hair out of his eyes. "I mean, why I made *you* drag *me* here. I thought . . . I don't know what I thought." She shakes her head. "I think I made some connection with David and the way he was that time we came here and the way he cries. . . . But I don't know, and that doesn't make any sense anyway. And even if it did, I've spent so long *not* crying, *not* feeling, making sure that I *can't* cry, so . . . why would I be courting it now?" She buries her head in her hands.

Guy puts his arm around her shoulders, but doesn't say anything.

"Maybe I was just supposed to run into Markie," Willow says. She lifts her head up and looks at him. "Maybe that's why we came out here." She shrugs. "I mean, it's not like I even knew that was going to happen, but . . . Whatever. . . . Look, I guess I'll just run the wash, and then I might as well get the *Bulfinch,* and then I don't know, do you want to wait here until the rain stops before we head back?"

"Okay, well, at least until the laundry's done anyway. But are you so sure that you're finished here?"

"I don't even know what it is I came to do," Willow says as she gets up from the stairs and dumps their clothes into the washing machine. "That'll take a while." She puts the detergent in and presses the on button. "So, let's go back upstairs, and I don't know, I'll just get the book. . . ."

She climbs up the steps dispiritedly. "You want to wait in here?" She gestures toward the living room. "I'm just going to go and get the *Bulfinch* . . ." Willow doesn't want Guy to go with her, because there is something she wants to give him, something from her parents' study, where the *Bulfinch* is, and she wants it to be a surprise.

"Are you sure that you want to be alone now?"

"I'm fine. . . . I just . . . look." Willow walks him into the living room. "This used to be my favorite place in the whole world to read." She climbs up on the window seat. "C'mere." She smiles a little as Guy sits down next to her. "I'll just be a second, okay?"

"Take your time."

Willow walks down the hall to the study, wondering if the room where her parents spent most of their time, where they did all of their work, will leave her as numb as everything else has. But as she opens the door and surveys the floor-to-ceiling bookcases and huge partners desk with the burgundy leather blotter, she realizes that once again she feels nothing.

She crosses to the bookcase and pulls out the *Bulfinch*. Then she looks for a few seconds until she finds *Tristes Tropiques*. She knows that if David ever finds out that she's given their father's copy away, a first edition in perfect condition, he'll kill her. But she can't imagine that will be anytime soon, and anyway, she's sure that it will have meaning for Guy. She desperately wants to give him something special.

Willow walks around the study for a few moments desultorily picking up random books. There is a fine layer of dust that covers everything like sand. She supposes that there's something fitting about the way the house now seems like an archaeological site. She sits at the partners desk and leafs through the papers on the blotter, morbidly curious to see what her parents had been occupied with on the last day of their lives.

There is nothing special, some notes in her father's barely legible handwriting, a few bills, and a letter to the housekeeper in her mother's bold script:

Hannah,
Thank you so much for staying late and helping with the party, I couldn't have gotten everything together without you. Don't worry about the vacuuming today, but when you go to the store could you make sure to get the calcium-enriched orange juice?

Calcium v. v. imp for Willow!

Willow takes the note—she thinks maybe that she would like to have it on her desk back at David's house. She has no other keepsake of any kind. She can't take a picture, David would certainly notice something like that. There doesn't seem to be another piece of writing to hand that might be more interesting, anything like that would be on the computer anyway. It's just a little thing, quite meaningless really, but she would like the small scrap of paper with her mother's handwriting on it.

She takes the books and the paper and leaves the study,

stopping on the way back to the living room to tuck the copy of *Tristes Tropiques* in her bag.

"Hey, what are you reading?" she asks Guy, who is flipping through a book as he sits on the window seat.

"You weren't kidding when you said that your parents had thousands and thousands of books," he says, gesturing at the shelves in the living room.

"Oscar Wilde." Willow sits down next to him and looks at the title he's holding. "He's pretty fun. I bet that tutor of yours must have given you a lot of his stuff to read."

"What are you holding on to, I mean besides the *Bulfinch*?" Guy asks, looking at the piece of paper in her hand.

"Oh just some note my mother wrote. . . . Nothing really." Willow shrugs. "I'm sorry that I made you drive me here. I mean, it was a lot to ask, and I don't know how much you minded missing school and . . . Well, it didn't accomplish anything. Thank you for doing it though."

"You don't have to thank me," Guy takes the paper from her hand. *"Calcium v. v. imp for Willow,"* he reads.

Willow doesn't realize that she's crying until Guy takes his hand and reaches over to wipe away her tears. And she knows then that she was right about her brother, that it takes unbelievable strength to feel this kind of grief, and she doesn't know if she can handle it, because it really hurts, hurts her more than the razor ever could. And she doesn't know why, after visiting the place where her parents lost their lives, after looking at the spot where she forged her unholy alliance with the screwdriver, that something so simple, so trivial should finally affect her so much.

Maybe it's because, as she listened to Guy read the note,

she realized as she did when she saw David with Isabelle, that she will never be anyone's child again. No one will ever worry about her the way that her parents did, or care about her the way they did. The only other time that Willow will ever experience a bond like that is when she herself becomes a mother. And even then she will still need her own mother, and she won't be there, she won't be there because she is *dead.* Dead. Decades too early.

And she is amazed, really amazed, that the razor managed to numb her so well and for so long, because the way she's feeling now is so overwhelming, so *overpowering,* that it would take a lot more than a few slashes with a blade to transmute her anguish.

She holds her stomach, afraid that if she doesn't she will double over from the pain. Guy doesn't say anything to her, he just holds her hair back from her face and occasionally blots her tears with his hand.

"I'm . . . I'm . . . not . . ." She chokes on the words. "I'm not anyone's *daughter* anymore!" Willow says this as if it is something that she has just figured out. "And I know . . . I know that I should be sorry for my brother, that . . . that . . ." She stops for a second; she's gasping for air so violently that she thinks she might hyperventilate.

"Can you breathe?" Guy asks.

"Yes, I mean no. Just give me a second." Willow wipes her nose with the back of her hand. "That was polite, I'm sorry." She laughs, a little hysterically. "I can't breathe when I cry really hard. . . . And I can't remember . . . the last time I cried like this. . . ."

She stops talking for a second and tries to dry her eyes. But it's useless, like trying to stem a tidal wave. Her hands get entangled with his and she grips his wrists and turns to face him as they sit side by side on the window seat.

"I should . . . feel sorry for David because he doesn't have parents either. And I know . . . I know that . . . that I should be sorry for my *parents* because they didn't wake up that morning knowing that they were never going to see another day. . . ." She squeezes his hands so tightly that she wonders why he doesn't cry out in pain. "But all I can think about is that I'm not anyone's *daughter* anymore. . . ."

She stops, once more overcome with tears, and gasps for breath.

"Do you need a paper bag or something?" Guy looks alarmed.

"No, no, I just . . . I never *will* be anyone's daughter again," Willow continues after a few minutes. "And I was right to be . . . to become a . . . cutter, because maybe you think this doesn't look so bad, that girls cry, people cry, but you'd be wrong, you'd be so wrong, anything . . . anything at all . . . would feel better than this does. I'm . . . sorry." She tries to catch her breath. "I'm sorry to be putting you through this. . . ." Willow wipes her eyes once more. Their hands are still clasped, and she feels the backs of his brush across her forehead. "This isn't what I had in mind when I said to take me here. . . . This isn't what I was expecting. . . . Or maybe it was. . . . I just . . . I don't even know."

"Willow, you haven't put me through anything."

"I need a Kleenex." She sniffs.

Guy disengages his hands from hers, takes the hem of his sweatshirt, and wipes her nose with it.

"That's romantic," she says, embarrassed.

"Well, it is sort of, because I wouldn't do it for anybody else in the world."

"I . . . I . . . well that's . . . That's the . . . the nicest . . . I . . ." Willow hiccups. "Excuse me. I also get the hiccups really badly when I cry." She takes his sweatshirt and wipes her nose again. "I'm a mess." She laughs shakily. "But guess what? There's no one else in the world whose sweatshirt I would want to wipe my nose on." She hiccups again.

"Do you want some water for those hiccups?"

"No." Willow shakes her head. "No, thank you. But you know what I would like? Could you get me my hot chocolate? I left it near the door."

"Okay." Guy shrugs. He gets up and is back within seconds. "Here you go." He looks dubious as he watches her take a sip of the now stone-cold drink. "Is that really good?"

"Well." Willow makes a face. "It depends on what you call good. It kind of tastes like river mud at this point."

"Is that something you've had a lot of?" Guy asks as he sits back down alongside her.

"I'm guessing." Willow puts the cup down on the floor. She leans back against the cushions with a deep sigh. "Thank you," she says suddenly.

"For what?"

"Thank you for bringing me out here. Thank you for not telling my brother about me. Thank you for being such a . . ."

"You're crying again." He shifts so he can take her in his arms.

"Yeah, I know. Gimme your sweatshirt."

"Okay, hang on." He wipes her tears away. "You going to start hiccupping again?"

"No." Willow shakes her head.

"Do you want to stay here and, I don't know, maybe take a nap or something? Or do you want to go back to your brother's house now?" Guy says after a few minutes.

But Willow wants neither of those things. And she's shocked by just what it is that she does want. The past half hour has hardly been conducive to passion. And yet, as she sits there with him on the window seat, with his strong arms around her, she knows that if she can survive crying, then there are other things that she can survive too. And that if some things are lost to her forever, there are others that she has not yet begun to experience. She knows too that what she wants is not because passion is the natural antidote to grief, but because it is the most natural, most perfect, most complete expression of what she feels for him.

"Do you remember when you first . . . when you first found out that I was a cutter?"

"I'll never forget it."

"But do you remember . . . Well, do you remember how I tried to bribe you?"

"I'll never forget that either."

"Well." She swallows. "I . . . well, I hope that now, maybe you would . . . I mean, I want to . . . If we could . . ." She stumbles over the words but looks at him expectantly, hoping that since he is so often able to know her better than she does herself, that he will understand what she is trying to say.

To her dismay he looks completely baffled.

"Oh, this isn't coming out right!" Willow exclaims, wonders if perhaps this isn't a good idea after all, if it will shock him, following as it does so closely on her breakdown, except she can think of nothing that she has ever wanted more. "Never mind!" she says dispiritedly. "This isn't how I imagined it would be anyway, not with my nose all runny."

"Imagined what?" Guy asks slowly.

Willow moves closer to him. "What do you think," she says finally.

"I . . . Well . . . I'm not sure *what* to think." Guy pulls back from her a little until she is at arm's length and studies her face. "And I'd really hate to make a mistake right now. Because, well . . . It sounds like you're saying that you want . . . Well, you want . . ."

"I've never heard *you* sound so flustered before." Willow laughs. She wipes the last vestiges of her tears away. She can't believe that he doesn't get what she's saying, and she can't believe that she can laugh about it either.

"Willow, are you . . . I mean are you referring to when . . ."

She decides to make things easy for him. "C'mere." She pulls him forward again. She has kissed him twice before. Once with disastrous results, once not nearly so catastrophic, but never with all that she feels inside. She hopes and believes that now, finally, she can show him how much she cares for him, but still, she is trembling slightly as she moves to close the gap between them.

"You're sure this is okay?" Guy whispers against her mouth.

"It's okay," Willow whispers back as she helps him find the buttons on her shirt. "It really is okay," she repeats, amazed and thrilled that it should be so. She pulls the tearstained sweatshirt off over his head.

"But you're so shy." Guy's breath is soft against her throat as he slides her bra off her shoulders. "And you're so vulnerable. Please tell me that you're sure."

"I'm sure." Willow reaches for the buttons on his jeans. "I'm sure, but . . ."

"But what? What's the *but*? What's the *but*? Why . . . Why are you saying *but* all of a sudden?" Guy stammers a little as he helps her shed the rest of her clothes.

"But . . . Well, have you ever done this with anyone else?"

"Never." He pulls her down so that she is lying on the window seat.

"Good." Willow is surprised that shy as she indeed is, she isn't embarrassed to be naked in front of him. Maybe this is because in every other important way she already has been.

"Have you?" Guy lies down on his side next to her.

"No!"

"Good." He kisses her hair, her face, her neck.

"Wait, wait a second." Willow pushes her hand against his chest. "I have to ask you something else. Do you . . . Do you . . . Umm. Do you have . . . *anything*?"

"What?" Guy frowns. "Oh! Umm-hum, I have . . . uh, I have something in my wallet."

"Good."

"Can I . . . Can I . . ."

"You can do anything." She shivers as his hands move over her body, but this time it is wholly unmixed with fear and she cannot believe how wonderful it feels.

"Wait a sec . . ." Willow sits up suddenly. "You do? Have something, I mean?"

"Well, aren't you glad that I do?" Guy sits up too and looks at her.

"Wait a sec . . ."

"*Again* wait a sec?"

"If I had something in my bag you'd want to know why . . . I mean, how *long* have you had *something* in your wallet?"

"Since I was twelve."

"No!" She hits him with the flat of her hand.

"Of course I haven't." He moves in to kiss her again.

"Well, tell me."

"Don't you want to stop talking now?" he says against her mouth as he pushes her gently back down on the window seat cushions.

"No."

"But if you keep talking, then I can't kiss you, and then we can't do what follows after that. . . ."

"But I like to talk to you. Because I can ask you *anything,* tell you *anything,* and no matter what I say to you, I know it will be all right."

"That wasn't fair." Guy sighs against the side of her face. "Now I have to answer." He props himself up on one elbow. "I've . . . had *something* in my wallet ever since I knew . . . Well, ever since I *hoped* that there would be a time when I would need to . . . protect you like this."

"And when was that?"

"If I answer that, *then* will you stop talking?'

"Yes." Willow bites her lower lip and runs her hands over his shoulders. "I will, because your answers are so perfect."

"Oh." He looks down at her and smiles. "Then would you believe me if I told you that I put it there after the first time I met you?"

"No."

"Okay." He pauses and Willow can tell that he is going to

tell her the truth. "I . . .Well . . ." He runs his hands through her hair and watches as it drifts back to her shoulders. "After I saw you in the physics lab."

"I don't . . . I don't get it."

"We'd already talked in the stacks, and I knew you were different from any other girl I'd ever met. And then you told me that your parents were dead, and I thought that you were so . . . lost and vulnerable. So when I saw you in the physics lab . . . and I saw you try and take care of someone that you thought was weaker than yourself, I couldn't believe that someone who had been through what you'd been through could be that . . . well, generous, and thoughtful . . ."

"But you hardly knew me."

"I know. And I don't want you to think that I rushed right out to a drugstore or anything. I didn't know that we'd even talk again, or that if we did, if we'd get along, or maybe you were seeing someone else. . . . I just knew that the way you tried to protect someone like that, especially given your situation. . . . I just . . . I thought that you had to be the most special girl I would ever meet. . . ."

"I'll stop talking now." Willow twines her arms about his neck.

"Isn't that interesting."

"Hmmm?"

"When you blush, it doesn't stop at your collarbone."

"Oh."

"I'll tell you something else."

"What?"

"I just figured out why someone would want to make the first mirror."

Willow blinks in surprise. That is not what she was expecting to hear.

"Why?"

"I think some lover wanted his beloved to see how she appeared to him. He wanted her to be able to see herself the way that he did."

Willow has nothing more to say. She watches him as he kisses her cuts and she hopes that her inexpert exploration of his body has the power to affect him the way that he's affecting her.

"Ouch." She winces as he inadvertently pulls her hair.

"Sorry, I . . ." Guy can't help crushing her as he leans over and reaches down to the floor. "I . . . um . . . I just um . . . need my wallet and it's in this pocket. . . ." He searches for the borrowed jeans.

"Are you nervous?" he asks as he finds the pants and fishes his wallet out of the pocket.

"Uh-huh." Willow nods. "What about you?"

"Very."

"Oh. Well, don't be, because I'm nervous enough for both of us." Willow wonders if what is about to happen will hurt, and she thinks how ironic it is that she of all people should have this concern.

It *is* painful, she flinches involuntarily, but it is Guy who cries out. "I'm sorry! Did I hurt you?! I didn't mean to, but . . ."

Willow covers his mouth with her hand. "Only for a second," she assures him. "Only for a second." And she realizes that this is true. Pain has somehow transformed into pleasure, and that pleasure is better than any pain could ever be.

CHAPTER FIFTEEN

Persephone dwells among the shadows in Hades, among them but not of them, she is . . .

Maybe talk about how her mother as a goddess of the harvest represents fertility, so that when she (Persephone) eats the pomegranate, it's kind of like an act of solidarity, since pomegranates are a symbol of fertility, even though it means that she'll have to stay in the underworld. . . .

Oh, who cares?

Willow looks at the notes she made in the library a few days earlier and sighs in frustration. They're absolutely useless. Still, trying to make some sense out of them is better than staring at a blank screen. She can't even bring herself to turn her computer on. But if she doesn't get something done soon, she'll be in trouble. The *Bulfinch* paper is due first thing in the morning, and she hasn't even written a sentence.

She'd thought that she'd had trouble concentrating on the subject before. But now that it's two in the morning of what has been, excepting the day of the accident, the most eventful twenty-four hours of her life, it's proving to be absolutely impossible.

Willow pushes her notebook away and reaches for her bag. She takes out the note, the innocent piece of paper that her mother had written to the housekeeper, and lays it flat on her desk. She finds it extraordinary that such a little thing has the power to move her so greatly.

Perhaps she had known all along that something of the kind was waiting for her at home, that to be confronted by such a thing would be to let loose with all that she had been suppressing for so many months. And perhaps even if she hadn't found the note, there would have been something else, something equally innocuous that would have set her off just the same.

Willow thinks back to the way she cried earlier in the day, the pain that she allowed herself to finally feel. She is staggered that she was able to process such overwhelming emotions, and wonders if she will be able to do so again.

Is she ready to part company with her constant companion?

Willow opens her desk drawer, takes out one of her many razor blades, and places it beside her mother's note.

Well, what's it going to be, then?

She looks at the dull metal blade, then shifts her eyes to the faded ink, wondering if the message will once again move her to tears, and if it does, if she will once again be able to withstand the onslaught.

Oh God I hope so!

But maybe her earlier tears have no implications beyond their immediate and obvious meaning. She was affected by her mother's letter to the housekeeper, by the small reminder that once her welfare was paramount in someone else's world, and for whatever reason, she was able to process that feeling without the alchemy of cutting.

Or maybe the reason is obvious after all. Maybe by allowing herself to care about somebody, to *love* somebody, she herself set the entire chain in motion, and maybe it is his love that enabled her to endure the grief that issued forth.

Willow pushes herself away from the desk and wanders over to the dresser, then looks at herself in the mirror that hangs above it.

She doesn't think that she looks any different. Shouldn't something so profound, so life-changing, mark her as visibly, as decidedly as her razors do?

Willow pulls up her shirt and examines the scars on her stomach. They are slowly fading, and in the dim light from her desk lamp, their shadowy outline is less vivid to her than the memory of the way that he kissed them.

Look at that. I guess when I blush it doesn't stop at my collarbone.

She drops her shirt and stares at her face again. Her hair is still down, she never bothered to braid it again. She wonders now if she had really been wearing it that way all these months because it was so convenient. Perhaps it had simply been an unconscious attempt to return to an earlier time. She pushes it back and focuses on her eyes. Maybe there is a change, albeit one that is invisible to her. Maybe there is something that would be immediately obvious to anyone else.

Would Markie notice? If she were to meet her tomorrow, would she see a difference? Will Laurie be able to tell?

Willow wonders if her mother would have noticed. And more, if her mother hadn't noticed, would she herself have told her?

Willow has no answer to that, but she knows this much is true: The rest of her life will be filled with moments just like this, moments when she will want more than anything to tell her mother something, ask her father a question, and simply not be able to. All the tears that she lets fall will never change that. And neither will the razor.

She walks back to the desk. She has to get some work done on her wretched paper, but as she sits down she hears a faint silvery sound, and this time she understands immediately just what she is hearing.

She should be accustomed to the sound of her brother weeping by now, but listening to his tears is even more painful than it was for her to cry herself.

Willow puts on her bathrobe, moves to the door, and walks out to the landing. She grips the banister, kneels down, and looks through the bars. If she cranes her head she can just see him seated at the kitchen table.

It is unbearable to watch.

She has a sudden urge, different from before, to go to him, confront him, *comfort* him if such a thing is possible. Now that she knows how weeping that way feels, she can't bear the thought of him there alone. But how can she possibly comfort him, when she knows that she herself is the cause of his tears?

Without thinking, Willow reaches into her pocket for her razor. She grips it tightly, but she doesn't cut. She can watch him without cutting. She has proven so to herself, but watching is no longer good enough. Can she go to him, can she face his pain, is she strong enough for that?

She takes a tentative step down the stairs, but this time she doesn't hide in the shadows. If David were to look up, there would be no way that he could miss her.

Willow reaches the bottom. She never takes her eyes off David as she grips the razor tightly. Without any choice on her part, the edge of the blade is already cutting into her skin.

Is this what she wants? To continue the same way that she has? Is this in fact the answer to her earlier question?

She sinks down on the stairs, unable to go to him yet unable to look away. She can feel the blood as it starts to spring from her palm. Willow knows that she should put her razor down. She should get up and walk the remaining few feet that separate them. But she is incapable.

And so Willow sits there, just sits there, waiting for David to notice her. Will he ever look up? Will he ever let her into *his* world of pain, even if only to lacerate her himself? And then David does look up. He does see her.

Willow slips the razor back into her pocket, and walks slowly toward him. Today has been a day of firsts, and she is desperate to connect, in some way, with her brother. She needs to let him know that she still loves him, even if she has forfeited his love, that she is made miserable by his anguish.

She watches his face as he watches her. She doesn't shy away from his tears. She doesn't turn away from his pain.

Willow stands in front of her brother. She sees him open his mouth, barely hears him whisper her name.

She leans closer, so she can hear what he has to tell her. Suddenly he grips her hand with surprising force, grips her so tightly that she can barely move.

"Oh Willow," he says. "Oh, Willow, what if you had died that night too?"

CHAPTER SIXTEEN

"Okay, I guess that's it. You need to do the footnotes, though, because I'm just not up for that right now."

"Are you sure?" Willow looks anxiously at the computer screen. "I still think we should put that stuff in about how ironic it is that the pomegranate, the thing that keeps her stuck in the underworld, is a symbol of—"

"Look, you don't want this to be too good, do you?" David gives her a look. "I mean, you don't want everyone to know that your brother did most of the work, right?"

"But you didn't come up with that, I did!" Willow protests.

"How about this, then." He pushes the chair back from the desk and stretches his arms over his head, then looks down at where she's sitting on the floor. "I'm done. I haven't stayed up all night working on a paper since I was in college, and I could really live without the experience. I'm not kidding, Willow.

You told me this thing was assigned three weeks ago, if you wanted help with it, couldn't you have come to me before two a.m. on the morning that it's due?"

"Okay, I guess. I mean, yes," Willow says between yawns. She still can't believe that she even asked him *this* time.

After she had come upon him crying, after his extraordinary statement, which moved her more than she would have thought possible, they had sat at the kitchen table and talked. Not, however, as she would have hoped, about anything of significance.

Certainly, after such a naked display of emotion, it had proven impossible for David to continue to act with his cold reserve, and his manner toward her had softened considerably. And yet the content of their conversation, to her intense disappointment, had remained on the most superficial level. And so, Willow found herself *not* speaking about how much she missed their parents, about how strange their new circumstances were, but talking to him instead, finally, about the French quiz, and also about the trouble she was having with her paper. David had suggested writing it with her, *for* her, really, as it turned out. Surely this is something that would not have occurred a few weeks ago, at least not as easily or as comfortably, and yet, as she leans back against the desk and watches him make the last few corrections, she feels empty inside. There is still something, *everything*, unresolved between them, and although talking to him like this is better than not talking to him at all, she still wishes for more.

"Anyway," she continues as she shifts her legs, which have fallen asleep from sitting still for so long. It is almost six thirty in the morning, they have been up in her room for the past four hours. "Thank you, I would never have gotten this done on my own."

"Yeah, sure, of course," David responds, but Willow can see that he's not really paying her any attention, he's looking at their father's copy of *Bulfinch,* which is lying on the desk, and which unbelievably enough, she has forgotten about. "Did you . . ." He trails off, picks the book up with a frown and flips through it. "This is . . . this is . . . from the . . . from the . . . *house,* isn't it?"

"Uh-huh." Willow nods. She can see how hard it is for him to even say the words. "I um, I uh . . . I took it that time I . . . that we went back for me to get some clothes. I knew I would need it. . . ."

"You did?" He glances down at her backpack lying on the floor.

"Uh-huh." Willow nods. "Sure."

"Really?" He looks at her in confusion. "But I keep seeing you dragging around some cheap paperback. Besides, I remember that day. Cathy gave you a huge lecture about the fact that your bag wasn't nearly big enough to fit anything. . . ." He frowns for a moment, then reaches down to the floor to pick up her backpack.

"Don't!" Willow says. But it's too late. She thanks God that her stash is inside a zippered pocket, she's sure that he won't open that, but for once she's carrying other contraband that is almost as worrisome.

David looks inside the bag. Maybe he's just trying to see how much room there really is, but that doesn't stop him from pulling out the copy of *Tristes Tropiques.*

"I . . . I hope you don't mind," Willow stammers. "But I want to . . . I'm going to give that to Guy."

Stupid! That was a stupid thing to say!

Okay, so maybe she hasn't been able to stop thinking about Guy all night, maybe she was trying to get David's mind off of whether she really did bring the *Bulfinch* back with her that time . . .

But it was still a stupid thing to say!

"There's no way that you've had both of these books with you the whole time you've been living here," he says slowly. "You've been back to the house."

"No, I . . ."

"Willow." David looks at her in alarm. "Please tell me, and please be honest, you didn't *drive* out there by yourself, did you?"

Willow knows that any attempts she makes at concealment are useless, that the truth is written all over her face for anyone to see. Not only that, but it is obvious to her that his main concern is not that she went out there, but how she got there. Clearly the thought of her driving by herself terrifies him, and she wants to spare him that anxiety.

"No, I didn't go out there by myself, and I wasn't the one doing the driving anyway."

"Pretty nice of someone to drive you all that way just so you could pick up a book. Sorry." He looks at the copy of *Tristes Tropiques*. "So you could pick up *two* books. Pretty nice of you to want to give him this too. I have an idea of what it must mean to you." He pauses and looks at her for a moment, deep in thought. "Willow, you can't tell me that's why you really went out there."

Willow stares at her brother in amazement. How could he

possibly know what she herself didn't. That her odyssey had a deeper purpose, that her desire to go out there for the *Bulfinch* had been nothing more than . . . And then she realizes that David's mind is elsewhere, he thinks she went out to the house with Guy—he *knows* that she went with Guy—just so they could have some privacy so that they could . . .

"Willow," David says suddenly. "You're bright red. *Bright* red. Go look in the mirror."

But Willow doesn't need a mirror to know that her face is flaming.

"Oh my God. Oh my God." He starts to laugh. "I am not equipped to deal with this, I'm just not equipped to deal with this kind of thing at all."

Maybe it's the lateness of the hour, or maybe it's just that he'd been crying the way he was, but for whatever reason, David seems to be thawing. He is looking at her, really looking at her the way he hasn't in months. He is finally connecting with her, teasing her the way he once would have. . . .

Okay, she wanted her brother to unbend toward her, to talk to her the way he used to . . .

But did it have to be about this?

"You would *not* be turning that color over a simple road trip."

"Fine. Just shut up already, okay?!"

"Sure. Look, I guess it had to happen sometime, and I think you picked the right person, because—"

"Gimme my stuff back!!" Willow snatches both the books and her bag from him.

"No problem. Just . . . look . . . Is there anything that you need to tell me?"

"No."

"Okay, is there anything that *I* need to tell you, or rather, explain to you about how—"

"NO!" Willow cuts him off.

"Well then, is there anything that maybe *Cathy* has to talk to you about? I want to make sure that you—"

"NO!" Willow cannot believe that she is having a conversation, or rather, trying very hard *not* to have a conversation like this with her brother.

"What's so funny anyway?" she asks belligerently after a few moments. She's sure that his laughter is not directed at the situation, but at *her*.

"Oh, I'm just thinking that when Isabelle is seventeen I'm locking her up."

"Will you stop it!" She hits his arm.

"All right." He is serious once again. "But Willow, I'm not joking about this. If you need me to explain anything, if you need me to talk to you . . ."

"I *do* need you to talk to me! I do need you to talk to me! I do need you to talk to me!" Willow startles both of them with her outburst. Unlike the day before with Guy, she is immediately aware that she is crying. "I do need you to talk to me," she repeats once more, burying her head in her hands.

"Willow!" David gets up off the chair, sits down next to her, cups her chin in his hand, and lifts her face to his. "What is it? What's happened? Did you . . . Did he . . ."

"I do need you to talk to me, and not about that kind of stuff. . . . I've known about things like *that* since I was in fifth grade. . . . You need . . . You need . . . You . . ." She can barely get the words out, she is hyperventilating so badly.

"All right, take a deep breath." David moves so that he is sitting next to her on the floor with his arm around her. He's trying to sound calm, but Willow can tell that he is, in fact, very worried by this sudden fit of tears and has no idea what it might signify. She is hardly less astonished than he is, and she can't help wondering if this is the way things will be from now on. That perhaps her grieving apparatus, frozen for so long, will now erupt at any moment, and, if that is indeed the case, if that is something she can tolerate.

"Give yourself a second," David continues. "Just take a second and then try and tell me what's going on."

"You . . . You . . . *We* need to talk about the way things were," Willow finally says. "We need to talk about *them.* Maybe they're dead, but they shouldn't be dead to *us*. They shouldn't be dead *between* us. You need . . . You need to talk to me too. You need to tell me how . . . how angry, how *furious,* you are with me about, about what happened. You need to talk to me too!"

"I . . . I do. I know that. . . ."

Willow wipes her face and turns to look at David in surprise. "You do?"

"Yes. And maybe I've done something very wrong these past months. I've wanted to talk to you, it just doesn't seem fair, I mean to make you relive . . . I never know how to talk about what happened. Or when. And I worry that if I do talk about things, then you won't be able to keep going the way you have, or that I won't. And I think that maybe it's just best to keep things contained. But obviously I don't know what I'm talking about." He pauses for a second, reaches up to the desk where she keeps a box of tissues, and hands her some.

"Thank you." Willow blows her nose very loudly.

"I . . . I'm even less equipped to deal with this kind of thing than I am the other. . . ." David sighs deeply and for a second he looks like someone twice, three times his age. "It's so hard for me to think about what happened and even harder to see what it's done to you. So I just try and focus on getting on with things, on taking care of you, which I don't know the first thing about. But I try and do one thing, I try and make sure that I don't constantly remind you, so that *you* can get on with things. And you *do* seem to get on with things. I'm so amazed at how well you've been dealing with all this, that I thought that bringing up the past would be cruel."

Willow doesn't know how to respond to this. He's said so many things that it's hard to focus and let them all in. She's dimly aware that he has alluded to what he considers her ability to deal with things well, and she is sure that she should disabuse him of this notion. But other thoughts are fighting for prominence, and she needs to reassure him that he has not been wrong. That even if she has wanted to talk to him, at times wanted that more than anything, that does not mean that he has failed her like she has failed him.

"But you do, you do handle things well," she stutters after a moment. "I know how hard it is, how hard it must be for you and Cathy to have me here and how hard it is financially, and how I barely contribute. It's all my fault. And I—"

"Oh Willow," David cuts her off harshly. "None of this is your fault. Did you ever think that maybe it was irresponsible for them to drink enough so that a sixteen-year-old with a learner's permit was forced to drive in what was one of the worst storms of the year? Did you ever stop to consider that if

I was on top of things I would sell the house, that it wouldn't matter how long the insurance was taking, and that if I did, we wouldn't have any money worries *at all*, for *years*? That the only reason you have to contribute *anything* is because I can't face doing that? That it's my fault that you have to give me all your money instead of spending it on yourself?" He looks angry, angrier than she can ever remember seeing him, and she can only be thankful that it seems to be directed at himself, because she doesn't think that she could handle him looking at her like that.

"I'm mad at myself for that, because with everything else that's going on, that should be one area where things are easy. And I know I'd better deal with it soon too. I need to sell our house before you have to start thinking about college."

"Okay, I guess I never did think about that exactly—I mean, make that connection about me having to work at the library and you selling the house." Willow puts her hand on his arm. "But still I think that—"

"And I get mad at other things too," David interrupts her once again. But Willow doesn't care because she can see he is about to say something very important. "I get mad at other things too," he continues. "I get mad that I'm forced to think about things like you going to college and putting the house on the market to pay for that college. I get mad that I can't have sex with my wife whenever I want because this apartment is so small and I don't want my little sister to hear us. I get mad that I can't walk around the house in my underwear and that I have to behave as if I am the parent of a seventeen-year-old and not just an infant." He pauses for an instant and takes a deep breath. "I don't ever get mad or hold you responsible for our parents dying. That would be worse than crazy. I meant what I said at dinner. It was a hideous accident, it was just an inexplicable event, and my first thought about it is *always, always, always* how hard it is for you. How hard the next ten years will be for you, ten years that I had parents to help me with, but that you won't. But you're right. I do get mad at you. I'm mad at you for the fact that almost every aspect of my daily life, every *stupid* aspect, has been irrevocably changed. And I'm mad that our relationship has changed too, that even though I still adore you and always will, it is not the same easy feeling that I had before." He holds on to her hand where it rests on his arm. "I have always been responsible for you. Just by virtue of loving you, I've had a responsibility to you and for you. You have that responsibility to me too, to anyone that you will ever love. But it's different now. Now on a daily basis, my responsibility for you has been put onto a practical plane, now I have to deal with French quizzes and teacher conferences, and there are times when it drives me crazy, when I know I'm not *old* enough to have these additional worries. And then, then I *hate* myself for thinking that, because I know how petty, how irrational, how unfair I'm being. And I look at you and I see how strong you are, and I'm amazed that you can be that way, and then I get even angrier at myself that I can't handle these little everyday problems, when you're able to handle so much more."

"But I'm not strong! I'm not strong," Willow cries. She takes her hand away and once more covers her face. She is so moved by what her brother has told her, she is so relieved by his emotional honesty, by his admission that he still loves her—an amazing thing!—even though he has been angry and frustrated and confused and conflicted, that she can't bear to sit there with him under false pretenses.

She should show him her scars, show him the razor marks, let him know that his image of her is fraudulent. Only his praise is like balm in Gilead, and she is terrified of forfeiting that. Neither does she want to add to the burden of his responsibility. She knows now, really knows that what she told Guy was true. It would *kill* him to learn this about her.

And she has not yet decided to give up her razors either. She realizes now that she is not quite ready to let them go. Yet she sits there next to him, takes her hands away from her face, holds her arms out in supplication, almost wishing that he somehow would take it upon himself to roll up her sleeves and discover the truth. And she thinks as she did before with Markie that it would be so easy. All it would take is for her sleeves to be pushed back, and the thing would be over, done, finished! She would be separated from her instruments, taken to a doctor, watched over, protected.

But she will not be the one who makes this happen. She will not put herself in a position of having this happen to her. She thinks that she still needs her blades, and she is sure that she can never tell her brother. That although he may love her, and although they now will be able to talk, they are still separated. His image of her is on one side, and the reality of what she has done, of what she chooses to do, is on the other.

"I'm not strong." She continues to weep. *"I'm not strong."*

"Willow." David grabs both her hands above the wrists, grabs them and holds them tight. He does not roll up her sleeves. Why should he? "You're trembling! You're just shaking all over! Was I wrong to tell you? Should I—"

"No! No! You were right, and don't stop talking to me, because—don't stop. . . ." She cannot talk anymore. She is too tired, she is crying too hard, and anyway, her brother is hugging her much too closely for anything she says to make much sense, because all her words are muffled in his shirtfront, and in any case, she has started to hiccup.

"Ssh." David tries to hush her much the way he would Isabelle if she were weeping so disconsolately. "Ssh, try and calm down. Willow, just try and . . . Goddammit, I hear the baby." He pulls away for a second. "Cathy needs to sleep, she's been up every night with Isabelle over this ear infection. . . . I . . . I should go downstairs. Are you going to be okay for now?" He holds her at arm's length and studies her face carefully. "Can we keep talking about this later?"

"Uh-huh." Willow swipes at her eyes with the back of her hand. And as she watches him go, go to his *daughter*, she is once again struck by the fact that she will never again be anybody's child, and that although some things in her life will improve, her relationship with David most certainly among them, that fact will never change.

❋

Willow walks out of the school building surrounded by dozens of other students. The day is over, and she could not be more thankful, not just because she is exhausted emotionally and physically, but because she is longing to see Guy. And since they don't have any classes together, the only time that she can be sure to find him is right after school.

She looks around a little worriedly. He's nowhere to be seen. But then she catches sight of him over near the gates.

And as she walks toward Guy, she can't stop thinking about the fact that she, alone among all the girls there, knows him, really knows him, in every possible way.

Willow wants to run up and grab him, run up and hold him, see if he feels as wonderful as he did the day before, but she's too shy, so she just walks over to where he's standing, and waits to see what he will do.

He grabs *her,* he holds *her,* and she realizes that he feels even better than he did the day before.

"Hey, you know what?" He holds her as closely as possible and looks deep into her eyes. "I really want to talk to you."

"Well, of course." Willow frowns. "I mean, what else? I don't get—"

"No, I mean, I need to talk to you about—"

"Hey Guy," Laurie calls from across the courtyard. "Take Adrian with you wherever you're going. You guys do something together, Willow can come with us." She starts walking over to them, Adrian and Chloe in tow.

Willow steps back from Guy reluctantly and stands at his side as she watches their approach.

"Seriously," Laurie continues. "Don't you and Adrian need to talk about rowing or something?"

"Adrian isn't on the team." Guy looks at Laurie in confusion.

"Yeah, I know," Adrian says in a wry voice. "And Laurie does too, she just wants to get rid of me," he explains needlessly.

"That's right." Laurie nods. "Chloe and I are going to a cafe. You too, Willow, if you want—we need to make a list of all the eligible—"

"Shut up, Laurie," Chloe interrupts her good-naturedly.

"Uh, sorry, Laurie," Guy says. "I wanted to be with—"

"You look different, Willow," Laurie says suddenly.

"Whaaa?" Willow jumps about four feet in the air. Out of the corner of her eye she can see that Guy is trying very hard not to laugh, and she knows that he knows exactly what she's thinking.

"What . . .What do you mean *different*?" Willow reaches for Laurie's hand and pulls her away from the rest of the group. "How different? What do you mean exactly?"

"Oh, I just . . . Well." Laurie lowers her voice a little. "You look like maybe you've been crying. I'm sorry, I shouldn't have said anything when everyone else was around, I just . . . Are you okay?" She squeezes her hand.

"Oh! Oh, sure!" Willow laughs. She gives Laurie's hand a return squeeze before letting go and moving back to Guy's side. "I'm fine. I was just up all night doing a paper for that class you liked so much. You know, the *Bulfinch* thing, but thanks for asking."

"Okay, so listen." Laurie turns her attention back to Guy. "Could you—"

"Forget it, Laurie." Guy shakes his head. "You'll have to drag him along with you. I feel like being alone with Willow, we're going down to the river. Besides, he probably has much better ideas than you do about who to fix Chloe up with."

"Yeah, I have no interest in this at all," Adrian protests.

"Deal with it." Laurie loops an arm around him. "C'mon. Maybe it's better this way anyway. Now you can pay."

"Did you really get your paper done?" Guy asks her as the others walk away. "I know I said I'd help you and I never did. . . ."

"Well, don't repeat this, because it's embarrassing and probably illegal, but my brother really did most of it."

"Really?" Guy looks at her in surprise as they walk out of the gates and down the street. "Does that mean that you, well, that you *talked* to him?"

"I did actually." Willow nods.

"So you're . . . I don't know, I mean you kind of worked things out? That sounds really stupid, but you know what I mean. You were so convinced that there was no way things could be okay between you. But you think that you can talk to him again, for real?"

"Umm-hmm." Willow feels that she owes Guy a fuller explanation of what exactly did transpire between her and David, but she can't give it to him, because she is laughing too hard.

"What's so funny?" He looks at her suspiciously.

"Oh, I don't know." Willow walks backward in front of him. "I just think that, maybe even though *I'm* more comfortable talking to him right now, *you* might not be."

"What, what do you mean, exactly?"

"I just have this feeling that you wouldn't be so comfortable around him right now, that's all." She falls back into step beside him as they cross the street and head into the park.

"Willow." Guy stops in his tracks. "You didn't . . . You didn't *tell* him that we slept together or anything like that, did you?"

"Oh, no!" Willow shakes her head vehemently. "I would *never* have told him that."

"Good." Guy looks vastly relieved.

"That's not to say he didn't figure it out on his own, though."

"Oh no!"

"What's the matter?"

"Oh, my God!"

"What do you care? Guy, I was joking about you not wanting to run into him, he doesn't have any problem with us doing—I mean, are you embarrassed about what we did? Or ashamed or something?" She looks stricken.

"You don't get it at all." Guy pulls her close to him. "It's not that, it's just . . . I do not want to know about this kind of thing with Rebecca, okay?"

"She's twelve!"

"Yeah, well, whenever it happens, I don't want to know about it. Oh, my God." He shakes his head. "How am I ever going to take another class with him?"

"I don't know." Willow starts laughing again. "But you know what? *You're* blushing!"

"Yeah, okay, I don't blush, all right?"

"You are!"

"Look, I'm not a girl."

"Oh, you don't have to tell *me* that! I mean if I ever had any doubts about that, they're gone after yesterday!"

"Thanks," Guy says dryly. "Listen, can we just sit here and talk."

"I don't like that wall." Willow bites her lip as they approach the water. "I really don't feel like falling in."

"You're not going to fall in," Guy says patiently. "I mean, unless you keep talking the way you have been, in which case I'll push you. C'mon." He gets up on the wall and helps her up beside him. "See, totally safe." They both sit down and swing their legs out over the water.

"So, what did you want to talk about so urgently?" Willow smiles at him.

Guy regards her steadily for a moment without saying anything. He leans in closer, and Willow thinks that he's going to kiss her, and she is disappointed when he reaches for her bag instead.

He opens it up and rifles through it until he finds the box of blades. "I was hoping that these would be gone." He looks back up at her. "I was really hoping, and you know what? I was halfway to being sure that they would be."

"Is that what you wanted to talk about?" She stares at him in surprise, but he is no longer looking at her, he is gazing out at the water instead. "You wanted to talk about me cutting?"

"That's right."

"But why?" Willow shakes her head at how stupid that sounds. "I mean, why *now,* this is nothing new, you've known about this, you've—"

"I thought things had changed."

"I see," Willow says slowly. "You thought it was just going to be that simple. That all it would take is me crying a little . . . and maybe us having . . ." She bites her lip. She can't, she absolutely can't bring herself to say anything that will cheapen what happened between them. "I guess, I guess you like happy endings, don't you?" she says after a moment.

"Everybody does." He puts the box of razors down between them on the parapet and turns back to look at her. "I don't believe that there are two categories for that—people who like sad endings and people who like happy ones. *Everybody* likes a happy ending."

"Well then, let me tell you something about happy endings," Willow says angrily. "I told you I talked to my brother. That's true. We did talk. We talked like we haven't since my parents died. Is *that* what you mean by a happy ending? 'Cause guess what? He still doesn't know about these." She gestures toward the small package of blades. "Even though we talked about everything else, I couldn't tell him about this. I can't tell him yet. It would just be too much for him. But maybe one day I will tell him. I'll tell him because I won't be able to keep having this secret between us, this wall. I'll tell him because enough time will have passed since the accident that maybe he'll be able to handle something like this. Does that sound happy to you? Does that sound good? Because, you know what? No matter *when* I tell him, it will hurt him so much. . . . It will be so painful for him. It might make me feel a little better, but it will make him feel so much worse. And you know what else? Maybe I haven't lost my brother like I thought I did, but my parents are dead. Gone. No matter how much I talk with my brother, no matter how much I tell him, from now until the end of time, nothing will change that. Is *that* what you mean by a happy ending?"

"No. Of course not. But you know what? You can't change that." He rolls up her right sleeve. "You can change this."

Willow looks down at her arm. The cuts on this side have faded considerably. More white than red, they look somewhat . . . innocent, like she might well have gotten them from scratching herself too hard, or coming into contact with an enthusiastic kitten. She starts to cover herself up again, but Guy stops her. She feels terribly exposed, but something else too: She has forgotten the sensation of sunlight against bare skin, and she makes no move to resist him.

"You said, that day in the library," Guy continues after a moment. "You said that if things were different, you would want to give them, it, the whole thing, up. Well, things *are* different now. Don't you *want* to stop?"

"I don't know!" she cries in genuine anguish, appalled to find herself bursting into tears once more. "I thought that I would, but it's not that simple. It's just not that simple!"

"Oh Willow, the last thing I wanted to do was make you cry again." Guy is genuinely upset. He moves closer to her and tries to put his arms around her. "I didn't—"

"You *should* want me to cry!" Willow pushes him away so that she can look him in the face. "You *should*! Because every time that I do, it's like . . . it's like . . ."

How can she explain to him that every tear takes her further and further away from the box of razors that lies between them. How can she explain that she is terrified of such a thing happening. That although she thought she wanted freedom from her implements, she doesn't know if she can handle what she's experiencing now. That she wants to know that she is still in charge of her grief. That her blades have always done her bidding.

"It's like what?" Guy says. He grasps her upper arms. "Every time you cry it's like what?"

"I . . . I don't know if I can take this," she says between tears. "You think cutting hurts? You don't know anything!" Willow picks up the packet of razor blades and presses it against her breasts. "These have saved me from *this*. From feeling like this! Yes! I thought . . . I did think that if I could cry like this, *feel* like this, I could let them go. But I'm not so sure now. . . ."

"Willow." Guy bites his lip. "I'm your lover now." Even in the depths of her misery the words give her a thrill, but he's not done talking. "That box of blades can't be your lover anymore, no matter how much they've been there for you in the past."

"You knew about this from the beginning," Willow says. "You've seen me do it. Heard me do it. What's so different now?"

"You have to ask me that after yesterday?" Guy looks at her incredulously. "All right, then. I'll tell you. Everything's different. Just everything."

Willow knows what he's talking about. They are no longer the two people they were yesterday. Her cutting and its consequences no longer affect her alone, if indeed they ever really did.

Her brother's words about responsibility come back to her, about what it must necessarily mean to love someone. And she knows that that responsibility must start with her, and that if in the past, cutting was the best way she knew of to take care of herself, there is a different way open to her now. And then, after that, she must extend that responsibility to Guy as well, because she cannot do everything to shield herself from pain while she forces the person she loves to endure even worse.

Willow looks down at the box and thinks about her other lovers nestled inside, about the pain that she exacts from them, so different from the pleasure that her flesh-and-blood lover gives her, and she knows that their lure is a pitiful thing against all that Guy has to offer. And that not only would renouncing that box of blades be the most responsible action, but it would also be the most beautiful, the most gratifying, the most rewarding thing that she could do.

And she knows these things, stronger than she has ever known anything, but still . . .

"I know I should get rid of them," she says finally when her tears have subsided just enough for her to talk more coherently. "I know I should, but I just can't do it. I can't. I thought I would. I thought I could. I thought about it when I was with Markie. I thought about it last night. I thought about it when I was talking with my brother . . . but I can't!"

"That's it, then?" Guy grabs the box from her. "That's it, then, you've chosen? You're going to be faithful to *them*?"

"I . . . I don't *want* to be!"

"Then get rid of them! Do it! Here, throw them in the water! I'll help you. Full fathom five, like it says in *The Tempest*!"

"You think that's all it would take?" Willow starts to cry again. "You think I couldn't go out and buy some more tomorrow, go to one of those all-night stores if I had to, improvise with a screwdriver if that's all there was around?"

"I know that," Guy says. He takes her hand and closes it over his as he clutches the box. "I know all about it, okay? Maybe you will get some more tomorrow, or maybe even tonight, but at least for right now, for right now, you would be free of them."

"All right!" Willow presses her face into his chest. She cannot stop weeping and she knows that her words are practically incoherent. "All right! I'll do it," she says against his shirtfront.

"What did you say?" Guy disengages himself and holds her at arm's length. He looks at her in amazement as if he cannot quite believe what he has heard. "Willow, what did you say? It's very hard to understand you when—"

"I'll do it, I will! You just . . . Give me a second. . . ."

An hour, a month, a year. . . .

"Look," Guy says. "I'm going to help you, okay? It's going to be easy. C'mon. I'll just hold our hands out over the water and count to three, and . . ."

But Willow doesn't even wait until three. She knows as she watches the box drift down to its watery grave, that although she can indeed go out and buy more anytime, that that part of her life is most probably over. The curtain is drawing closed over the past seven months, and her brave new world with Guy beside her is beckoning. And that if this is not a happy ending, it is perhaps a happy beginning.

Acknowledgments

I am very happy to thank the following people, who helped so much and in so many ways:

Andrea Haring, for her unfailing support and faith. David Damrosch, for his time, energy, and suggestions, each one of which made the book better; and Jenny Davidson, who answered many eleventh-hour queries with grace and enthusiasm.

At Dial Lauri Hornik not only bought *Willow* but teamed me up with the extraordinary Kate Harrison. Kristin Smith provided a beautiful and inspired cover, and Regina Castillo caught countless embarrassing inconsistencies.

And finally to the wonderful Erin Malone, of the William Morris agency, to whom no thanks could ever be great enough.